Leona Stewart

THE SEALED VERDICT

Lionel Shapiro

THE SEALED VERDICT

Doubleday & Company, Inc.

GARDEN CITY, NEW YORK, MCMXLVII

This book was written for the millions who,
like Thémis and Lashley,
know that our triumph of arms over Nazism
was the merest of beginnings.

CONTENTS

MONDAY

I

THE SMALL, ALMOST EMPTY COURTROOM WAS DIMLY LIGHTED by a single electric bulb that dangled from a strand of wire stretched across the ceiling. Even the commission in Reschweiler was not excepted from the town major's stern warning against the use of full lighting when it was not essential.

Under the dull brassy glow the courtroom looked like a country church interior when the crimson of twilight begins to merge with dark of night. The fourteen rows of seats were deserted save for a motionless person here and there.

At the head of the center aisle a low gate led into the well of the court. The bench of justice consisted of a long dais, newly constructed, behind which stood nine armchairs. Above the bench was a clock, and under the clock a huge American flag was tacked flat against the wall. To the left of the dais two park benches, ludicrous in faded green paint, marked the prisoners' dock, and adjoined in singular contrast were seven small desks for defense counsel.

Below the dais and slightly to the right stood a massive mahogany table. At this table there was a single chair and in it, facing the slumbering courtroom, sat Major Robert Lashley, the American prosecutor.

He felt like a schoolmaster supervising a few laggard students as they completed their examination papers. These were people who awaited the verdict with as much patience—or was it impatience?—as he. Idly he counted them. There were nine; ten with himself.

Three military policemen, their white lacquered helmets pulled over their eyes, sprawled in the back row. He could not see their faces but he recognized the flashes on their sleeves. They were part of the MP detail assigned to guard the defendants in the basement cells of the courthouse.

Halfway down the aisle the *Burgemeister's* wizened wife sat primly beside her grown daughter. Lashley could guess why they persisted in remaining in the deathly silent room. They and the *Burgemeister* were the only Germans who counted for anything in Reschweiler and they liked to demonstrate their privileged position by sitting where only Americans were usually allowed to sit.

Far on the left, sitting beneath the high windows which admitted the last glimmer of daylight, was Captain Jacques Gribemont. Unaware that he was under scrutiny, he popped a biscuit in his mouth and munched it sadly. Lashley watched him with amusement. Gribemont was a ceremonious fellow, as behooves a French staff officer who finds himself living among Americans, and he played heavily on the gray solemnity of his appearance which was, as far as Lashley was concerned, his only asset as official French observer at the trial.

The Czech, Rodal, and his pitiful little companion, Maria, sat in the second row almost directly facing Lashley. He understood the implacable calm with which they waited out the awkward hours. Rodal had been his best witness, and empty-eyed Maria his most poignant exhibit. They sought vengeance. He hoped they would get it soon. The panel of judges had been in closed session three hours now.

The ninth person was the Delisle woman.

Lashley wrinkled his forehead suddenly and fiercely, and the creases ran down the channel between his black full eyebrows. His precise mind rebelled against her presence. He could not bear not fully understanding anyone and anything that came within the range of his work. He had been like that in Harvard Law School, and before that during his undergraduate days at Ohio State. He had even been bothered by things mysterious and beyond his reach before he graduated with honors from high school. It was one of the qualities which contributed to his success as a lawyer, but took away from his happiness as a man.

He did not understand Thémis Delisle: neither her character, nor her background, nor the pull she exercised on his attention. Not that she appeared to demand or want attention.

During the past days he had had plenty of opportunity to study her. His eyes were familiar with every curve of her graceful body. She was not a tall woman, but a slender one, so well proportioned that she seemed taller than she was. Most of the time she sat motionless, but whenever she moved Lashley found his attention drawn to her. There was something exciting to him about the way she raised her arms to adjust the tilt of her hat, about her long narrow fingers holding a gold-encased lipstick. The economy of her motions fascinated him. Most women, he thought, were awkward when they crossed one knee over the other. Most women should never cross their knees.

She sat in the front row. One hand was tucked under her chin, the other swung her brown leather purse in a short arc. Lashley could not divine what her eyes were seeing. They were looking at him now, he thought, but they were not seeing him. Their green depths seemed to close over their own secret. The inward curve of her face between cheekbone and jaw was white against her brown hair and dark fur collar. She had a wide, mobile mouth. In the course of the trial Lashley had seen on it briefly the flicker of a smile, a sudden look of determination, a reflection of sheerest innocence, a disdain, a supreme obliviousness. It was, he told himself now, the mouth of a sensitive, high-strung but finely balanced woman. Perhaps it was that about Thémis Delisle which piqued him whenever his glance fell on her. She did not look what his reason told him she was.

Roughly he pulled up his chair and drummed his long square fingers on the table. To his ears the noise was like a rumble of thunder in the deadly quiet room and he was content to hear it. The dimness, the silence, and the brooding people were too much for his tired mind. He sought by drumming his fingers to break the collusion. He was a trifle light in the head, he conceded. There could be no doubt that he was exhausted. This was the forty-third day. It had not been an easy case. Seven Germans on trial simultaneously presented a multitude of technical problems, of which the most annoying was the need for translation. The pause after each sentence, so the inter- preter could echo the words in German, distressed him and bored him, for he was fluent in German. But he understood why it was necessary, and whenever he understood he could practice great forbearance.

Lashley turned his head to look at the clock.

Five past five. They couldn't be much longer. There was so little leeway for discussion, even on penalties. He had proved guilt in each case. Old Colonel Macklin was probably giving his colleagues a short course in law. Macklin knew his law; before the war he had been an outstanding jurist and had earned respect for his sound opinions. The others were not qualified, Lashley thought; especially the artillery captain who had sat blankly on the right of the bench for forty-three days. A year after the war the army was still full of men like that, detailed to odd jobs while waiting for sailing orders; odd jobs like deciding whether seven Nazis should live or die.

His eyes swung back to the woman in the front row. They caught and rested on the bronze arrow piercing the crown of her brown hat.

The arrow reminded him of Ginny, who had a piece of costume jewelry like that which she wore on her lapel or some- times in her berets. He began comparing the two girls in his mind—Ginny with her wide blue eyes and deceptively inno- cent expression and this expensive-looking Frenchwoman whose green eyes told him nothing.

He'd been going around with Ginny ever since sophomore year in high school, although when he went away to college he forgot all about her. Then there was that picnic the summer after he finished law school, when he had taken her out in a canoe and discovered her all over again. Well, that was some time ago, and as soon as this filthy job was over he'd go back to Erie and ask her to marry him.

There was nothing unpleasant or mysterious about Ginny, he mused, none of that sullen, explosive quality he found in the French girl. Perhaps "bitchy" was the best word for it.

He remembered Ginny as he had last seen her, saying good-by to him in the Union Station. It was at the end of his embarkation leave. She was laughing cheerfully, telling him to get the job done fast and come back soon. Then all at once she was crying, the train was pulling out, and he was kissing her self-consciously.

He'd taken it for granted, of course, that she'd be waiting for him.

Lashley smiled a faraway smile. He stretched his shoulders and returned to reality.

Through the open doors he saw people gathering and talking in the brightly lighted corridor. He flicked his sleeve and looked at his wrist watch. It was five twenty-five. Macklin and his judges had been out nearly three and a half hours.

People were trickling in now. Three GIs whose uproarious laughter preceded them through the doors became inordinately quiet as they walked down the aisle and took seats in the third row. A tall gray colonel, extremely erect, came in with a Red Cross girl who walked as though she had stilts instead of legs. Two second lieutenants, escorting a pair of awe-stricken USO girls, slipped into the back row.

Van Tyne of AP and Gubbins of UP ambled importantly through the enclosure into the well of the courtroom and took their seats in the press section. Lashley's eyes followed them. He wondered why it was that newspapermen are the only people in the world who can amble importantly. The slender girl from the New York *Times* seemed to skate in after them, nodding primly to Lashley as she sat down.

Captain Lance Nissen, sandy-haired and of athletic build, came through the gate and walked to a desk on the defense side. Lashley smiled at him briefly. Poor Lance! he mused. Mostly because he was junior in grade he had drawn the bitter end of the assignment. For nearly two months they hadn't spoken to each other except across the well of the courtroom. Without discussing it they had tacitly agreed it would not look well, nor would it sit well on their minds, for the American prosecutor and the American defense liaison to be seen together. He missed Nissen's acid humor, and he relished the imminent end of the trial for the promise it bore of a renewal of their evenings together.

The big hulk of Kinsella, captain of the courtroom guard, trundled out of the door leading to the chambers and leaned over Lashley.

"About ten minutes, Major," Kinsella said. He smelled of sweat and bad cognac. "They're taking the last ballot now."

"Thanks, Captain," Lashley murmured without looking up.

"And, Major, don't worry about one little thing. I've got twelve men inside the room and eighteen in the halls. Nobody's gonna start a rumpus here."

Lashley said sharply, "I'm not worrying, Kinsella."

"Swell, Major. I just thought you looked worried." He wiped the sweat from the back of his neck. His ruddy flesh squeezed out of his tight collar like shaving soap from a tube. "Also I wanted you to know. We're letting about forty krauts in for the show. Frisked 'em all outside, checked 'em all too. No relatives."

Scowling, Lashley looked up. "Very well."

Kinsella leaned closer. "Just one more thing, Major. The old man wants me to see that the French sweetie pie gets on the train for Paris in the morning. You know, the one sittin' there in the front row——"

"Talk to Nissen about her. She's his witness." Lashley turned away his head and looked toward the courtroom. The bright lights were being turned on and the benches were almost filled.

"Don't be that way, Major," Kinsella purred. "I just wanted you to know I'm taking *that* job on myself. Not bad, huh?" He winked.

Lashley whirled around. Kinsella backed away, grinning. "Okay, Major, okay. Just wanted a laugh on the job. I always say if you can't have laughs on the job it ain't worth workin' at." He guffawed all the way to the door.

Lashley studied the woman once more. He felt an intense curiosity to know what transpired behind her eyes. She had a generous face, a compassionate face. He suddenly felt he would like to have seen her when she was happy.

It was not that she made any difference in the case. He was sure of that. The trial had gone well before she came. For thirty-nine days he had raised his structure of guilt brick by brick with the sureness of a builder who knows he works from a perfect blueprint. He could see the lines of conviction set in Macklin's face. And Macklin was the only one who counted on the bench.

She had arrived four days before the end. The trial continued well, just as well, he thought, after her appearance. Her testimony had been worthless. It would take more than her strange little story to break his case against Steigmann. She had testified that he saved a French Jew from execution—in 1944—when Steigmann was deputy town commandant in Paris. Her story was so vulnerable. Lashley recalled the zeal with which he approached her for cross-examination. He had wrung from her an admission that she had known Steigmann when he was stationed in Paris. That was all. He hadn't pressed the point. It was a nice bit of courtroom strategy. He had left it to the imagination of Macklin and his fellow judges how well she had known Steigmann. She was beautiful and that was enough. He recalled how deliberately he had smiled when he motioned her abrupt dismissal from the stand. And then he called the Czech, Rodal, in rebuttal; Rodal with the discolor of suffering on his sunken face in devilish contrast with the chic beauty of the young woman. Rodal was magnificently effective. He had been a prisoner in the foreign workers' camp in Reschweiler when Steigmann was made commandant later in 1944.

Not for a moment did a misgiving, legal or moral, cross

Lashley's mind. It was only that the woman was an enigma, the one enigma, in an otherwise straightforward case. She created a tiny rebellion in the ordered ranks of his thinking. She presented him with a mystery, and this he could not long abide. Why had she come from Paris to testify? Because she loved Steigmann? Lashley rejected that. It was too simple an answer. It didn't ring true. It couldn't be so. Not Steigmann and this poised, sensitive woman.

Lashley twisted his knuckles against the wood of the counsel table. Why?

Then he relaxed. It was a superficial question with a thousand possible answers. He caught himself shrugging his shoulders and he looked around self-consciously.

Kinsella's white lacquered helmet gleamed under the lights. He walked with ludicrous precision across the well of the court, like a lonesome overgrown boy playing soldier by himself. At the railing he stopped.

"The commission!" he shouted. Then he turned about and stood facing the bench, his chunky legs spread apart, his hands locked behind him.

As he rose to his feet Lashley glanced across the well toward the defense desks. Six of the German lawyers wore black robes. One, the gray-haired patriarch who was Steigmann's lawyer, wore purple. Their arms dangled disconsolately from their sagging shoulders. Nisson stood by their side. He was wistful to the point of sadness. Behind them the prisoners' dock was empty.

A military policeman opened the door behind the bench and the judges came through in the order of their seating. They looked aloof and wise. All except Macklin, who was fifth in line. His mouth drooped sternly at the corners. He leaned forward, glanced left and right to see that his colleagues were properly placed, then nodded toward the courtroom. Amid a vast shuffling of feet the crowd settled itself.

This was the moment, Lashley told himself. He must remember it. He had prosecuted cases before, but not a capital case like this. It was something to recount someday. He felt good. He enjoyed the exhaustion of work accomplished.

"Gentlemen," said Macklin quietly, "it is customary——"

"*Meineherren*——" began the interpreter.

Macklin waved a finger at him. "No, no, Sergeant. This is not part of the record. I am merely arranging something with opposing counsel."

Lashley and Nissen looked inquiringly toward the bench.

"It is customary, gentlemen," Macklin resumed in a low voice, "for the verdicts and possible sentences to be announced to each defendant in the alphabetical order of his name. I propose to change the procedure slightly for the purposes of convenience. The—uh—journalists attending this trial have explained to me their anxiety to have the verdict on the defendant Steigmann as promptly as possible because of his—uh—prominence as a figure of public interest and because of certain technicalities connected with the dispatching of their reports to America. I intend to accede to their wishes in this matter. We will deal with the defendant Steigmann first and proceed with the others in alphabetical order. Uh—Captain Nissen, I wonder if you would be good enough to explain this to counsel for the defendants. There is nothing irregular about it. It is merely a change in customary procedure for purposes of convenience. Have them understand that perfectly."

The German lawyers looked confusedly at Nissen. He stepped into their midst and held a whispered conference. Then he turned to Macklin.

"They understand, Mr. President, and they have no objection."

Macklin turned toward Lashley. "I assume the prosecution has no objection."

Lashley shook his head.

There was a brief silence as Macklin arranged the documents in front of him. Without lifting his head he said, "Captain of the guard, bring in the defendant Otto Steigmann."

Kinsella clicked to easy attention and marched up the aisle. The courtroom was noisy with whispers. Macklin, apparently still deeply concerned with his documents, tapped lightly with his pencil. The whispering subsided.

The clatter of shoes on marble was heard in the corridor. Flanked by two military policemen, Steigmann marched into the courtroom. Kinsella followed behind, his jowls shaking in counterpoint to the thump of his boots.

Inside the well of the court Kinsella murmured, "Halt." He stepped forward, grasped Steigmann by the arm, and led him to a point six feet in front of the bench. Then he stepped aside smartly and stood at ease. The sergeant interpreter took his place on the other side of the prisoner.

Lashley glanced briefly at the young woman. Her purse had stopped swinging, but her manner was unchanged. Her face retained the vast emptiness of a desert by starlight. She was not looking at Steigmann.

Standing alone in the glare of lights, Steigmann looked shorter than Lashley's fixed impression of him. When he had sat in the dock and the witness box these last weeks Steigmann had held his solid frame defiantly erect.

Lashley now realized that he was a full head shorter than Kinsella. Long body, short legs. Not like most Germans, he thought. His hair was sparse and stringy and even careful combing did not conceal a growing baldness. Lashley saw through the thin strands beads of perspiration making highlights on his scalp. But the shape of his head was pure German. And his eyes, blue and small, were German. So was his nose: straight but too slight for the size of his head. The nose, Lashley figured, would have looked pretty on the woman.

Macklin turned his eyes on Steigmann with the bored expression of a man reading a newspaper in a streetcar.

"As president of this commission . . ." He paused.

"*Als Präsident dieses Gerichtshofs . . .*" the interpreter shrilled in a voice that lacked timbre because it lacked calmness.

". . . it is my duty to inform you . . ."

"*. . . ist es meine Pflicht sie davon in Kenntnis zu setzen . . .*"

". . . that the commission in closed session . . ."

". . . *das der Gerichtshof in Geheimer sitzung . . .*"

". . . and upon written ballot . . ."

". . . *und in urkundlicher Geheimer Abstimmung . . .*"

". . . two thirds of the members present at the time the vote was taken concurring in each finding . . ."

". . . *bei Übereinstimmung von zwei dritteln der Abstimmung anwesenden mitgleider . . .*"

". . . find you of the specifications and charges guilty."

". . . *sie der tat Gemäss der Anklage in allen Punkten schuldig findet.*"

Steigmann's eyelids fluttered. There was no other reaction. He continued to look squarely at Macklin.

"And again . . ."

"*Und ferner . . .*"

". . . the commission in closed session . . ."

". . . *das der Gerichtshof in Geheimer sitzung . . .*"

". . . and upon written secret ballot . . ."

". . . *und in urkundlicher Geheimer Abstimmung . . .*"

". . . two thirds of the members present at the time the vote was taken concurring . . ."

". . . *bei Übereinstimmung von zwei dritteln der zur zeit der Abstimmung anwesenden mitgleider . . .*"

". . . sentence you to be hanged until you are dead."

". . . *sei zum Tode durch hängen veruteilt.*"

The interpreter's chin quivered as he spoke the last words. He gulped, glanced at Steigmann, and quickly looked away.

Kinsella moved a step toward the German and half extended his arm in readiness.

It was unnecessary. The prisoner's legs were steady. He appeared paralyzed in a posture of attention. Only his fingers were outstretched as though making ready to grasp the thighs in case his legs failed him. His mouth and chin were rigid. His face was drained of color until it attained the gray depth of fine marble. His eyes continued to stare straight ahead.

Macklin had turned unconcernedly to his papers and was rearranging them.

Kinsella moved quickly behind Steigmann, grabbed his arms above the elbows, and twisted him around. The prisoner's shoes might have been soled with ball bearings, so mechanically did he turn.

"March," grunted Kinsella.

Steigmann took a few steps. He stopped and jerked his head from side to side. It was as though the action of his legs had released him from a hypnotic spell. He looked confusedly toward Lashley, realized he had lost his sense of direction, and turned his head toward Nissen. The American apparently knew what Steigmann intended. He darted to the prisoner's side. They whispered a moment. Lashley could not hear what they were saying.

"Mr. President!" Nissen's deep voice cut through the sullen atmosphere. Macklin looked up inquiringly.

"Mr. President. The defendant would like to make a statement."

"You mean the prisoner, Captain," Macklin said dryly. "Tell him he must be brief."

Steigmann nodded impatiently to indicate he understood the instruction. He walked to the gate at the head of the aisle and turned toward his counsel. Lashley saw that he stood almost directly in front of the Delisle woman. The German did not look at her. His head was turned toward the bench. She was watching him intently but without visible emotion.

His words came fast, as though rehearsed from a prepared manuscript.

"Ich winne den letzten Sieg!" he declaimed in a voice pitched high with excitement, almost exultation. "I win the last victory. The pattern of my life is complete. I lived without pity and without fear. Now I die without regret. Quick and full! Quick and full! That is the pattern of my life. Only battle and decision count in life! Even in death I am forcing a loathsome decision upon these reluctant victors——"

Macklin's dust-dry voice interrupted. "That will be enough," he said with vast unconcern. "Captain, remove the prisoner."

Kinsella held open the gate and pointed along the aisle.

Steigmann twisted his head down and looked at the French-woman. She met his glance. Her lips moved though no sound came from her. Lashley could read in her face neither love nor hate. It seemed to him that her voiceless gesture was one of recognition touched with pity.

The German moved to go, then paused. Still looking at her, he said in a low voice, "I am not afraid."

"Captain, remove the prisoner," Macklin ordered sternly.

Kinsella grasped Steigmann by the arm. The German tried to hold his ground, but two military policemen grabbed his elbows and roughly propelled him along the aisle. For a brief moment he resisted, then marched in quickstep. As he neared the door he turned his head once more.

"Leb' wohl, Liebling!" he cried.

His words echoed in the corridor.

Van Tyne of AP and Gubbins of UP darted unobtrusively up the aisle. They broke into a run when they reached the door.

The shattering silence that ballooned in the wake of the German's words was pricked by Macklin's nondescript voice.

"Captain of the guard. Bring in the defendant Johann Bacher."

II

IT WAS JUST AFTER SEVEN O'CLOCK WHEN LASHLEY LEFT HIS office on the first floor of the courthouse.

The sentry in the rotunda was leaning against a bronze plaque bearing the names of Germans who died in the 1914–18 war. He looked up from his copy of the *Stars and Stripes* and saluted limply.

"I suppose that's it, eh, Major?" he said. "No more late nights."

Lashley said, "I hope so. Good night, Buckley."

"Good night—sir."

Gusts of wind muttering around the colonnades on the portico struck his face. He flipped away his cigarette and watched its glowing tip bounce from stair to stair like a performing firefly. Smoking in the crisp April air seemed somehow sacrilegious. He threw back his shoulders and breathed deeply.

The courthouse stood on the heights of Reschweiler and from its portico Lashley looked upon the sullen city falling away to the banks of the Auer River. Darkness hid the ruins and the dull street lights failed to reveal the pockmarks of bomb and shellfire. Night had its magic for Reschweiler; the city was invested with the illusion of wholeness. Only the irreverent autopsy of daybreak would betray the frightfulness of its wounds. Now he could scarcely see the twisted girders of the two broken bridges rising out of the Auer; between them the fast-flowing river capered in gay communion with the glint of starlight.

In Erie, Lashley estimated, it was early afternoon. The Hammermill Paper Company plant next to the lake would be getting into full stride again, after the lunch-hour break. There would be women pushing baby carriages in Kahkwa Park and kids ordering ice cream sodas at Pulakos's. In his own little office on Peach Street, Reginald Matthews, the senior partner, would be leaning back in his swivel chair and lighting his third cigar.

So different, Lashley realized, from Reschweiler with its shattered streets and its empty-eyed people.

He did not linger on the thought, but wondered instead how soon the *Times* and the *Dispatch-Herald* could carry the story, and he tried to picture what prominence the verdict would be given. There were more important matters in the news—the Security Council, the Trieste business, and the endless war in China. But six men sentenced to be hanged and one sentenced to life imprisonment was also news—especially when the prosecutor is a local man.

He wished the magic of science could transport him quickly to Erie. He could picture his father dodging friends on the street. The old man would be embarrassed by the news, but he'd be awfully proud and pleased too. Lashley had felt very close to his father in the four years since his mother's death, though the two men never discussed the deeper and more personal aspect of their lives. And yet Lashley always had the feeling that his father knew what he was thinking. It gave him a sense of comfort and security.

Tomorrow morning his father would be waiting impatiently for the first edition of the Erie *Daily Times*. It might even carry a picture of "Robert Lashley—young Erie lawyer" with a flattering story. He hoped they would use the picture he had taken in uniform just before he sailed. It made him looked scrubbed and stern and successful.

Even now in the tight military hierarchy of Eleventh Army Headquarters he had become someone in the last hour. Its commanding officer, General Joshua Marriner, possessor of the efficient military brain that had led the Eleventh Army from the Normandy beach to the Elbe, had called up the moment the trial was over and asked him to his house for a drink. It was common knowledge that Marriner, in war and in peace, was as shrewd a military mind as was ever produced by West Point. An invitation from him was a high accolade for a field officer. Tonight was the first time, as far as Lashley knew, that the general had been conscious of his existence. He had said, "I shall expect you at seven-thirty," in the crisp tones of a man who is accustomed to being obeyed.

Lashley realized he was late. He hurried to the far corner of the courtyard where his jeep was parked, climbed into the driver's seat, reached for the padlock on a heavy chain that secured the steering wheel, and unlocked it. As the chain dropped to the floor boards he groped for the starter.

His boot stopped short of the button. The clatter of the chain reminded him of something. Six condemned and a seventh who would die in prison languished not twenty-five yards from where he sat. For a moment he looked at the light from the tiny windows of their basement cells edging over the top of the cobblestones. Then he stepped savagely on the starter, threw the gearshift, and the car careened out of the gates.

He admired humility. And he had not practiced it. He had been thinking not of what he had accomplished for humanity, or for his country, or in pursuance of his duty. He realized for the first time how much he had indulged his vanity, and without knowing it he began to drive more carefully.

The house General Marriner occupied as his private residence was the finest left standing in Reschweiler. A dirt road marked *"Eingang strengst verboten"* veered off the main highway at the eastern outskirts of the city and one traveled it for nearly two kilometers before reaching the massive iron gates that gave entrance to the grounds.

A sentry stepped out of his box, flashed a light on Lashley, and saluted. He then threw his light on a typewritten card tacked on the side of the sentry box and called out, "Major Lashley, sir?"

"Yes."

The sentry hammered on the gate with his rifle butt and shouted, "Open up!"

An aged German appeared in the glare of the jeep's head-lights and pulled open one gate, then the other, panting and muttering, *"Ja wohl, ja wohl."*

As Lashley drove through, the sentry saluted again.

Two staff cars were already parked in the driveway behind the general's gray-green Cadillac. Lashley jumped out with-out stopping to chain his steering wheel, and ran up the stone steps two at a time.

A Frau immaculately uniformed in black dress, white cap, and apron answered his ring and led him through a great oak-paneled entrance hall and across the foot of a beautiful stair-case to a massive double door. In his first quick glance after she opened it Lashley saw a huge room furnished with delicate magnificence. The far wall was lined with french windows. Four men were seated in front of a fireplace.

He recognized Marriner and paused to make a gesture of coming to attention.

"Major Lashley, sir. I hope I'm not late."

Marriner reached for his horn-rimmed spectacles on a side table and examined the newcomer. He rose almost immediately and extended his hand.

"All right, Lashley, quite all right. Evenings here we're in-formal."

Lashley came forward and they shook hands. He felt im-mediately that he would like Marriner. The man's appearance denied his reputation as a ruthless field commander and an austere disciplinarian. His figure was slight, his clean-shaven face pleasant to look upon, and his shrewd gray eyes beneath a vast expanse of brow reflected a lively intellect. Except for a burst of decorations on his blouse, he might have passed for a fashionable physician in his late forties.

Marriner said, "You know some of these gentlemen, I think. Our French friend, Captain Gribemont. Major Lashley."

Lashley said, "Of course. How do you do, Captain."

The Frenchman shook hands a little stiffly, Lashley thought, considering the fact that they had consulted together every day for two months.

"A happy moment for both of us," said Gribemont.

Marriner led Lashley by the arm. "And Colonel Pike, my G-1. Major Lashley."

Pike was stubby, gray, and fifty-five. He put down his glass and chuckled for no apparent reason. "Glad to know you, Lashley. Grand stuff you've been doing. Just grand stuff. Yessir."

Marriner said, "You know—of course you do—Lieutenant Parker."

Lashley knew Parker. The sallow young man combined the functions of aide, secretary, and confidante to Marriner, and he had become a power in the politics of the Eleventh Army.

"Sit down," said Marriner, "and tell us something about the trial. What will you drink?"

"Whisky and water, if you have it, sir."

Pike bellowed, "Have we got it? Hell yes, man, we've got it." He jerked his thumb toward a rolling bar that stood in the corner of the room. "A man who does a job deserves the best in the house. And you've done a job, man. Agree, General?"

Parker bustled to the bar.

Marriner said, "All right, Pike. You confine yourself to drinking and let Lashley here do the talking."

They settled in deep chairs around a spanking fire. Lashley sipped his drink. He felt extraordinarily well.

Marriner said, "I want to congratulate you, Lashley. Gribemont has been telling me about the trial. I understand you did a very effective job in court."

"My God, yes," Pike chuckled. "I was there this morning. Jesus, he was wonderful. Great gift of gab."

Lashley began to feel even better.

"The summation was easy, sir," he said. "There was plenty of evidence to build on."

"Easy or not," said Marriner, "you've accomplished an important mission. More important perhaps than you know. Gribemont here is especially grateful."

Gribemont said, "Indeed, General. We were concerned, as you know, about Steigmann. His crimes against France were abominable. Had he been acquitted here, we would have had to try him in Paris. Major Lashley has saved us the trouble—and expense."

"Haw!" boomed Pike. "You mean, saved *us* the expense, eh, Captain? The French never spend their own money. Borrow it from us. *Oui, oui* or no?" He chuckled.

The Frenchman flushed, then lifted his glass toward Pike. "We Frenchmen know who are our friends."

Marriner ignored the colloquy. He looked thoughtfully into the fire and said, "I'm a soldier, Lashley. Have been most of my life. I suppose a great many men have lost their lives by my command, one way or another. But I've always felt their fate was touched by destiny, never by me. You feel the same way, I imagine, when you send six men to the gallows."

Lashley stared. The general's quiet remark stirred him uncomfortably, and he was silent. For months he had thought of this as only a legal problem. Not until this instant had he considered himself in the role of executioner.

He said after a moment, "Not quite, sir. You see, I didn't sentence them. Colonel Macklin did."

Marriner smiled. "Well, that's a fair extension of the old army game. I'm sure nothing bothers Macklin."

Lashley rubbed his forehead in reminiscence. "He reminds me, sir, of my professor in criminal law. Twice as wise as an owl and nearly twice as ugly. He used to say, 'Some of you will undoubtedly become judges someday—God save the bench—and you will probably feel a catch in the throat when you sentence a man to be hanged. As for myself, I have always found it convenient to reserve the catch in the throat for the murderer who is about to hang.'"

Pike guffawed. "Rich! That's rich." He drained his glass, held it out, and said rudely, "Thanks, Parker."

The lieutenant took the glass and went to the bar.

Marriner turned to Lashley. He said, "I'm sure Macklin has the right idea. The men are murderers. They deserve no second thought. I'm proud of our CIC people who brought them to justice, and I'm proud of you—well, for having brought justice to them."

"Hear, hear," grunted Pike.

Lashley tried unsuccessfully to think of a graceful rejoinder. But the pleasure he had felt earlier was enhanced by the drink and the fire, and words eluded him.

Gribemont said, "I can only add my felicitations." He turned his glass slowly in his hand. "And express my regrets."

"Regrets?" Marriner put on his spectacles and looked up brightly as though anticipating a *bon mot*.

"Yes, General," said the Frenchman. "I regret, particularly in view of our special interest in Steigmann, that the only person to appear in his defense should have been a French-woman."

Pike came alive. "My God, yes. And pretty, as I remember. Odd name, too; Thémis something, wasn't it?"

The woman marched across Lashley's complacent mind like a company of fifes and drums. He stared into the fireplace, puzzled that into this quiet moment of triumph she had again intruded the enigma compounded of her mission and her character.

"Thémis Delisle," he said carelessly. "She really had no effect on the case."

Gribemont said bitterly, "Maybe not on the case. But on me—definitely."

The doors opened and the housekeeper tiptoed in. The conversation stopped until she had drawn heavy brocaded curtains over the french windows, curtsied, and tiptoed out.

Parker said in an aside to the general, "You remember, sir. You made a note about the Delisle woman."

Marriner rubbed his chin. "Oh yes. Curious thing, Lashley,

talking of your fine handling of the case. I made a memo about this woman. I was a little disturbed at the time."

"Disturbed, sir?" Lashley said unhappily.

"I'll tell you why," Marriner continued. "Well, you know something about the way our public safety people operate. They have a very comprehensive set of criteria and graphs on civilian behavior, and every now and again, when the underground pokes up or the civilian black market goes bullish, they recommend that we tighten the screws a bit. A few days ago my G-5 indicated strongly that a capital conviction of this fellow Steigmann would have a salutary effect on the whole area. He was a big man around here, no doubt of it. I think"— he rubbed his forehead—"that was the day the Delisle woman was put on the stand."

"The day after, sir," Parker corrected.

"Quite right. I read a report on the court proceedings just before I called the regular staff meeting. In view of the G-5 recommendation, the appearance of the Delisle woman tended to upset me."

Lashley said, "Her testimony meant nothing, I assure you, sir."

"So we found out," said Marriner. "I had Colonel Macklin to dinner that night and I asked point-blank what the chances were of Steigmann hanging."

Lashley's brow darkened. "How did the colonel react to that?"

Marriner raised his highball and pretended to be intent on drinking, but he was studying Lashley from behind the shelter of his oversized spectacles.

"You know Macklin. He's a crusty old bird. He said—a little abruptly, I thought—it would depend on the development of the case. I can tell you I was in a bit of a quandary." As he watched Lashley stiffen in his chair, Marriner smiled reassuringly. "Well, it turned out Macklin was having his little joke. Before the dinner was over he got around to saying that you were building as fine a prosecution case as he'd seen in twenty-seven years on the bench."

"Yessir," chuckled Pike.

Gribemont muttered, "That blasted woman."

Lashley leaned forward like a pointer. "Did you tell Colonel Macklin about the G-5 report?"

"I think it came out sometime during the dinner," Marriner said.

Lashley's mouth tightened and the muscles around his eyes contracted slowly.

Marriner added quickly, "It's of no importance now. The woman intrigues me, though. Who is she?"

"Yes, who is she?" Pike echoed. "Come on, Frenchy, don't spare the details."

Lashley only half listened to Gribemont's reply. He was thinking of the general and Macklin, and wondering how much importance the G-5 report had been given at the dinner. Almost immediately he dismissed the suspicion that crossed his mind, for he knew Macklin's stern reputation as a jurist was too great to allow even a hint of collusion. It struck him he was being too sensitive about his first capital conviction.

Gribemont was saying, "I can tell you very little about the miserable creature. She took us all by surprise. Isn't that so, Major?"

"Yes," said Lashley absently. "She meant nothing."

"Come now, Lashley," said Marriner brightly. "A beautiful woman witness at an important trial. You can't let her down so cheaply."

Pike chuckled. "Let's have the inside stuff, Major. Was she Steigmann's sweetie? Bet she was."

For some reason Lashley found himself not wanting to discuss her.

"I suppose she was," he said.

"Undoubtedly," said Gribemont. He pushed himself to his feet. "And, gentlemen, I can promise you this. We will know more about her—much more. I have already been in touch with Paris. The Deuxième Bureau is most interested. I understand she is being put on the train tomorrow. When she reaches our

zone at Mainz she will find she has company the rest of the
way and for some time thereafter. The case of Mlle. Delisle is
not closed. It is, as a matter of fact, merely opening."

Marriner said pleasantly, "There you are, Lashley. You
might get a Legion of Honor out of this."

Furrows formed between Lashley's eyebrows.

He said, "Surely you're not going to arrest the woman."

The Frenchman threw forward his hands. "But obviously.
Her testimony clearly implied intelligence with the enemy. We
must detain her."

Parker spoke up. "I think he's right, sir. It seemed to me she
almost upset the case—I mean, against Steigmann. He might
have got off with prison if it hadn't been for that Czech,
Rodal——"

"Parker!" said Marriner quickly. "Get the major another
drink."

Lashley stood up slowly. In the firelight he looked taller than
his nearly six feet as he moved with thoughtful deliberation to
the back of his chair. The changing reflections of the fire high-
lighted his dark hair and played on his tired face. He leaned
over his chair as though it were a lectern.

The Frenchman was still standing. Pike sat deep in his chair.
Parker was at the bar, holding a bottle in his motionless hand.
Marriner had an expectant look on his face, like a theatergoer
at the rise of the curtain. They watched Lashley as though
attracted by the intensity of his hazel eyes. In contrast to his
eyes, his words were calm and cold.

"This was an American trial. Under our concept of law
even the most forlorn cause has a right to be heard in court
without let or hindrance." His voice rose in pitch without sac-
rificing its quiet tone. "Without let or hindrance, Gribemont,"
he repeated. "We cannot dispense justice if witnesses are subject to persecution. The woman may have been misguided but
I think she was honest. I know she had courage. She volunteered to appear. She was as much a part of our process of justice as the Czech." He paused and looked away.

Gribemont turned toward Marriner. He said with a trace of annoyance, "My dear Lashley, this is not the occasion——"

"You made it the occasion," Lashley said.

Marriner threw his cigarette in the fire. In the low, almost benign voice which had become recognized at headquarters as reflecting his most vicious mood he said, "It seems to me the captain is right. The woman has brought herself under suspicion."

Lashley swept around toward the general. "We have a certain responsibility toward her."

Marriner's voice became even quieter. Parker studied his chief with a troubled face.

The general said, "What the French do with a French national on French soil is completely beyond our responsibility. I don't think it is proper for an officer from this headquarters to make any recommendations."

Lashley said sharply, "My opinion is my own responsibility. Gribemont is privileged to ignore it."

Marriner drew deeply on a new cigarette. He said nothing. Parker looked appalled.

Gribemont shook his head unbelievingly. "You are a curious person, Lashley. You regard this as a game, a contest. You have just sent six men to the scaffold and now you are being magnanimous. France cannot be magnanimous. With us it is a matter of life and death. For a man who has displayed such magnificent thrust and attack during the last six weeks, I find you incredibly sentimental."

"God damn it, yes. I am sentimental," Lashley cried. "I am sentimental about compassion and courage. I am sentimental about my integrity, about my responsibility to myself."

Gribemont said, "And the Nazis. Are you sentimental about them?"

Lashley fixed his eyes on Marriner. "Sir," he said, "you asked me what I feel about the six men who were sentenced tonight. This is what I feel." His voice became savage.

"I feel for the millions. The helpless millions, the wailing millions, the damned and the tortured millions. The dead mil-

lions. I've been to the camps. I saw and I smelled. I threw up.
I feel for them all. The French, the Jews, the Czechs."

Lashley paused. His wide, full-lipped mouth was compressed
and he breathed hard. "I hate Nazis. As for the six Nazis
who are going to be hanged—I say God damn them. God
damn them to hell!"

Lashley lowered his voice. "That too is sentiment. My
kind of sentiment. Compassion is the quality we display when
we punish the cruel and lift up the wounded. It is an important
thing to feel and to know."

He looked to the Frenchman. "I don't know who this woman
is, what she has done, or why she is here. I do know by the
very act of her coming that she has compassion and I cannot
stand by and see her crushed by a process that should be reserved for the evil and the vicious."

Gribemont shook his head slowly.

Lashley said, "Sir, may I be excused now?"

Marriner walked with him through the big hall.

"You didn't win the argument," the general said sharply.
"The Frenchman wasn't convinced. Neither was I."

Lashley grunted, "Sorry, sir." He picked up his cap and coat.
"I'm sorry I broke out."

Marriner said, "Spirited men make good soldiers, but only
in the front line. Remember that."

They stood in the open doorway, Lashley an inch or two
the taller, and they were silent. Then the general said, "How
long before your time for separation?"

"Three or four months, sir."

Marriner said, "I spoke to Frankfurt tonight. They were
very pleased about the verdict on Steigmann. Of course they
would be. God and the JAG willing, there may be an extra
grade in this for you."

"Thank you, sir."

"And, Lashley. I would advise you to forget about the
woman. Leave her to the French. They know her kind better
than we do."

"I'll—I'll try, sir."

"Good night, Lashley."

The Excelsior Hotel where Lashley had his quarters gleamed in downtown Reschweiler like a lighthouse in a dark and angry sea. Across the street the opera house was a fire-blackened ruin rising above a tide of masonry, rubble, and fallen statues. Next to it the Hotel Ritz existed only as a sign hanging askew by a single hinge. There had been no Hotel Ritz since the first thousand-bomber raid in March 1943. The store fronts along the streets were boarded up. Only the light of a small apothecary represented the business life of what was once Reschweiler's main thoroughfare.

By a miracle the Excelsior had escaped heavy damage. It was here that many officers of Eleventh Army Headquarters were billeted in single rooms. A few suites were reserved for colonels.

When Lashley went to get his key the sergeant behind the desk said, "There are two people waiting for you, sir." He jerked his chin toward the far corner of the hall.

The Czech, Slava Rodal, and his desolate little companion, Maria Romanek, sat together. Rodal was stroking her lank, tan hair and whispering in her ear. Lashley had long admired Rodal for the kindness he lavished on the girl. She was perhaps eighteen and obviously demented. Rodal had befriended her in the foreign workers' camp where they had been prisoners, and she had remained with him since liberation. Lashley thought he understood why Rodal took care of her. Although she was his link with the bitterness of the past, the girl was also his instrument of adjustment to the world of the living.

"Tell them to come up," said Lashley.

Rodal sat on Lashley's bed with Maria Romanek beside him.

"I would like very much thank you, my major," he said. Maria watched Rodal's face as he spoke. Her lips moved silently and almost imperceptibly and her pale blue eyes were wide with inquiry. She seemed to marvel at the miracle of speech.

"What for?" Lashley sat on the arm of a chair.

Rodal looked around the simple room. When his eyes focused on the bureau he saw a bust of Hitler which Lashley had picked up as a souvenir.

"This man he is Hitler?" Rodal's voice shook with indignation. As she watched him Maria's breath emerged from her mouth in little moans, like an eager dog panting.

"Rodal," Lashley said, "don't worry about him. He's dead."

The Czech tossed his chin in the air contemptuously. Maria mimicked him wonderingly. Lashley was amused.

"Now," he said, "you didn't come here to thank me. What is it?"

Rodal played with his thin lower lip. His dark cadaverous face was set in contemplation. Then he blurted, "I like know when beasts will be killed. I like from you *laissez-passer* for me and for Maria to watch beasts killed." He lowered his voice and quickened his speech. "Also I like little money."

Lashley looked up, startled.

"I don't know when the men will be executed. The date will be set by the commanding general—after the record has been reviewed. As for a pass, you must apply to the general's office. His name is Marriner. I'll write it down for you."

Lashley glanced at the narrow stooped little man out of the corner of his eye.

"As for money. What money do you refer to?"

Rodal jerked one shoulder and fingered a strand of Maria's disheveled hair.

"Money," he said. "Marks."

"How much money have you received so far during the trial?"

"A day twenty marks."

"And your room and food."

"Yes, also."

"You received that every day."

"Every day. From the *Leutnant* of the second floor in the courthouse. That is finished. The *Leutnant* said that is finished."

"You are returning to Pilsen?"

Rodal nodded vigorously. "The *Leutnant* he says he arranges it—for me and for Maria."

"Then why do you ask for money?"

Rodal squirmed in impatience with the question. "Journalist last week here give me hondred marks."

"What for?"

The Czech waved an open hand, palm outward, in front of his forehead. "I give exposition of camp of concentration." He tapped his skinny chest. "Me myself regard it. Four years." He held up four fingers.

"I understand that," said Lashley slowly. "Now you want money from me. What for?"

"Little money, my major. Two hondred marks. Like that."

Lashley leaped from the arm of the chair and stood over Rodal. "What for?" he cried. Maria crushed herself against Rodal and whimpered.

The Czech stroked the back of her head. "For live here and watch beasts killed," he said.

"I don't care why you want the money. Tell me why you came to me for it." His mouth tightened angrily over the words.

"I not worth two hondred marks?" said Rodal, sucking his teeth and looking away.

"Rodal, this is important. Listen carefully. Why do you come to me for money? Why should I give it to you?" He put his hand on the Czech's shoulder. "Now answer me!" he demanded.

Rodal looked tenderly at Maria. He rubbed her ear with his thumb. As he did so he said, "All beasts *schuldig*. That good. Good for Americans. Good for you, my major. Small money. Not big importance." He jerked his shoulder again. "Must live see beasts killed."

Lashley stepped back and leaned against the door. He pressed his hands against his temples. His voice was quiet

now. "It is very important to you to witness the executions?"
he asked deliberately.

Rodal turned to Maria and whispered in her ear. The language was of Slav derivation, Lashley thought. Maria's eyes
lighted and her mouth quivered into a smile. She squealed like
a small bitch in heat.

"Maria wants see beasts killed. Also me," said Rodal.

"Have you asked someone else for money?"

Rodal shook his head vehemently. "God'n heaven truth
no."

"Tell me, Rodal. Why did you come to me? Why didn't
you ask Colonel Macklin? Why didn't you ask the lieutenant
in the courthouse? Why me?"

"You good man, my major. Make beasts *schuldig*. You my
friend. I help you. You help me." Rodal nodded thoughtfully.

Lashley walked across the room, then back to the door,
then across and back again. Each time he turned in the constricted space he saw Rodal gazing at Maria as though there
were pictures to be seen in her empty face.

Suddenly Maria spoke in a high, cracked voice. She spoke
in German. "My hands are clean, are they not, Rodal?" She
looked at her companion appealingly and extended her hands.
Lashley had heard her ask that many times before. It was the
only thing he had ever heard her say. Once he asked Rodal
what it meant and Rodal had replied, "Nothing. She has suffered much."

Now Rodal stroked her hands and answered in German,
"Yes, Maria. They are clean. Fine and clean." Lashley saw
that her hands were filthy and her scraggy fingernails clogged
with dirt.

Lashley stopped at the door and turned abruptly to face
the Czech. "Rodal, I am not going to give you money," he
said, each word hard and distinct. "Not a single mark. Do you
understand? Not a single mark."

Rodal shrugged his shoulders and got to his feet. Maria
shuffled beside him.

Lashley opened the door and stood aside. "If you want to

remain in the American zone you will have to ask permission of the lieutenant in the courthouse. I advise you not to ask him for money."

Once more Rodal shrugged his shoulders in a quick gesture of resignation and stepped toward the door. Maria snuggled against him as though his muscles controlled her movements.

"Before you go," Lashley said, stepping into the doorway. "I want you to answer one question. Listen carefully. Why did you testify against Steigmann?"

Rodal made a spitting noise with his purple-gray lips.

"He's beast!" he cried. "Pig, murderer. German pig!" He pushed frantically at his left sleeve to show his worker's number tattooed in light blue on his forearm.

"I've seen that," said Lashley.

The Czech moved his head up and down as though reviving grim memories.

"Then it pleases you Steigmann is going to die," Lashley muttered.

Still holding back his sleeve with his right hand, Rodal worked the fingers of his left convulsively. "Killing not enough! Not enough!" he shouted. Maria whimpered in sympathy with the excitement in his voice. "Give him to me. I kill beast myself. With my hands. Me, Rodal. I tear out his eyes. His tongue. *Langsam. Langsam.*"

"I understand that too, Rodal. Now tell me this. I prosecuted him and proved him guilty. That pleases you?"

"Yes. Much."

"Then I helped *you.*"

Rodal's disconsolate voice revealed his comprehension of the trend of Lashley's questioning. "Yes, my major."

Lashley barked, "Then why do you want money from me?"

Rodal and Maria moved toward the door where Lashley stood. "It's nothing. Forget, my major. Forget, please."

The men stood face to face.

"One more thing. You swore on the Bible that you—personally—saw Steigmann in the punishment cell when Davilov had his two legs broken by the guards and then was hanged by his thumbs until he died. You swore that. You swore it in court."

Lashley grasped Rodal's lapels with both hands. The thin high sob that escaped from Maria sounded like a lyric soprano singing far away and off key.

"Tell me, Rodal. Do you swear it now?"

Rodal's eyes opened wide. The pupils were like two small-caliber muzzles aimed at Lashley's forehead.

"Yes, my major," he cried. "It's true! True! I swear now. God'n heaven I swear. Yes, my major. Yes, yes!"

Lashley's knuckles trembled against the man's chest.

"Now get out!"

Lashley threw himself on the bed and lay a few minutes forcing his tired mind to calm itself, to think. Then he reached for the phone.

"The provost marshal," he ordered. "Get me the provost marshal."

When the connection was made he said, "This is Major Lashley of the JAG office. There's a woman billeted somewhere in town. Her name is Thémis Delisle. . . . Have you got it? Thémis Delisle. . . ." He spelled it out. "Kinsella is keeping an eye on her. . . . Yes. . . . She is supposed to leave tomorrow morning on the Paris train. . . . I want you to get in touch with Kinsella or the woman or both. . . . Now listen. I want you to keep her here. Don't let her take the train tomorrow. . . . Do you hear me? . . . It's important. . . . My orders, yes. . . . I don't care how you hold her. . . . Don't let her take the train tomorrow. . . ."

III

TALL, BLOND HEDY HUMMED A PASSAGE FROM "STAR DUST" AS she came across the dining room of the Excelsior Hotel. Her apron was spotted with grease and her face shiny from frequent attendance in the steaming kitchen but her walk was supple and provocative. Patently she was happy.

Supper hour in the officers' mess was over and ordinarily Hedy would have been chagrined to see a table still occupied. Now there was something freshly eager about her as she approached the corner where Lashley and Captain Lance Nissen were deeply engaged in conversation.

Carrying a coffeepot high, like a spear carrier, she stopped at their table and simulated an aloofness which scarcely concealed the quick coquettish glance she threw at Nissen.

"Frischen Kaffee, meineherren?"

Nissen looked up at her calculatingly. *"Bitte, Liebling,"* he said.

She pursed her lips to smother a pleasurable little smile, refilled both cups, and mumbled a very professional *"Bitteschön."* Catching up the tune of "Star Dust" with discordant abandon, she turned about quickly and flounced toward the kitchen doors. Nissen looked absently at the movement of her buttocks under her thin cotton dress.

Lashley rested his elbows on the table. He drew deeply on

a cigarette and watched the steam curl from his coffee cup. After a moment he crushed his cigarette and turned his tired eyes on Nissen.

"You think I'm a fool," he said.

"I think you're an idiot," said Nissen promptly. "You have brains and no common sense. That kind of an idiot."

Lashley passed his hand over his forehead. "You don't seem to understand, Lance. Why would Rodal——"

"Never mind that. I've heard it all," Nissen interrupted. "How long ago did you phone the provost people?"

"About an hour. Just before you called."

Nissen said, "Well, phone them now and tell them to forget it. Tell them you were drunk, which in a way you were. Tell them anything."

"I'd like to sleep on it," Lashley said disconsolately.

Nissen threw up his hands. "Fine," he moaned, "just fine. Tomorrow will be a beautiful day. Marriner will hear about it, and in his nice, quiet, humane way he'll ruin you, you idiot! Call the provost people and forget about the whole thing. Take Hedy to bed. She loves me dearly but she'll sleep with you. All sex and no conscience. Just what you need."

The suggestion passed by Lashley's ears like cigarette smoke.

He said, "Marriner has no jurisdiction. He can't do anything to me. Remember, we take our orders from USFET in Frankfurt."

Nissen snorted. "Listen. You don't go kicking a general in the slats—any general. Sure, he's got no control over the War Crimes Section, but he's still in command in this area—and does he know it! He can ruin you, brother. And for what? Don't you know how lucky you are?"

"Lucky?" Lashley snapped.

Nissen stood up and leaned on the table. "Yes, lucky. Five years out of law school and you make the front pages back home. See those correspondents run like hares after the sentence? They were running with money to the bank. Money in *your* bank, brother. Know what it means? Everything! A good partnership, a county appointment, a political start, write your own ticket. Steigmann was big news. No Goering, but big enough. When do you go home?"

Lashley said, "Three or four months. But I've got a lot of accumulated leave."

Nissen slapped his hands against his thighs.

"Go home now, you nitwit," he pleaded. "Take your leave and go home. By air, even if you have to pay for it. Go home and make speeches. The Kiwanis, the Rotary, Chamber of Commerce, Ladies' Morning Music Club—set 'em up and mow 'em down. Tell 'em about the Nazi scourge and how it must be eradicated, smashed, wiped out, torn up by the roots. You're big, you're made—if you play it right. There's a tide in the affairs of Lashley and this is it. Christ, man, I'll be your campaign manager. Me. Nissen. The poor bastard who sits around here and defends 'em."

Nissen walked around the table in his excitement.

"My God, Bob, you can do it. You're an orator, a spellbinder with a conscience. That summation of yours this morning was fine, really fine. Wasn't such good law, but who cares? It was great emotional stuff. Even that pinhead of an artillery captain listened. He looked positively human for the first time——"

Lashley crashed his fist on the table. His half-filled cup fell on its side and the coffee made dark stains on the tablecloth.

"What do you mean—it wasn't such good law? What do you mean, Lance?"

Nissen stiffened where he stood. For a moment his face was covered with chagrin. He recovered quickly.

He said, "For God's sake, Bob, stop play-acting. I'm not talking about the trial. It's finished and done with. I'm talking about the future you're tossing away. And for what? That's what I want to know. For what?"

Lashley watched the spilled coffee moving slowly toward the edge of the table. When he spoke again his voice sounded old and tired.

"I wish I could tell you in a way that would make sense. Three hours ago I walked out of the courtroom feeling"—he smiled miserably—"almost as elated as a bridegroom. Since then—all I know is, now I'm not at peace with myself. Something is wrong—wrong—wrong!"

Nissen studied him as a doctor studies a feverish patient. "I know how you feel. It's not easy to realize that you've had a hand in sending six men to their death." He sat down and looked into Lashley's tired face. He said, "For just so long they're just so many legal problems. They're perjurers, liars, evaders, connivers, bastards, murderers. You're against them. You're fighting them. Then the judge says, 'Until you are dead,' and they suddenly become human beings. It does something to you where your throat meets your chest."

He looked at his watch. "What you need is a drink. Let's get over to the Winter Garden. New floor show tonight."

Lashley shook his head. "I couldn't enjoy a drink. I'm tired —desperately tired."

Nissen frowned. He said tartly, "I could enjoy a drink. That's because I'm not tired, I suppose. Hell, all I've done for six weeks is catch the bullets you fired across the courtroom."

Lashley put his hand on Nissen's arm. "I'm sorry, Lance. Your job was miserable. And tough. Much tougher than mine."

"Don't be sorry, my friend," Nissen said. "That's what is technically known as the Nissen nemesis. Runs through the family like the hound of the Baskervilles. That and alcoholism and sex. We're thoroughly depraved, we Nissens, and proud of it. Now will you come to the Winter Garden?"

"I'd like to go to sleep."

"What!" exploded Nissen. "And wrestle in the bed sheets with that dark little mind of yours? I'd rather see you in bed with a man-eating tiger. You need five or six drinks. Develop a hangover. Then you won't have to wonder why you're unhappy. You'll know."

Lashley got up. "Maybe you're right, Lance," he said.

As they walked across the deserted room there was a flutter of skirts at the swinging door leading to the kitchen. Hedy emerged. She stood morose and sensuous against the wall.

Nissen said, "Pardon me. My paramour awaits like an Indian in ambush."

When he rejoined Lashley in the lobby he muttered, "She's suffering from an overdose of spate and spermatozoa. That's been the trouble with the Germans since the fifth century." He pulled on his coat. "Let's go."

The April night had whipped itself into a biting temper. Lashley and Nissen turned up their coat collars as they came out of the overheated lobby of the Excelsior. They crossed the street and took a short cut through the driveway of the opera house toward Bahnhofstrasse.

On the rubble-filled portico of the opera house they saw a gaunt man sitting at the base of a statuette which was shrapnel-spattered beyond recognition. He was hatless and he wore an ankle-length black leather coat in the style of Wehrmacht officers. With a pocket knife he was paring cement from a salvaged brick. Beside him a wheelbarrow filled with clean bricks attested the length of his labor in the stinging cold. Nissen eyed him as they passed. He said, "Look at him. He probably commanded a battery of 88s in the war. No wonder the Germans beat history every twenty-five years."

In Bahnhofstrasse there was more life. A Red Cross club for enlisted men occupied the most important building still standing in the street, the former Palast Kino. Just beyond the lights that brightened the entrance to the club, each dark doorway of the boarded, fire-gutted shops was populated by one or two girls. They were mostly children of thirteen or fourteen, and the rouge that was lumpily applied to their cheeks made them look like Halloween pranksters rather than apprentices on the dreary night watch of the camp follower. Some, heedless of the cutting wind, wore GI shirts boldly unbuttoned to the precipitate whiteness of their child breasts. Others had skimpy neckpieces of squirrel or cat fur over polka-dotted blouses. A few, those with an expectant smile frozen on their lips that connoted a longer experience in the trade, were wrapped in short fur jackets.

As Lashley and Nissen passed they heard giggles interpolated by a whispered word, "*Offizieren.*" GIs shuffled back and forth, pausing at each doorway. Here and there they saw in the glowering dark a khaki-jacketed back tightly enclosed by two white hands. A little man with sunken cheeks appeared at Lashley's elbow and walked with them briefly, whispering, "What got to sell? *Zigaretten? Amerikanische* dollars?" He fell away in the darkness and a boy, perhaps ten, took his place. "Want girl? Pretty girl. Young. No sick." He too slunk away. As they crossed in front of the Red Cross Club two MPs saluted briskly.

They walked another block and were about to turn into Münchenerstrasse.

Suddenly the brooding night was pierced by a girlish voice screaming German epithets with the shrill hysteria of violent heartbreak. Then there was the sound of a shot, followed by a high-pitched cry that tailed off like an air-raid siren abruptly gone dead.

Harsh shouts and the patter of running feet echoed up and down the street.

When Lashley and Nissen reached the scene, two MPs were already elbowing their way through a crowd of some fifty soldiers and civilians. Whatever tragedy had occurred was centered in the doorway of a boarded-up Woolworth's store directly across the street from the Red Cross Club. Above the excited chatter in American and German, they heard a curiously childlike voice sobbing fitfully.

One of the MPs stumbled out of the crowd and ran across the street into the Red Cross Club.

The other MP shouted from the doorway, "Back! Everybody back! A man's been shot. Get back now!"

The growing crowd pushed in all directions. Newcomers racing to the scene shoved forward eagerly. Others backed away as though terrified by what they saw.

"GI! He's dyin'!"

"American!"

"The girl shot him!"

"Where's the ambulance?"

"They got 'er!"

"A GI! Christ!"

"He's covered with blood!"

"Lousy Fräulein!"

"Get a padre!"

"Back there! Give him air!"

"I saw it. She was waitin' for him with a rod!"

An ambulance and an MP jeep screamed into the street. Four military policemen, their pistols drawn, jumped out and shouldered their way through the crowd. A machine gun mounted on the back of the jeep was trained on the scene. A weapons carrier brought a new squad of military policemen. They locked arms across the doors of the Red Cross Club and closed off hundreds of hatless soldiers who flailed at them and shouted. Red Cross girls hung out of the upstairs windows of the club.

"Make way for the medics!"

A stretcher was trundled out of the ambulance by two soldiers wearing Red Cross bands on their sleeves. They cut through the crowd.

Nissen grabbed Lashley's arm. "Come on," he said. "We'll hear about it in the morning."

They darted across the street and disappeared into Münchenerstrasse.

A five-piece string band led by a white-haired German violinist was playing "Symphonie" in the little musicians' gallery overlooking the foyer bar of the Winter Garden. A sign tacked on the wall identified the place as the "official night club operated by the Eleventh Army for officers and their Allied escorts." The tune was almost lost in the confusion at the crowded bar as officers waved their chitbooks and shouted for rye, cognac, scotch, and bourbon. Three German bartenders frantically splashed drinks into tumblers and passed them to eager hands. An American sergeant sat on a stool behind the bar and read a colored comics magazine.

At one end of the bar there was still a small space. Lashley and Nissen checked their coats and moved into it.

"What'll you have?" said Nissen, running his thumbnail over the edge of a new book of chits.

"Rye, with water," said Lashley.

"Hi, Fritz! Two rye. Doubles."

The drinks came sliding along the bar. Nissen picked up a water decanter and said, "How much?"

"Half full."

"Avoiding the issue," muttered Nissen. "I take mine straight." He snapped his fingers. "I must escape from myself. Away, away. Far away. Into delirium. Into love." He sighed a mournful sigh. "Last time I escaped from myself I wound up in a black dungeon, hacking away at the wall and screaming to get out. It turned out to be my own stomach."

"You should be on the radio," said Lashley.

"And you," retorted Nissen, "should be in a padded cell. When are you going to call the provost people?"

Lashley made a slight movement with his shoulders. He lifted his glass.

"God bless you, Lance." He drank lightly.

"You." Nissen swallowed his drink in a gulp and waved his chitbook.

A steady stream of people moved through the foyer into the big room. Many of the officers had girls on their arms. They were mostly American girls, nurses and Wac officers; a few were British girls working at headquarters or with UNRRA. A sprinkling of them wore dinner dresses. The rest were in uniform.

The string band in the foyer retired and now the deep-throated harmony of saxophones came from the big room. The fourteen-piece GI dance band of the 35th Infantry had begun operations for the evening.

Nissen swallowed his second drink. "Polish that off," he said, "and let's get a table inside before it jams up."

Before the war the Winter Garden must have been the most popular cabaret in Reschweiler. The dance floor was huge, occupying almost half the floor space, and the bandstand was garishly lighted with blue, green, and white neon tubing. Two small doors on each side of the bandstand gave entrance to the artists' dressing rooms. Tables along the side walls were elevated from the dance floor and protected by chromium railings.

Nissen surveyed the room with a practiced eye and moved quickly ahead, dodging revelers like a fullback, to take possession of a small table facing the floor. By the time Lashley reached the table Nissen had snared a distracted Fräulein and was ordering a quantity of drinks.

The chatter and laughter were oppressive to Lashley. His mind felt cluttered. He had been under a strain for six weeks and the reaction was beginning. He wished devoutly he had not succumbed to Nissen's well-meaning invitation, that he were somewhere quiet so that he could sort out the day's events. He had a sense of foreboding which he could not explain. Perhaps he was only overtired. "What do you know about the Frenchwoman?" he asked suddenly.

Nissen smirked with satisfaction and set down his glass. "I knew you were thinking about her," he said. "I would have put a month's pay on it."

Lashley said, "I shouldn't ask it, Lance. It would be proper for you, professionally, not to answer. But I've got to know. I've got to make up my mind tonight—now." He found himself shouting in order to be heard above the music and the noise.

Nissen played with his glass and shook his head slowly. He said, "It's not a matter of professional ethics. The fact is, you found out more in your cross-examination than we ever knew."

"For God's sake," Lashley said, "she was your witness. Surely you talked with her before she testified."

Nissen laughed lightly. "She turned out to be *your* witness."

Lashley leaned hard across the narrow table. "This is important to me, Lance. What *was* she to Steigmann?"

The band ended a dance number and it was as though hearing had suddenly returned to their ears.

Nissen said, "This is all I know. When we were preparing

the defense Steigmann gave us a list of about a dozen people
we could call as witnesses. Nobody turned up, not even his
wife, who lives here in Reschweiler."

"I didn't know he had a wife in town."

"It isn't important," continued Nissen. "I saw her. She refused to have anything to do with him. Well, in telling us
his case history, Steigmann mentioned that he'd been transferred from Paris because, among other things, he was under
suspicion of having helped a Jew called Flanders—Pierre Flanders, I think. He didn't labor the point, just mentioned it. It
was my idea to get Flanders to testify. We put through a routine request to Western Base in Paris to see if they could locate the guy. Nothing happened. Then one fine day this gal
appears in my office and tells me she knew both Steigmann
and Flanders in Paris and is willing to spill it on the stand.
That's all I could get out of her. Whatever else she told was
under your cross-examination."

"Has she been living in Paris till now?"

"That's what I gathered."

Lashley said, "Then how did she get here? You just can't
wander into Germany. You've got to have military orders."

Nissen threw back his head and laughed. "You're naïve,
Bob. A woman can go anywhere she wants—if she's pretty
enough and there are soldiers around."

A roll of drums thundered through the room. The band
leader announced with inordinate enthusiasm, "The 'Jersey
Bounce'!" and a blast of trumpets raked the room.

Conversation was impossible. Lashley reclined in his chair
and surveyed the dance floor. The "Jersey Bounce" blended
expertly with the mood of the room. Elderly colonels swung
their awkward hips and glared with sleazy eyes into the necks
of their partners. Youthful officers lashed their girl friends
around the dance floor with an all-consuming enthusiasm.
Lashley regarded them with a touch of envy. He wished he
were capable of such violent escape from reality.

The place was now crowded to overflowing. A large table
off the dance floor was occupied by twelve roistering fliers.

One was drinking champagne from a bottle. Their raucous laughter made Lashley wince. He knew he shouldn't have come tonight. The mood was foreign to the dark turnings of his mind.

Nissen touched his hand and said, "I know what's wrong with you. By God, I know." His face broke into a grin. "It's not Steigmann and it isn't Rodal either. What's happened is that you've fallen for the woman."

Lashley looked up. His face broke into creases of sudden amusement.

"Don't laugh," said Nissen doggedly. "Crazier things have happened in a courtroom. You've been looking at her for four days. I've watched you." He slapped the table and guffawed. "You've got a yen for her."

Lashley laughed and said, "That kind of nonsense is just what I deserve for applying a serious problem to that lecherous mind of yours."

Nissen said knowingly, "I can smell the symptoms on top of this lousy rye. You're going down the line for her—all the way."

"Don't be idiotic. I'm not doing anything for her. I've got to live with myself and I don't want to see her pushed around, though she's probably just a high-class Paris whore."

Lashley felt inexplicably ashamed even as he uttered the words. If the woman had to be dismissed from his mind, this was a gauche way of dismissing her.

"I wouldn't go that far," said Nissen. "But I think she's a whore at heart. You noticed how well turned out she was."

Lashley thought of the arrow in her hat and of Ginny. The chain of association amused him. He said, "Some of the most magnificent women in the world are whores at heart."

"Anyway, I'd like to sleep with her," said Nissen bluntly. "What's wrong with Hedy?"

Nissen shook his head with mock sadness. "Hedy is a nymphomaniac," he said, and he added in an exaggerated whisper, "Nymphomaniacs are notoriously without passion."

A fanfare of trumpets cut across their conversation. The

lights dimmed. From behind the bandstand a pretty girl in a blue-sequined evening gown fluttered into the spotlight that played on a microphone. She was greeted with applause and yowls. "Now, folks," she announced with a trace of Teutonic accent, "we present for you our new show—the Winter Garden Follies." She threw up both arms and smiled widely, like a politician accepting a nomination.

The fliers at the big table howled in unison and slapped one another on the back. She threw a kiss to them and held up her hand. "We open our show with Gerta and Elena—two girls on the flying trapeze. Thank you!"

Lashley turned his eyes from the swinging torsos of Gerta and Elena.

"You think the Delisle woman is passionate?"

Nissen sighed. "I'm sure of it. She has great courage. Women with great courage have great passion."

"Unless they're nymphomaniacs," parried Lashley.

Nissen swallowed the last of his drink.

"D'accord. Unless they're nymphomaniacs."

The trapeze act of Gerta and Elena was followed by a pair of agile tumblers. They worked with an aplomb which was hardly dented by lack of applause and the not infrequent shouts of "Get the hook!" and "Where are the women?"

The tumblers were taking an enormous number of unsolicited bows in the grand manner of European artists when Nissen put down his glass with a thump of finality and said, "I'm leaving. Promised Hedy I'd drive her home."

Lashley said, "You don't like Hedy."

"I don't. It's just that I correct my perspective on life when I get in bed with her."

"Soulless bastard." Lashley was smiling now. This was the Nissen he liked, tart and wholly lacking in restraint.

"On the contrary," said Nissen. "I've got more soul than sense. When we go to bed she feels triumph. I can tell that. She's conquering me. And don't forget, I'm supposed to be conqueror."

"You sacrifice yourself," said Lashley.

"Certainly. It makes her feel powerful, both as a woman and a German. Mostly as a German. Same as these performers. Their pay isn't important. They love being dominant in a company of the conquerors. A hundred thousand women in Germany are conquering tonight as their men could never conquer on the battlefield."

For the first time in longer than he could remember, it seemed, Lashley laughed heartily. He said, "You're the only person I know who carries his study of practical psychology to the *lit d'amour*."

"I would say you're the only person in the world who doesn't," Nissen said. "Only a fine whorehouse is a *lit d'amour*, as you put it, as simple as it's purported to be."

Nissen stood up and grinned. "Well, I've got a date with Hedy," he said, then seriously, "Don't forget to make that call to the provost. Save yourself a headache in the morning."

"Sit down a minute, Lance," Lashley said.

He closed his eyes wearily for a moment and leaned back so that his chair rested on two legs. "Tell me something frankly," he said, opening his eyes and leaning forward again. "You were on the defense. You were close to the man. Does Steigmann deserve what he got today?"

As he asked the question Lashley felt suddenly foolish.

Nissen scratched the back of his head.

He said, "That's a hell of a question to ask me. As you say, I was on the defense. I'm subject to bias. Anyway, I don't see how it affects you. The verdict was Macklin's, not yours."

"Do you want to answer my question, Lance?"

Nissen stood up again. He looked toward the spotlight and blinked. A violinist was now contending with the howls and whistles.

"The six others were bloody killers," said Nissen. "Even the one who got off with life deserved to hang."

"And Steigmann?" Lashley looked sternly into his friend's eyes.

Nissen blurted, "I loathe Steigmann. He's a Nazi through and through. If you ask me, I say he's guilty as hell. But I don't think Rodal's evidence was reliable enough to convict him. Does that answer your question?"

Lashley's muttered "Yes" was drowned amid the derisive cheers that greeted the end of the violin solo. He felt the squeeze of Nissen's hand on his shoulder, then watched him dodge between tables on his way to the doors.

He summoned a waitress. "Get me a double rye—no, make it two doubles," he said.

The statuesque woman who came to the floor drew Lashley out of himself. She must have been a great attraction in other days, he thought. He could tell by the grace and confidence with which she moved into the spotlight and by the way the cacophony of drunkenness seemed to subside even before she began to perform. She was fifty at least. This much was revealed by the deep lines that ran down the sides of her mouth and the wrinkles that formed themselves like lace on her thin neck. Her hair was shimmering blond except close to her head, where it grew dark gray out of her scalp. Her narrow nose bespoke sensitivity. Her evening gown, as neatly faded as its mistress, must have been handsome ten years ago.

In a small, well-controlled voice but with considerable difficulty she began to sing in English, "Yours Is My Heart Alone." Only a piano and a violin accompanied her out of the gloom beyond the spotlight. This nostalgic music warmed Lashley and he realized how dearly he had missed its comfort during these years away from home.

She was halfway through the song when there was a flurry of commotion at the big table where the fliers sat, and amid hoarse shouts a young officer walked unsurely across the floor. He clasped a champagne bottle in his hand. When he came within the radius of the spotlight he held out the bottle to her. The audience whistled and shouted hilariously.

She continued her song as though oblivious of the disturbance. The flyer swayed there a moment, shrugged his shoulders, then let himself down on the floor directly in front of her. Bringing the bottle to his lips, he drank deeply. Six more fliers staggered from the same table, each carrying a bottle of champagne. As the crowd cheered and laughed they seated themselves Indian style in a semicircle around the singer, looking up at her with amused innocence. The woman began the second chorus although she could scarcely be heard above the clamor.

Lashley felt deep chagrin. He despised Germans because he despised the infliction of unhappiness. These youths were not German. They were Americans. He hated to see them inflict even this harmless unhappiness.

The woman finished her song and fled. The fliers yelped and slapped one another on the back as they scrambled to their table.

Lashley almost wished he had departed with Nissen. But he admitted that he wanted to be away from Nissen and what Nissen was thinking. He realized how considerate Nissen had been tonight, how deliberately glib and gross Nissen had made the conversation. Nissen knew what was plaguing him. Nissen had scarcely mentioned Rodal. That was good of Nissen. The very goodness of Nissen surged through his mind and made him angry. Nissen had wanted to ask, "Now—what do you think?" Nissen hadn't done so. That was considerate of him. It made Lashley resentful. He didn't want consideration. He wished Nissen had snarled, "Rodal was your star witness. A little mad, isn't he? And not too scrupulous." Nissen hadn't said it. Nissen was a good friend. Nissen was mocking him with his goodness. He was glad he was alone. He knew why he hadn't left with Nissen. He didn't want to be with Nissen.

He swallowed his drink—straight. And then another.

"Now, boys," announced the mistress of ceremonies, smiling impishly, "our grand finale! We bring you what you've been waiting for!" She winked. "Our Winter Garden girls in—the Hungarian dance!"

Eight girls bounded to the floor, four from each side. They wore tights and brief halters and they carried tambourines. Lashley's head thumped with the tumult of cheers and whistles.

The orchestra appeared to be making the proper motions but no music could be heard above the bedlam.

Now Lashley hated the place. The girls whirled and stamped and whirled again in their flimsy costumes. They shook their heads proudly and laughed madly, lasciviously. There was one whose halter slipped under the bounce of her full breasts. The audience screeched. She threw her head high and laughed crazily. The other girls glanced at her and laughed too. Young officers at the front tables whistled and made signs with their hands. The conquerors, Lashley thought; these were the conquerors. Not in 1946! Surely not in 1946. Surely not Americans. Yet this happened here every night. Perhaps it was an excusable release for men who had been through the fighting. He consciously checked himself, for he knew conscience had made him inordinately sensitive tonight.

He shoved back his chair and made for the door, pushing people roughly out of his way.

He plunged into the line-up before the checkroom. They thought he was drunk. He was, a little; it didn't matter. He wanted to get out, to leave behind the clamor and the coarseness, to walk away quickly from this place that was compounding the confusion in his mind.

He pushed his ticket toward the girl, grabbed his coat and cap. Now he was out. The MP at the door said, "Better put your coat on, Major. It's frosty."

It didn't matter about his coat. He was out in the sharp, quiet air. The harder it hit him, the better. He felt the cold bite against the sweat of his face. He breathed deeply.

Then he saw her. She sat in the front seat of a weapons carrier, staring ahead. The low-built truck stood at the curb directly in front of the Winter Garden. He couldn't help noticing her. Her mouth was tight. Her face chalk-white against dark fur. Kinsella sat beside her, his left arm draped over the steering wheel and his thick body twisted toward her. His overseas cap dropped low over his right eye. At the sight of Lashley framed in the lighted doorway, he made a halfhearted comedy of saluting.

"Hiya, Major."

Lashley frowned. The woman was looking at him now and he felt the cool envelopment of her gaze as he had felt it many times during the trial. Now as then it made him acutely self-aware; it focused, alerted him. He had the disturbing feeling that this mysterious and remote Thémis Delisle knew more about him than he knew about her.

Kinsella grinned sheepishly. "We're having a little argument, Miss Delisle and me. What do you know, Major, about a dame that don't drink, don't do nothing? French, too. I'm just through tellin' her it ain't natural."

It struck Lashley there was unconscious irony in the ex-policeman's comment. So much about this woman was not "natural." Her attitude to Steigmann, for one thing. He found it incredible that she loved that gross, hard man with the cruel mouth. Yet Steigmann had cried out to her before they took him away: "Farewell, dearest." The woman who could inspire that kind of devotion at such a moment was no ordinary one.

He said sharply, "What are you doing here, Kinsella?"

"Like I said. Takin' her home. Only I thought we'd get a few under our belts."

Mlle. Delisle disentangled herself from Kinsella's arm, slid out of the seat, and stepped down. Now she was standing between Lashley and the weapons carrier, facing him.

"Hey, come back here," Kinsella growled. "I'm gonna keep my eye on you tonight, lady. I told you." He tried to reach for her. "The colonel's orders. Gotta put you on a train first thing tomorrow."

Lashley looked at the woman. Her white face was empty. But her eyes seemed to plead. He heard himself saying, "All right, Kinsella. I'll take over."

The captain pushed back his cap and leaned across the empty seat. In a whisky-scented whisper he advised: "Confidentially, Major, she stinks. Doesn't give. Get yourself a Fräulein job. Sure-fire."

Lashley stepped swiftly to the curb, putting himself between the woman and Kinsella's foulness without thinking. He spoke curtly: "I'll be responsible from now on, Kinsella. That's an order."

Immediately he knew he should not have said that; he had no authority. He added swiftly: "Something's come up since I saw you this afternoon. I've got to talk to this woman."

A guffaw came from inside the weapons carrier.

"Okay, Major. Big brain you got. Heavy thinker, huh? Like your piece same as us plain Yanks." He cackled loudly. Lashley sprang forward. The twirl of the starter was caught up in the roar of the engine.

"Okay, Major. Try an' get it." The weapons carrier rolled away.

They stood on the sidewalk a few yards apart. Men and their girls emerging from the Winter Garden walked around and between them.

Lashley jerked on his coat, for suddenly he felt miserably cold. He said stiffly, not looking at the woman, "I'm sorry if the captain annoyed you. He was probably drunk. That's not the way we do our duty around here. I'll have him charged, if you like."

There was a perceptible pause. Then she said quietly, "Please do not bother. It is not important."

He nodded. "All right."

She said, "I know you can be hard. But you are not evil. It was kind of you to send that man away." Her lips trembled. "There is not much kindness in Reschweiler. Or elsewhere."

"No. Perhaps not."

He was confronted with the immediate problem of what to do with her. It was true what he had told Kinsella; he had to talk to her, though the necessity for this had come to him only when he caught sight of her. But where?

Behind them the Winter Garden's door opened and let raucous voices out into the night. He dismissed the thought of taking her in there. He could not see himself with her, facing the battery of curious eyes, overhearing the inevitable whispers: "Isn't that the woman who testified at the trial? The witness for the defense? Steigmann's woman?"

Steigmann's woman.

It was he who had fastened that label to her. His lips twisted, thinking of her gratitude for what she called his kindness.

He said, "It's true what I told Kinsella. I've learned something which affects you very closely."

He heard her catch her breath.

"Something dangerous?"

"Possibly. I can't say. But under the circumstances I think you should be informed."

"Ah, m'sieu, I was right. You are kind."

Behind them the Winter Garden's doors swung again and half a dozen of the young fliers pushed out onto the pavement. They stood, arms locked, swaying, blinking. Suddenly their befuddled gaze took in the two figures at the curb. A shout went up.

"What a dame!"

Quickly Lashley drew the woman's arm through his. They crossed the street. The fliers' hoots followed them.

"Where are you living?" Lashley asked.

"Up the hill. I live in a billet and you are not allowed to come up this late."

They walked slowly toward Bahnhofstrasse. Her hands were lost in the fur-trimmed pockets of her coat and she held her head high and straight as though she were on parade.

The street was deserted. The Red Cross Club was dark and only a few persistent German girls remained huddled in doorways. The wind whipped at Lashley's legs above the ankles. He looked toward the lights of the Excelsior Hotel and said, "That is where I live. We can talk there. Do you mind?"

She gave a slight shake of her head. "It doesn't matter. I will go with you."

They walked across the Operaplatz.

IV

A BLANKET OF PULVERIZED STONE LAY LIKE CRISP SNOW, covering the mounds of rubble that filled the Operaplatz. A moon just past the full was caught on the rim of the sky and cast a silver glint upon this grotesque design of silence after Armageddon. In the distance a single lamp gleamed beneath the marquee of the Excelsior Hotel.

Wordlessly they walked the narrow pathway between heaps of crumbled masonry which were all that remained of the baroque opera house, once Reschweiler's pride.

Thémis paused before an undamaged granite column which supported a bust of Schumann. The moon's dimness gave both the calm marble features and her uplifted face the same pale radiance, so that she looked like a new statue in that impoverished park. It made Lashley start to see how beautiful she was.

In the courtroom, during the dragging hours of Steigmann's trial, he had been aware—at times to the point of exasperation—of how incongruous her appearance was in that stark setting. Her self-possessed aloofness was an affront. He thought sardonically how the staggering contrast between this woman and other witnesses like Rodal and the vacant-eyed Maria must have weighed heavily against the defendant.

But now her face was invested with a gravity which was

impersonal and remote. It gave her beauty a timeless quality. It made her strangely a part of this shattered, lifeless scene. Here the mystery that enveloped her was no longer an affront, but her proper raiment. She was woman, as the serene, faintly smiling Schumann was music.

"Do you know music?" she asked suddenly.

"I like music," he replied. "I don't know it."

She turned her head to look at him.

She said, "If you do not know the music of Schumann and Wagner and Richard Strauss, you cannot know the Germans."

Her precise schoolroom English was softened by the low, throaty quality in her voice. It was a different voice, he noticed, from the lifeless one in which she had given her monosyllabic replies to his questions on the witness stand. That voice had been drained not only of emotion but seemingly of all capacity for emotion. This had timbre and made him uncomfortably aware of certain qualities he did not want to believe she possessed. He had been trying for days to convince himself she was calculating, brittle, the kind of woman a man like Steigmann could possess.

Well, any number and all classes of Frenchwomen had crept into the arms of the German conquerors. This woman would not be alone in that. He could understand why this was so, ugly and dishonorable as it seemed to be. Ten months spent in the wake of war had opened his eyes to a lot of things.

He muttered, "Damn their music. Damn them."

As though she did not hear, she turned again to examine Schumann's face. She observed dispassionately, "As a race Germans have never ceased to be children. They are energetic, vicious, sometimes beautiful, always illogical. Words have no meaning when they are used to describe Germans. Music offers better clues."

Her words brought him smartly to attention, driving in upon him facts about her that he felt suddenly he had been in danger of forgetting. He said, and his voice had a cutting edge, "There are words to describe evil—good short strong words. Only people prefer not to hear them. I hate Germans.

I know why I hate them. Their music can teach me nothing about them I don't know."

Deliberately he moved on away from the column and its imperturbable, ironic survivor. She moved at his side, but a step behind him. He heard her voice, but now it was bitter. "You know a great deal about hate, Major. Hate is cheap and easy today. It is the only thing of which the world has a surplus."

He said, "We can't stand here talking. What I have to say to you I must say privately and quickly."

"Then let us go to your place. There is no other," she said.

The sergeant behind the desk smirked and turned away as they walked through the dim empty foyer. A night watchman, his eyes filled with the blindness of broken sleep, ran the elevator to the fourth floor.

It was a small room and its original none too lavish furnishings had been depleted to equip other apartments in the overcrowded hotel. When Lashley flicked on the electric light in the ceiling bulb the room's unredeemed meagerness struck him more forcibly than ever before.

There was but one chair, a stiff straight one in front of the window. He motioned Thémis to seat herself less uncomfortably on the bed. She sat close to the head of it and rested her back against the post. The walk in the cold had brought color to her cheeks. Her lips needed fresh rouge. Suddenly he found himself wondering if Kinsella had kissed her.

"What is it you have to tell me?" she asked.

Standing in the middle of the room, he told her bluntly what Gribemont had said. "The order has been given to arrest you when your train reaches the French zone at Mainz."

She took it silently, without flinching.

"I expected no less," she said without emotion.

"You knew it would happen?"

She murmured as if to herself, "It doesn't matter——"

"Then you will submit?"

She breathed deeply and stretched her shoulders on the pillow.

"Without regret," she said. "One does what one has to do."

Lashley shoved his hands in his pockets and paced slowly between the bed and the door. He was remembering the bitter look on Gribemont's face in the general's house that evening. It was not a look he liked to remember.

Presently she said with great calmness, "You brought me here to tell me this? Why?"

That was a question he had been asking himself ever since he had dismissed Kinsella.

"I have no intention of inquiring into your reasons for coming to Steigmann's defense," he said stiffly. "Your relationship with him doesn't concern me. Your coming did him no good, but I understand you came on your own initiative. Well, the trial is over. My case is won. Steigmann has been proved guilty and he will die. That is justice. But I feel a certain responsibility toward you, at least to the point of letting you know the danger that confronts you."

"Danger?" Her lips had a look of disdain. "I am no longer afraid of danger."

"Perhaps not," he said stolidly. "But I believe I should warn you. You can't leave Reschweiler now."

She said: "You do not know the French as I do. More than anything else, more than justice, more even than liberty, they love a spectacle. You will not deny them. They will have me —and their spectacle."

It was as though she welcomed the thought of it. As if she found a bitter satisfaction in the prospect.

He said abruptly, "I'm not going to let the French have you —not now."

"But the order has been given—so your Captain Kinsella told me—that I must leave Reschweiler in the morning."

He said slowly, not looking at her, "That order has been canceled."

"Who canceled it?"

"I did."

Her eyes probed his. "May I ask why, m'sieu?"

Without reply, and with elaborate courtesy, he took a packet of cigarettes from his pocket and offered it to her. She drew one out. He snapped his lighter and held the flame to the cigarette between her lips.

Her eyes looked directly into his. She said, "You have just said the case is closed. Why do you wish me to remain in Reschweiler?"

Pondering his answer, he slowly lighted his own cigarette. He hadn't told quite the whole truth when he said he didn't care what she had been to Steigmann; he was curious.

"You've been out in the cold," he said, "and this room isn't warm. Would you like a drink?"

"Thank you. I would enjoy it, if you please."

He said, "I have American whisky and armagnac. Not a very good armagnac, I'm afraid."

She shook her head slightly is if it did not matter.

"I prefer the armagnac. Anything to take the stench of your Captain Kinsella out of my nostrils."

He felt her eyes follow him as he went to the closet. When he turned around with the bottle in his hand she was looking at him with surprising tenderness.

He placed a glass of the amber-brown liquor on the bed table beside her. She unbuttoned the fur collar of her coat and laid it back against the flat of her shoulders.

"Won't you take off your coat?" he said. "Now that you're here, I'd like to talk to you."

She bowed her head. It seemed to him mockingly ceremonious. He wasn't sure whether he saw her briefly smile or not. She walked to the closet carefully, draped her coat on a hanger, and placed her hat on the upper shelf among the bottles. The implications were not lost on him.

Her green wool dress was plain but finely tailored. The upper half was styled as a doublet and buttoned along the length of her left shoulder. It must have cost a great many francs, Lashley thought, because its simplicity gave verve to her slender body and its severe modesty subtly enhanced the curve of her breasts and the long line from armpit to knee. She returned to her place at the head of the bed.

"Will you pardon me, m'sieu?" she said, drawing a compact from her purse. She looked at herself in its tiny mirror and her mouth gestured distaste. He watched her as she applied lip rouge.

Robert Lashley had always been slightly in awe of women. Unfortunately he had had no sisters and his mother, who had been an invalid most of her life, was a saint rather than a woman. When he was ten she had tried primly to explain to him the differences between the sexes and the eternal verities of begetting children. The conversation had bogged down in the middle and had never been resumed. Two months later Lashley found out all about it from one of his young friends, replete with gestures and dirty words. He had been shocked and disgusted.

As he studied Thémis now he thought of the first time he had put those ugly words to the test. It was during his sophomore year in college. He'd been going around with a leggy blonde from Muncie, Indiana. Her name was Gloria and she was an expert in the art of necking. One night he had taken her dancing at the Deschler; he had his roommate's car. On the way home he had said, "Let's," and she had said, "Why not?"

They had driven out of Columbus and parked in a deserted lane. Gloria had been willing, but she'd been inexperienced. His eyes came back to Thémis and he wondered what she would be like making love. Not like Gloria certainly. Not like any of the American girls he'd known. He couldn't imagine her engaging in anything so halfway as necking. With her, he thought, it would be all or nothing at all.

There was something provocative and explosive about her. And an air of maturity.

In the harsh light he saw that her features weren't entirely perfect. Her nose was too large for the strict standards of beauty. But it suited the generous fullness of her lower lip and the height of her cheekbones. It was a face that revealed courage, daring. Her light brown hair was parted deep on one side and flowed in a single wave almost to her shoulders.

She took a final, impersonal look in her mirror, then snapped the compact shut and dropped it in her purse.

"Must we have this searchlight?" she said, pointing to the ceiling bulb. "It does not compliment your tired face. Nor mine."

Lashley lighted the lamp on the bed table and turned off the ceiling light. The room became suddenly warmer, more intimate.

"And now, m'sieu," she said, lifting her glass, "I drink to the tranquillity of your heart."

Lashley gestured with his glass and barely wet the inside of his mouth. He had not been prepared for this new side of her nature. He did his best to meet it.

"That's a graceful toast," he said. "I like it."

She was unsmiling, but not grave.

"I meant it," she said.

He countered, "What makes you think my heart is not tranquil?"

"I did not say that. I merely wished for the continued tranquillity of your heart. Is it not proper?"

He said, "Not only proper and lovely, but also a trifle pointed."

"I intended no hidden meanings," she said. "But this is your day of triumph."

Her courteous tone was a bitter mockery of her words. He felt himself flush.

"I had an unpleasant duty to do. It is done and I am glad. But not triumphant."

"Ah!" She regarded him over the rim of her glass. Her eyes were somber, not mocking. "You are sensitive to what happened today. I knew it when I saw you coming out of the cabaret. You were not happy."

"Let's not overestimate my sensitivity," Lashley said, annoyed that she had understood him so clearly; "this is not the first time I've acted in a criminal case. It's an ugly duty, but not unclean. I am not ashamed to say I'm sensitive to the responsibility of sending six men to execution. But don't believe for a moment that I regret what I have done, or feel sorry for any one of them."

He thought, If she loves Steigmann, that will hurt her. It surprised him to discover that he hoped she would be hurt.

It was time to end this fencing. He came to the edge of the bed and looked directly down at her. "Why did you come to Reschweiler?" he said.

She looked up at him, unmoved by this direct approach.

"A little while ago you spoke of your duty. Obviously it is a word you understand. I had a duty to perform here that was important to me."

He pressed his question. "Why? You knew you couldn't save him."

There was a touch of steel in her voice as she replied, "Some things only the heart finds logical. I cannot tell you why I came to Reschweiler. I can only say that I am content with what I have done."

"You're in love with Steigmann."

She smiled. "That is what you tried to show in court, is it not? It was amusing—like a fifteen-franc *roman policier*."

"It's true."

She shook her head ever so little. Her eyes were inscrutable.

"Whatever you say," she murmured. "What does it matter now? You have said the case is closed."

He saw that he was no nearer the truth of her than he had been in the courtroom. That truth continued to elude him. The mystery that surrounded this woman, which fascinated and yet tormented him, was like a wall between them.

He sat down on the bed beside her. She did not move.

"Did you bring me here to ask me that question?" she said.

"Yes. I felt I wanted to talk with you."

"That is better," she murmured.

"But it has nothing to do with the trial. Or with Steigmann," he said quickly. "It has to do with you."

"You wanted to help me?"

He felt her hand on his. Her fingers were light and cool and strangely exciting. Suddenly nothing was so important as the nearness of her.

"What more do you want?" She said it softly, as if it had nothing to do with what had gone before.

All at once he knew what he wanted. What he had wanted all along, though the realization of his demand only just now occurred to him.

Covertly watching her in the courtroom, his mind had been challenged by her mystery. His body too. He knew it now. Nissen had suspected it long before he had. What was it Nissen had said? "You've got a yen for the girl." That was one of Nissen's typical exaggerations, but now he knew he had been resisting her appeal all the hours and the days he had studied her as she sat on the front bench. Only now, in his suddenly acquired awareness, was he able to recognize his feeling for what it was—desire for her.

He had been drawn to women before. But not like this. This woman had challenge and she had beauty. She harbored a secret and she mocked him with it. The rebellion that had been growing in his mind merged now with the urges storming through his body. He leaned over, bent down with a quick aggressive movement, and kissed her.

He didn't care now about the bond which linked her with Steigmann. The past was torn away like the leaves of a calendar, leaving only the present moment. And that moment was filled with his urgent need of her.

"Thémis," he said, using her name for the first time, "I can understand why Steigmann——"

"Let's forget about Steigmann," she said, moving so that her head lay on the pillow and her body was nearer the wall.

She touched his hand beside hers on the bed. "He's not important now."

He swung his legs up from the floor and lay beside her. In the soft lamplight he saw the quick rise and fall of her breasts and the darkening of her eyes.

His right arm went under her shoulders and his left hand rested against the buckle at her waist. For a moment he tried desperately to remain master of the situation, to remember who they were in Reschweiler: the American prosecutor, the French witness. But alone with her in this stark little room, all he could be aware of was that he was a man and she a woman.

She was smiling now, whether in triumph or in tenderness he didn't know. Then with a quick graceful movement she turned toward him. He reached over and drew her close, feeling his whole body strain to hold her closer. He was aware of her pliability, of her knees, her thighs, her breasts, all yielding to his urgency.

"The lamp," she whispered against his mouth.

He swung the pillow out from under their heads and aimed it at the table. There was the sound of breaking glass and then darkness.

There was no longer a world outside—no longer a tomorrow or a yesterday—he was lost in a rising tumult such as he had never known. And yet in the tumult there was an acute awareness, a seeking and then a finding of which he was a part and not a part.

He had been asleep and in his dreams the face of Steigmann kept reappearing, alternately glaring at him and laughing. When he awoke Thémis was still beside him. He could feel the warmth of her there in the darkness, guessed that she was awake too.

"Thémis," he asked, "did you imagine this would happen when you came up here?"

"My poor silly American—I didn't have to imagine it, I knew it."

He realized that she had turned her face toward him and he could feel the force of her eyes even though the dark hid them. She seemed remote once more, as mysterious and unapproachable as she had been before.

"I knew it, my dear," she repeated and added slowly, "as surely as I knew the verdict."

Her words brought him back to reality. He remembered now his dream and the taunting face of Steigmann.

"Are you reminding me," he said with some bitterness, "that you were once Steigmann's woman?"

She didn't answer him, but he could feel her moving away from him in the dark. Now she was on her feet, a white blur against the deeper gloom.

"Thémis," he demanded, "tell me what this man is to you."

Still no answer, but instead the soft rustle of clothing quickly drawn on, the scuff of high heels as she stepped into her shoes. She came close to the edge of the bed, so close that he could have reached out and held her. Some instinct warned him not to try it. That she had given herself voluntarily to Steigmann's defense did not mean that she would readily give up her secret. Moreover, if he forced it from her now, the release and the fulfillment he had known with her would end swiftly in disillusion.

She moved away from the reach of his arm. He heard the click of a latch, then the tiny rattle of one wire coat hanger against another, telling him she was taking her coat and hat from the closet.

"Thémis," he said, "don't leave without a word."

"But I leave you happy." She spoke from across the room. "You have reached the end of your great day."

"It is you who have given me happiness," he said, and meant it.

Her answer was almost defiant. "Enjoy your triumph. The prosecution is now perfect. You have won everything. You have had your German and possessed *his woman.*"

The door into the hall opened. He saw her briefly silhouetted against the light. Then the snap lock clicked and she was gone. The unmistakable sound of sobbing reached him from outside the door, followed by the fast receding tap of high heels.

TUESDAY

V

THE BROWN ENVELOPE WAS ADDRESSED TO "MAJOR RM LASH-ley, AA–JAG, Courthouse Building," and across the top in inch-high letters it was rubber-stamped: RESTRICTED.

Lashley turned the envelope loosely in his fingers. He swiveled his chair to face a wide window which looked out of his office in the courthouse. It had become habit for him to turn toward the window when he was thinking hard, for his office was narrow and exceedingly drab. Its furnishings consisted of a steel desk, a filing cabinet, and a visitor's chair, and its bare walls were covered with stained plaster. But the view from the window gave him a sense of space and height.

This Tuesday was gray and the hills beyond the river were ghostly beneath a thin mist. On the Auer a tug billowed black smoke from its funnel but the three coal barges it was pulling seemed to be making no headway. Rising from the river, the broken city was lifeless. Not a smokestack breathed. Across the street a queue of women stood bent and immobile before the door of a sausage shop. Even the children who clung to their mothers' sides were frozen like trained dogs in an attitude of endless patience.

Lashley glanced again at the envelope that was turning between his nervous finger tips.

"So you did it, after all," said Nissen.

The blond captain, his arms akimbo, stood in the doorway

with the gratified air of a man who is about to collect a friendly bet.

Lashley turned quickly around.

"Did what?"

Nissen said, "Kept the Delisle woman in town."

"How do you know?"

The captain smiled elaborately. "For two good reasons, the foremost of which you now hold in your hands. Look at it."

Lashley saw the neat lettering on the flap of the envelope. "Commanding General, Eleventh Army."

"When did it arrive?" he asked.

"About a quarter past nine, by courier," said Nissen. "Been waiting ever since for you to come in. What the hell time did you leave the Winter Garden?"

Lashley gestured with the envelope.

"This may have nothing to do with the Delisle matter."

"You're hoping," said Nissen grimly.

"If it came at a quarter past nine, it must have been written yesterday."

"You don't know Marriner," said Nissen. "He's one general who gives the taxpayers a break. He's up at six-thirty and at his desk at eight. By nine o'clock he knows how many Fräuleins were sneaked into officers' quarters last night and at ten he can tell you which of 'em is pregnant. Come on, open the damned thing."

Lashley put his finger under the flap and ripped open the envelope. He paused.

"What's the other reason? You said you had two."

Nissen said, "The provost marshal called."

Lashley frowned in real anxiety.

"What did he say?"

"Just about everything I was afraid of. He went through the train before it pulled out this morning, found the girl, and returned her to her billet—as per your orders, you silly idiot."

Lashley's lips tightened. It was as if he had been waiting for a blow to fall, and now it had fallen. The thought of Thémis had been constant in his mind since she had left him in the night. He had hoped she would not try to leave Reschweiler and now this was her answer.

His eye fell on two cables that lay unfolded on his desk.

> HEARTFELT CONGRATULATIONS STOP
> YOUR PICTURE ALL PAPERS STOP MUCH
> LOVE   GINNY

> YOU'VE DONE A FINE JOB AM VERY
> PROUD   FATHER

He read them, but his mind refused to take any meaning from them.

"Come on, Bob," urged Nissen. "What's the old man say?"

Lashley unfolded the letter and read it carefully.

From: Gen J. Marriner
To: Maj RM Lashley, AA-JAG
Subject: Prosecution of German civilian

1. At approximately 2030 hours last night a German civilian, one Erika Wagner, accosted a soldier of the U. S. Army, Pfc. Clay Hockland M087936, in the vicinity of Red Cross Club on Bahnhofstrasse in Reschweiler and attacked him with a .32 Mergler pistol which she apparently carried in her possession.
2. Pfc. Hockland has been admitted to 135th Station Hospital, Reschweiler, where he lies dangerously wounded. Civilian Wagner is now being detained in Headquarters Stockade, 11th Army, Reschweiler.
3. Information now available indicates that Pfc. Hockland was friendly with Civilian Wagner over a period of months.
4. It is desirable that necessary action be taken in this **case** with utmost dispatch due to current unrest and lawlessness among German civilians of the 11th Army area. (See Public Safety section, G-5 report to Chief of Staff, restricted file, 6th inst.) It is also desirable that lengthy proceedings be avoided in this case due to unfavorable publicity accruing to U. S. Army of Occupation in stateside newspapers.
5. The Commanding General, 11th Army, has specifically requested the Judge Advocate General that you be assigned to the prosecution

of Civilian Wagner. Confirming orders from the JAG will doubt-
less arrive promptly. Meanwhile it is directed that you proceed
with the investigation at once.

6. For your immediate attention and necessary action.

J. Marriner
Commanding General, 11th Army

Lashley tossed the letter to Nissen.

Clever, that Marriner, Lashley thought, quiet and clever.
When troops show signs of mutiny the procedure is to throw
them right back into battle. Make them fight hard and maybe
they'll forget their squawks. That was the textbook procedure,
neatly packaged, nicely delivered. Marriner was using it on
him now.

Nissen whistled. "This must be the shooting we saw last
night."

"I wish that were all," murmured Lashley.

"Well, get going; get over to the hospital," said the captain.
"Don't get caught off base on this one. This is an order."

The 135th Station Hospital occupied what was left of the
Reschweiler civic library. One wing of the medieval Gothic
structure had cascaded away under the impact of a blockbuster
and from its naked wall jutted three rounded huts of corrugated
steel which provided wards for the hospital. The effect assailed
Lashley's eyes. It was like the hind end of a dachshund grafted
to the head and chest of a shaggy St. Bernard. American effi-
ciency and resourcefulness took precedence over beauty, he
thought. The French would have done it differently. They
would have preserved the ruin for its poignant beauty and sent
their wounded to languish in the dust and drabness of a factory
building.

He parked his jeep beside a row of ambulances.

The sweet, sickly odor of ether came to him as he approached
a nurse sitting at a desk in the reception room. This must have
been the librarian's office, for old manuscripts yellowing in
glass cases hung along the oak paneling.

"I want to see Pfc. Hockland," he said.

She sawed vigorously at her thumbnail with a long nail file.

"Enlisted men two to four weekdays, three to six Sundays," she parroted.

Lashley said, "This is official business."

She suspended the file in the air and looked up. She was a tall girl with a long, narrow face, and she wore very careful make-up which had the effect of robbing her of all expression. Her khaki shirt was open two buttons at the neck.

"Oh," she said. "What's the name?"

"Mine or his?" Lashley said absently.

She smiled archly.

"Don't be silly, Major. His, of course."

"Pfc. Hockland. Clay Hockland."

She leaned across the desk and flipped the crimson-tipped fingers of one hand through a card file, carefully holding her other hand against the open neck of her blouse. Lashley wondered irritably why she didn't button up properly and be done with it.

"Hockland . . . Hockland," she mumbled. "Hockland. Ward 3."

She shot a sidewise glance upward to catch Lashley's eye. She said: "Ward 3, straight along the hall through the fire door. Turn right."

As Lashley turned sharply away she shrugged and returned to her filing.

There were about thirty beds backed against the walls on both sides of the ward. From a table radio near the door Crosby's voice floated softly into the room. Most of the men in the beds slept. A few leaned on one elbow and read. One sat on the side of the bed, his legs dangling, and regarded the floor morosely. It was hot in the room. Lashley unbuttoned his coat.

He walked to the nearest patient who was sitting up.

"Where's the nurse?" he said.

The soldier jerked his thumb back of him.

"Behind the screen. Must be somebody dyin', poor bastard."

They always put up a screen when somebody's dyin'. Makes yuh feel lousy. Why'n't they take 'em someplace else?"

Lashley saw the screen that closed off a corner at the far end of the ward. He tiptoed toward it.

A temperature chart was hooked on the outside of the screen. On the top line was written "Pfc. Clay Hockland MO87936."

He rapped lightly on the wood of the screen.

A nurse looked inquiringly from behind it. She saw the bronze medallion on his epaulette and she came out noiselessly. She was a handsome woman, prematurely white. The grave look on her efficient face caused Lashley to wonder if he had arrived in time.

He whispered, "I'm from the JAG office."

She raised a finger to her lips and murmured, "Better talk to Captain Bossin."

The doctor came out. He was short, slight, and spectacled. He wore a white surgeon's gown over his uniform. He took Lashley by the arm and walked him down between the beds.

When they had gone a dozen paces the doctor said, "You're JAG."

Lashley nodded.

"Fräulein trouble, I hear," said the doctor.

"Looks like it," said Lashley. "How is the man?"

"Man." The doctor laughed shortly. "He's a boy, a kid, nineteen. He should be buying sodas for the girl next door, playing basketball Saturday nights. I'll bet he comes from a town called Pleasantville. In Iowa or Kansas. That kind of a kid."

He dug his hands deep in his pants pockets. "What the hell connection has he got with the grand passion and a bullet in his chest?"

"How is he?" said Lashley.

The doctor played with the thongs on his stethoscope.

"This one is up to God," he said. "The bullet smashed his right clavicle and deviated into his lung. We can't touch it yet.

It's imbedded in the tissue near his fourth dorsal vertebra. All we can do is wait. We'll know more tomorrow."

"Can he talk?" Lashley asked.

"How important is it?"

"Depends whether he's going to live or die. If he's going to live, I can get the information another time."

The doctor said, "I'll give you five minutes. Better get your ear down so he can whisper. And try not to get him excited."

They edged behind the screen. The nurse was leaning over the boy, wiping perspiration from his eyes and forehead. He seemed unable to move.

When she turned away from the bed Lashley looked at the boy's face. As the doctor had said, he was just a high school kid. His tawny hair stood up straight from his scalp like fine wire. His eyes were clear and blue, and beneath the pallor of shock his skin was firm and bronzed. One arm lay on top of the bed sheet. It was a long arm, thin and muscular, the kind of arm that can make the long throw from the outfield. Pfc. Hockland himself was straight out of a Norman Rockwell picture. Lashley bent over him.

"How are you feeling, son?"

The boy swallowed hard and twisted his mouth into something resembling a smile.

"Okay, sir," he murmured. "Guess I'm okay."

"Does it hurt you to talk?"

"I'm all right."

"Do you think you can tell me what happened last night?"

The boy's eyes shifted from side to side.

"Nothing much—to tell. I was edgin' along—on the other side of the street. I figured she'd be watching for me. Didn't want to see her——" He stopped abruptly and eyed Lashley's insignia. "You're not from the MPs, eh, Major?"

Lashley shook his head.

The boy licked his dry lips.

"Good, Major. Don't want—get Erika in a jam. Poor kid. It's tough enough on her—way it is."

"Tell me, Hockland. Was she your girl?"

Lashley couldn't tell whether it was a tear or perspiration that showed for an instant just below one of the boy's eyes. The nurse wiped it away.

The boy said, "Could she go—a minute?" His eyes indicated the nurse.

Lashley looked meaningly at the white-haired woman. She caught his signal and tiptoed out.

"Can't talk in front of—ladies," Hockland mumbled.

He looked away from Lashley toward the high, tiny window without seeing it.

He said, "She was the first girl I ever had——" He coughed weakly. "I mean—that way. You know. Erika really loved me —gosh, yes. Not like the girl back home—it's sorta different— hard to explain. Erika's strictly an occupation job—if you know what I mean, sir——"

He paused. His breath came short and fast. Lashley looked anxiously toward the doctor. Bossin frowned.

"Sir——" the boy whispered.

"Yes, Hockland."

The boy moved his head painfully from side to side.

"Sir, would you see please—she doesn't get into a jam? I'm awfully sorry about Erika."

Lashley looked into the boy's face.

"I might be able to do it, Hockland, if you tell me why you don't want the girl to get into a jam."

"Well, sir——" the boy mumbled. He could scarcely be heard. "I've been thinking most—the night. Erika's German— and all that—with the war and all, she never had a break. But her people aren't much—and I guess she's like any other girl— she's got feelings. Not her fault—it had to be this way."

Lashley nodded. "I'll do my best, Hockland."

He let the boy rest a few moments. Then he said, "Do you feel as though you can answer one more question? Just a short one?"

The boy nodded.

"You wanted to avoid her last night. Will you tell me why?"

The boy bit his lips.

"Like this, sir——" His voice was muffled in his mouth. "I was going home in—couple of days. I told her. She cried—terrible. Said she's carrying my baby. Maybe so. She wanted —to go with me. I couldn't make her see——"

His eyes rolled feverishly.

The doctor tapped Lashley on the shoulder.

"That's enough for now," he said.

Lashley turned to go.

"Sir——" the boy whispered.

"Yes, Hockland."

"One thing—sir." Tears were rolling from his eyes now. "Tell them to say—it was—accident. My mother—father—wouldn't understand. You know—sir—how it is back home—not like this. Folks there don't know——"

Lashley felt a lump in his throat.

"All right, son. You'd better rest now. I'll see you tomorrow."

Lashley and the doctor walked through the ward together.

Bossin said, "The kid is right. The folks back home don't understand. What do you think'll happen when the War Department notifies his parents? I'll tell you. The father will say, 'God damn that German bitch,' and in five minutes he'll have his congressman on the phone screaming at the government to hang her. Am I right, Major?"

Lashley said, "I suppose you are."

"God damn right, I am. But the boy—he knows better. You heard what he said. 'Don't let Erika get in a jam.' The kid's grown up. He's touched life. He knows everything isn't right or wrong, take it or leave it, black or white. Nothing is black or white. It's something in between. It's the grays, Major. The grays are important. If you know your grays, you understand life. Most people don't."

They reached the door of the ward. Crosby was singing "April Showers" on the radio.

Lashley said, "Thanks, Doctor, I'll be in tomorrow."

"What happens now?" Bossin asked.

"I don't know. I'm going to see the girl." He looked at the doctor quizzically. "As you say, this one is up to God."

It was nearly noon when Lashley piloted his jeep into the forecourt of the old Reschweiler central police station. A wooden sign, "Headquarters Stockade," was suspended on wires from the beaks of two Reich eagles that glowered over the main entrance.

In a low rotunda musty with age an MP sergeant sat at a table. He was fiddling with a Luger. His feet straddled a radiator and his chin rested against his chest.

Lashley came up to the table quickly. He said, "I'm from the JAG office."

The sergeant's eyes reached only as high as the hem of Lashley's short officer's coat before he unscrambled himself and came to attention.

"Yessir," he said.

"You've got a girl here—Wagner."

The sergeant winked coarsely.

"You betcha we have, Major," he said, "and I'm prayin' for someone to come and take her off our hands."

Lashley said, "What's wrong? Is she trouble?"

"Well, it's this way, sir. This here is a stockade—and me, I'm a sergeant. I ain't Mr. Ant'ony. All mornin' this girl is cryin' her head off. Me, what can I do? Can't even speak kraut. And another thing, Major. She got a belly like the Graf Zeppelin. Any minute I feel I'm gonna go pagin' Dr. Kildare like crazy. Look, Major, the JAG or somebody has gotta take 'er off our hands."

"I'll do my best, Sergeant. Where are you keeping her?"

The sergeant jerked his thumb in a wide sweep toward the staircase.

"Upstairs, sir. Turn left at the head of the stairs, then double back—never mind, sir. I'll show you."

They climbed a narrow staircase warped with age and usage.

"Seems like a guy can't never get away from some things,"

the sergeant remarked confidentially. "Take me. I'm doin' all right, drivin' a cab, livin' with my old man in the Bronx. Not a care in the world. Not married. See? One day there's a woman gets in my cab. On the Grand Concourse it was. Says she wants to go to Beth-El Hospital. You a New Yorker, Major?"

"I'm from Pennsylvania—Erie," Lashley said.

"From Erie, huh! Well, this hospital this dame picked out is down near the East River Highway. A helluva way from the Grand Concourse. I seen how she was pregnant and I didn't want nuttin' to happen in my cab. Not me. I'm a bachelor, see? So I drove kinda easy. Moochin' along.

"Just below Ninety-sixth she taps on the glass and says, 'You'll have to hurry up. I ain't got much time.' So I step on the gas. A couple more blocks and she starts in groanin' and screechin'. I shoot up to fifty. 'We'll make it, lady,' I says. 'Just you hold on.' The sweat is comin' out all over me, Major.

"Pretty soon the screeches get worse. I take a look over my shoulder. She's down in the bottom of the cab. I don't go for no hospital. I head for the nearest exit and the first cop. Him and me deliver that baby at Forty-eighth Street. Christ!"

He paused, reliving it. Lashley grinned.

"When the ambulance come and took her away, do you know what happened? I get home and I see I'm drafted. Me, I'm glad. The only guy on Governors Island who's glad.

"And now that damn stork's trailing me again. There just ain't no gettin' away from some things, is there?"

They proceeded along a dark, airless passage.

"Is she alone up here?" said Lashley.

"No, sir," the sergeant said promptly. "We managed to borrow a Wac to help out. A real good annie. No Dorot'y Lamour, mind yuh, but she is got a heart as big as 'er—well, anyway, sir, she's okay. An' she chews kraut like it was candy."

They stopped at a door at the far end of the hall. The sergeant knocked.

There was the muffled sound of feet. The door opened, revealing a girl in Wac uniform. Her plump, plain, but kindly face wore a scowl for the sergeant.

"Be quiet, you," she hissed. Then she caught sight of Lashley and she added hastily, "Excuse me, sir. I've just got her off to sleep."

Lashley entered the room. On an army cot Erika Wagner lay on her back. Her eyes were closed and she was breathing heavily.

Once she might have been pretty in a pert, snub-nosed fashion. But now the sockets of her eyes were swollen, her cheeks were bleary with dirt and tearstains, and her matted black hair fell stiffly across her ears.

She had the physique of an emaciated child, and her pregnancy protruded from her like a starvation bloat. The bones of her narrow shoulders showed through her faded print dress. Her chest was flat as a boy's, but below it the abdomen was enormous. She looked like a caricature of the succession of life, Lashley thought.

He beckoned the Wac to step out of the room with him.

In the hall he asked, "Has she been asleep long?"

"Not ten minutes, sir. Ever since I came over here she's had hysterics. I thought I'd never get her quieted down."

"What did she tell you about last night?"

The Wac's face grew troubled.

"I didn't take any notes or anything like that," she finally said. "I'm not used to this kind of work. They sent for me this morning because I speak the language. You see, my mother was from Germany. I've never been in a jail before. My regular job is checking on the kitchen help at headquarters. But that girl's nothing but a kid, sir. Breaks your heart——"

Lashley held up his hand.

"I know. Now tell me, did she say she shot the soldier?"

The Wac clasped and unclasped her hands.

"Well, yes and no. All the time she keeps moaning—like, 'What did I do? What did I do?' Things like that. And then she cries and says, 'If he dies I want to die. And if he lives I want to go with him wherever he goes. Because I love him so much.' All in German, of course."

She paused. Then she added in an embarrassed way: "She's awful pregnant."

"How old is she?"

"In her papers it says she's nineteen."

"Did she say anything about her family?" Lashley asked.

"Oh, didn't they tell you? Her people were here this morning. I talked to them."

"What did you think of them?"

The Wac shook her head. "They didn't say much," she said. "It's like they were numb. If a house fell on them they couldn't care less. Her father's a postman, but he hasn't worked for over a year. And they got four other kids. They live in a kind of cellar down by the river. Thaelmannstrasse number 17. The mother takes in washing for soldiers in the barracks near there. That's how Erika met this fella. She goes up to the barracks all the time to pick up the wash. And from then on—well, you know. What's a girl like that got to lose? Her happiness? She hasn't got any to start with."

A violent sobbing was heard from inside the room. The Wac said mournfully, "Now she's started up again. That means I'll have to sing to her again."

Lashley said, "What do you sing?"

"Oh, *Kinderlieder*. Same as Ma used to sing to us kids." She hummed a bar from what Lashley recognized as Brahms's "*Gute Nacht.*" "Those songs made me the champion baby sitter at Central High. I never thought, though, I'd be singing them in a jail in Germany."

"The girl goes to sleep when you sing them?" Lashley asked.

"Sure. She's just a kid if she is nineteen. That's what gets you."

He said: "Better get back to her. And thanks."

When Lashley came downstairs the sergeant stood up and said, "Well, Major, are yuh gonna take her off our hands?"

"Maybe later this afternoon," Lashley said.

"I sure hope so," grunted the sergeant. "We ain't set up to

handle people like her. All the guys we get in here are smart cookies. Every one's his own shyster lawyer. They know all the answers." He shook his head from side to side. "But that kid. She ain't smart. No, sir, she ain't smart. Boy, is *she* pregnant!"

A great many thoughts crossed Lashley's mind as he drove through the lacerated streets toward headquarters and a late lunch. He recalled the easy-flowing phrase as Marriner must have dictated it ". . . assigned to the prosecution of Civilian Wagner." He thought of the pregnant girl who was "Civilian Wagner" being lullabied to sleep.

But mostly he thought about Thémis sitting somewhere within the murky, uneven walls which glowered above the pavement.

VI

HEADQUARTERS OF THE ELEVENTH ARMY OCCUPIED A GLEAMING glass and granite building on the eastern edge of Reschweiler just beyond the city's outermost blocks of houses. It was a modern structure, squarely utilitarian, built during the early years of war to house the head offices of Wolff Electrowerke and it had fallen intact except for a few blast-shattered windows into the hands of the Americans.

A driveway swung through spacious grounds to a canopied entrance beside which four parking spaces were reserved by placard for the automobiles of: COMMANDING GENERAL, CHIEF OF STAFF, VISITING GENERAL, V.I.P. The Stars and Stripes fluttered lazily on a flagstaff jutting from the canopy.

On the perimeter of the grounds clusters of two-story dwellings lay in ruins, their roofless structures open to the skies. The usual rumors existed about how the *Electrowerke* building had come to escape destruction. A number of soldiers hinted darkly that Big Business had arranged with the air forces to spare such buildings as this and the I. G. Farben place in Frankfurt as well as other symbols of the international cartel system. A few officers attributed the apparent miracle to the shrewd brain of General Marriner, intimating that back in 1944 he had reserved the building for his headquarters after examining air photographs, and had removed it from the target list.

From time to time Lashley listened to these conjectures and

their variations and was puzzled by them. He could understand the need to destroy a country because it is the home country of the enemy, and also the pleasure in discovering that somehow a useful building has been overlooked. And yet he couldn't digest the contradiction in his mind any more than he could fully digest the quick moment of a cease-fire order when everybody suddenly stopped destroying and raced madly to preserve. This inconsistency was clearly reasonable in the logic of war, and even children understood it, but for him it made sense only if he was willing to admit that the human race was fabulously inadequate. And since he was unable to accept that premise he remained puzzled.

There was the time he was sent up from Paris to the Ruhr front to take evidence from a captured SS general called Von Scheinmetz. He traced the general to an American field hospital close behind the lines. The American effort to destroy the notorious Von Scheinmetz had very nearly succeeded. The man's left arm had been sheared off by a shell. Three army surgeons hovered over him in a resuscitation tent, and blood plasma was being poured into him from little bottles that hung on wires over his bed. Having sought desperately to destroy him, the Americans labored feverishly to preserve him. And having succeeded in preserving him, they shot him as a war criminal a month later after a brief court-martial. The fact that this was all supposed to be logical infuriated Lashley and made him morose for several days.

Now as he propelled his jeep toward the headquarters compound the same puzzlement assailed him. Erika Wagner was an enemy national and she had shot a soldier of the United States Army on occupation duty. She would have to be punished. She was nineteen, therefore she was an adult. She would probably be executed. That's the way it was—simple and concise as the arrow sign on the roadside which carried the lettering, "11th Army HQ 1000 yards ahead. Show your pass."

It was so simple a child could understand it. A child could but he couldn't in any real sense. That was the devilish part of it. His precise mind recognized the bald facts but rejected their face value; he could trace the clear logic but it failed to impress him. Between the tidy habits of his mind and his natural compassion there was a deep and utterly mysterious chasm and he could not traverse it. And this circumstance made him exceedingly unhappy, especially during the years of conflict, because the incidents of war had pointed up the problem with cruel clarity and the tedium of war had given him much opportunity to wrestle with it.

At the gateway to the *Electrowerke* grounds he braked the jeep and reached inside his coat for a headquarters pass. A sentry with a ruddy face eyed him, saluted mechanically, and waved him on, shouting, "Okay, sir."

He parked his jeep in a big lot behind the building and walked disconsolately along a gravel path toward the side entrance. A few feet away he paused, then headed for the small snack room in the basement rather than the huge headquarters mess on the first floor. He had little appetite for food and none at all for chance acquaintances.

He was showing his AGO card to a sentry inside the door when he heard a familiar voice.

"By the way, Major——"

It was Lieutenant Parker. Lashley turned impatiently, knowing he was going to be short with the man, knowing too this was an impolite thing to do. Because he was General Marriner's confidante Parker was in a position to obscure certain matters on the general's agenda or to underline them. Even full colonels recognized this fact and curried his favor.

"Yes, Parker," Lashley said quickly.

"I was wondering whether you received the general's directive this morning," Parker said. "It was rather important."

Lashley answered sharply, "If you dispatched it properly, obviously I received it."

Parker's narrow face flushed and his shoulders hunched forward like a fighter who has taken a blow and is inviting his opponent to try another.

He said firmly, "I just happened to see you and I thought I'd check. The general was pretty much concerned."

Lashley almost shouted at him, "God damn it, of course I got it. Is that all?" He didn't like the man's smugness and his assumption of responsibility for Marriner's official business.

For an instant Parker was disconcerted, but when he spoke again he had regained his usual composure.

"I've been looking over the provost marshal's report for the last twenty-four hours," he said. The simple statement was as innocuous as a booby trap.

"Well?"

Parker continued with easy confidence: "You issued an order last night—about the Delisle person—on rather shaky authority."

"Does the general think so?" Lashley demanded.

"The general hasn't seen it yet," said Parker. "He doesn't see everything, you know. A lot of paper comes into the office."

Lashley studied the man's face.

"Then *you* think my order was on shaky authority?"

Parker nodded wisely.

Lashley said, "Look, Parker. When I became a second looie I stopped taking orders from sergeants. Don't forget it."

Before the lieutenant could reply Lashley walked past him and down the steps to the snack room. He felt an unmistakable sense of elation rising out of his encounter with Parker. There were Parkers in all walks of life and he had happened across a good many of them. They were produced from a single character mold, and readily identified after you had known one. Like the secretary of a dean at the university who expected and received lavish gifts each Christmas from professors of the faculty. And like the nurse-companion to Ginny's rich grandmother who tried to tyrannize the family because she knew what was in the old lady's will and could put notions in the old lady's mind.

He knew what Parker would hasten to do. The order involving Thémis would be brought to Marriner's attention. It didn't matter. Marriner could not take precipitate action without recourse to the JAG in Frankfurt, or without an official French request for extradition. That would require a few days. A few days would be sufficient for his purposes one way or another.

He pushed away his half-finished sandwich and lingered over a pot of coffee. The room was reasonably quiet. Three British girls, civilian workers, sat two tables away and chatted over their tea. The German girls who stood behind the sandwich counter and the coffee urns were dressed in blue smocks, a pleasant relief in a room filled with khaki. A bespectacled lieutenant colonel sat at a far table, engrossed in a copy of the Paris *Herald Tribune*. Judging by the fit of his uniform, which would have looked no worse on Professor Einstein, he was probably a scientific researcher. Some men were soldiers, others weren't. But there was no rule of the thumb. Lashley considered that he looked smart in a uniform, although he knew he wasn't a soldier. He asked himself now whether he was even a lawyer. Lawyers were shrewd men, inflexible men, and their inflexibility was fused with their shrewdness. They could battle hard for what they thought, or what it was in their interest to think, and they could defend and advance the cause in which they were engaged. They could afford no misgivings, and their minds were so arranged that they harbored no misgivings.

He did not possess that kind of mind. He knew that after yesterday. He had prosecuted Steigmann vigorously, zealously, because not for an instant had he doubted either the righteousness of his cause or the proof of Steigmann's guilt. He had fought for what he believed to be justice. But now there was a doubt in his mind. No longer was it the brief question raised by a friend's quietly uttered remark over a drink, or the disturbing implications of a witness's demand for money. These he might have dismissed. But he could no longer still the clamor of the conflict set off by the silence of a woman he had known and yet had failed to understand.

What was there to rest his case on? Rodal's testimony? That had seemed to him trustworthy until the man came whining to him for money and seemed to expect to get it. Rodal had almost hinted that he was owed two hundred marks for proving the case.

If Rodal's testimony were set aside as perjury, where was his case? He had no doubt Steigmann had committed crimes of cruelty; the man was a Nazi through and through. But aside from Rodal's story as an eyewitness, actual proof was lacking. Steigmann was intelligent and thorough. There were probably very few witnesses still alive who could testify against him.

A lawyer had to have facts, not hearsay, not suspicion. He was supposed to present a tightly woven case; one with no loose ends sticking out. He had thought he had such a case until that slight doubt began to work in his mind.

That was where Thémis came in. She held the key to the truth about Steigmann. Naturally she would know whether he was guilty or innocent. Unless he could get her to talk, unless he could understand why she had volunteered to testify, he would never know the truth. That wasn't going to be easy.

As for Erika Wagner, she was clearly guilty. No doubt there. But hang her! She didn't deserve to pay the same penalty as Steigmann. No, but she probably would—that was the law. He realized again that he was not thinking like a lawyer. Perhaps he should have gone into the tool and die business like his father.

That reminded him of the day he had decided to go to law school: it wasn't an easy decision to make, because he knew his father had been expecting him to go into the small company which he had been running for twenty-five years.

"Dad, I don't know what you're going to think about this," he had said. "But I've got my heart set on being a lawyer."

His father's face had looked blank and he had replied, "If that's what you want, Bob, it's fine with me. You know, it doesn't make much difference what business you go into, but it makes an awful lot of difference if that business is strong enough to make you back your own beliefs. If you're going to be a lawyer, be a good lawyer and I'll be proud of you."

As he wrestled with his thoughts, here in Reschweiler, Lashley wished that his father were not four thousand miles away. He had learned the meaning of the word "integrity" from his father. He had known that the tool and die company might have been far more successful if the old man had been willing to cut corners here and there. But Lashley, Sr., had never been willing to compromise with truth and honesty. Perhaps that was why his son had wanted to become a lawyer.

He caught himself wondering what his father would think about the case of the United States Army against Civilian Erika Wagner.

A significant clearing of the throat brought him out of his reverie. He looked up. The bespectacled lieutenant colonel stood over him.

"You're Lashley," the man said.

"Yes."

"My name's Elson. I'm covering the area for stolen art."

Lashley nodded and pushed out a chair.

The man shook his head.

"I know when a man's thinking," he said. "Spend a lot of my own time at it. I just came over to tell you this: About twenty years ago Clarence Darrow lectured in Denver. My father took me to hear him. I thought of Darrow when I heard your summation yesterday. You've got a lot of his humanity. You made me feel hopeful for the first time since I looked at Monte Cassino. I was down there a couple of months ago."

He paused for a moment by the table. Then he said, "That's all I wanted to say, Lashley. Good luck." And he went away.

Lashley felt suddenly strong. Elson couldn't have come at a better moment. Lashley made a mental note of the name, for here was one officer who might understand what was bothering him. He wished now that he had asked Elson to stay. It would have been a great relief to talk over his troubles with a man like that. Lashley turned and looked toward the door, but Elson was gone. The room was quiet except for the clatter of the dishes. The German girls were putting out the pastries and cokes for the midafternoon rush. Lashley looked at his watch. It was nearly three o'clock.

There was nothing he could do at present on the Wagner case. The boy's fate would not be known for twenty-four hours or more. And the girl was in the last stages of pregnancy. She couldn't be properly questioned until after she had delivered her baby. A preliminary report was all he could possibly make to Marriner.

He should go back to his office. But he was put off by what he knew awaited him there: a summons from Marriner to explain his authority for keeping Thémis in Reschweiler. He couldn't face it now, not at this moment. He would keep away from the office as long as possible.

Thémis was somewhere in the city. He could find her easily enough by phoning the provost marshal. Perhaps she would be more tractable today. Perhaps there was no mystery about her at all. Perhaps she was just the hard-boiled mistress of a Nazi criminal and he was only imagining the other side of her nature. After all, there was nothing unusual in French camp followers who stood beside their Nazi consorts until the end. Women had done that over and over again in the early days of the Normandy invasion. Perhaps Marriner was right about her.

But every instinct told him it wasn't so. She wouldn't have made love to him if it were so. If she had been Steigmann's woman of her own free choice she would never have betrayed the German's love. Gang molls went down the line with their men, into hiding, into gunplay and death. Thémis's relationship with Steigmann was on a different plane altogether—she had even seemed bored by the verdict.

No, he decided, she was neither Steigmann's woman in the complete sense, nor was she immoral. Well, not really immoral. Otherwise she would not have spoken of a duty she had had to perform, a duty which embraced her defense of Steigmann.

He would not seek her out. There was nothing he could say to her that he hadn't already said. He had finally made up his mind to trust her and he could do no more. The next words would have to come from her. He would wait for her to seek him out again. She would, just as naturally as she had gone with him last night. He was certain of it.

Laughter and the murmur of voices interrupted his thoughts. People were coming in for an afternoon snack. A middle-aged major, erect and sedate, moved his tray along to the pastries. He was followed by an American girl, a civilian worker, whose khaki skirt emphasized her trim waist but was too tight around her thighs. Three lieutenants hovered around the door and were joined by three Wac officers, two of whom were pretty and the other consciously coy. They were all laughing over some joke. A one-star general joined the line and the three lieutenants glanced at him uneasily.

Lashley looked at his watch. It was precisely half past three. He had been sitting alone a long time. The girls squabbled amicably over their orders.

"What are you having, Madge?"

"Just salad, coffee, baked apple."

"I think I'll have the chocolate cake."

"Alma! It's six hundred calories at least. Think of your shape."

"Oh hell!" The girl called Alma hastily withdrew her hand from the direction of the mound of chocolate cake.

The lieutenants chuckled.

"That's right. You girls have to think of your figures as long as we're around."

"Boy!" sighed one of them. "What wouldn't I give for a bottle of milk!"

"Me too. I wrote my wife, when I get home she's got to meet me with a cow."

Jostling one another, they came away from the cashier's desk and carried their laden trays to a table near the window.

All at once Lashley knew what he wanted to do. He had seen Erika Wagner, but he had not seen her parents. He got up quickly from the table, retrieved his coat, and shouldered his way through a group of officers just outside the door.

The day was a shade grayer. He drove his jeep through the gates, slowly a moment so the sentry could check him through, then faster along the wide, deserted street until he came to the Bahnhofstrasse. Traffic was heavier here and he rolled slowly past the Red Cross Club and continued toward the river front. The buildings on both sides of the street became successively more scarred as he approached the docks, for the docks had been a primary target of the Air Forces. One block from the river he turned into a narrow street and parked his jeep between two gigantic heaps of rubble which blocked the roadway.

This was Thaelmannstrasse.

Jumping out quickly, he climbed the pile of loose masonry and looked down the short street. It seemed impossible that anyone lived here. Not a building had been left standing from the point where he stood to the ruined warehouse which marked the end of the street. Near him a jagged wall about ten feet high stood upright and from it swung a rusted ironwork sign which read, "Hofbrau Bensinger." The remainder of the *Hofbrau* was an avalanche of brick and plaster and twisted steel which seemed to have come roaring down from the sky and torn through the roof. Next to the *Hofbrau* there was nothing but an open cellar and the broken end of a bathtub to indicate that a dwelling had once stood here.

Lashley climbed over the rubble and made his way carefully along the street. He came to a wall two stories high. Its windows were just squarish holes and behind the wall there was nothing. Farther along was the ruin of a church, as evidenced by a great stone arch which must once have contained massive doors. Now there were no doors and no church. Only an arch.

At the end of the lifeless street, abutting the warehouse, a dwelling had burned to street level. Lashley found a set of narrow steps leading down into the basement of this house and went down them.

There was a door made of corrugated metal at the bottom. Nailed to it, a weather-beaten card with writing on it: "Thaelmannstrasse No. 17. Emmerich Wagner."

He knocked on the door with the heel of his hand. There was no reply. He pushed on the door and it opened inward.

His first impressions were the heavy smell of cooked cabbage and the sound of childish coughing from somewhere in the gloom. The room was dimly lighted by a coal-oil lamp hanging from the ceiling. It was a tiny room, not quite so wide as his hotel bedroom and, as far as he could see, without any means of ventilation. Frayed blankets were hung on the walls, apparently to keep out the cold, and in one corner was a small charcoal burner. Between the old frame doors which had been used for flooring he saw wet clods of earth. The ceiling, scarcely high enough to allow him to stand erect, had a tarpaulin suspended from it and damp stains on the canvas indicated the necessity for it. The room was unfurnished except for the stove, a chair, and a huge washtub over which a woman was bent almost double.

She straightened up to look at him. She was a gaunt, gray, large-boned woman dressed in a man's woolen trousers and a shapeless sweater of unrecognizable color.

She said mechanically, "*Washen nicht* finish. *Morgen.*"

Lashley shook his head. "I want to see Emmerich Wagner," he said, enunciating the name clearly.

She pointed to a chair and bent again over the washtub.

Someone coughed again. Instead of sitting down, Lashley walked carefully across the floor boards toward the room beyond. It was a small enclosure with cement walls and ceiling, apparently intended as a storage closet. He saw first a double bed which almost filled the place, then behind it against the wall a straw mattress stretched on the floor. It was too dark to see clearly the two lying there, but he heard their coughing and knew that they were children. The air was stale and the dampness made him want to sneeze.

He turned and went back into the main room. The woman seemed to take no notice of him. He sat on the chair and looked at the remains of a rag doll that was wedged in the mud between two of the floor boards.

After a while there was a noise outside, the door opened and a short, wizened man came in. He wore no hat. His gray hair was as short-cropped as the stubble on his expressionless face. He was wrapped in an old overcoat several sizes too large for him. It suspiciously resembled American issue but it was dyed a dirty purple and its pockets bulged. His jack boots were old and cracked.

He stopped inside the door and looked inquiringly at Lashley, his arms hanging limply and his head turned slightly askew. Then he walked across the floor boards and disappeared into the room beyond. He came out and handed Lashley a paper. It was a copy of his *Fragebogen*, the questionnaire every German was required to fill out for military government inspection.

While Lashley glanced at the paper the man went to the stove and drew from behind it a wooden box. From his coat pockets he dropped pieces of coal into the box. When he had emptied his pockets he took off the coat and held it carefully upside down over the box so that the coal dust at the bottom of the pockets would not be lost. When he had completed this task he hung the coat on nails against the wall at a place where the blankets didn't quite come together.

The *Fragebogen* told Lashley almost everything he wanted to know. Wagner was forty-seven, a veteran of the first war, and a postman by trade. He had joined the Nazi party in 1938; "by force," he had indicated. He had not worked since April 1945, when the Americans entered the city. He had five children of which Erika was the oldest. His wife, Anna, took in washing from American soldiers and earned an average of fifty marks a week. A note written at the bottom by an MG official stated that he could not resume his work as a postman until he had been cleared by a denazification court.

Lashley watched him move about the room. Both he and his wife seemed oblivious of a stranger's presence. It was as though privacy was something they neither understood nor cared about. The woman labored mechanically at her washing. The man shuffled across the room and examined a leak in a corner of the ceiling tarpaulin. Neither seemed disturbed by the coughing which came from the other room.

They did not even speak to one another. Lashley wasn't surprised at that. He had known others like these who were beyond tragedy. They were dumbly concerned with living, like soldiers in the heat of battle who scarcely notice those who fall.

He got up from the chair and handed the paper to Wagner. Taking it without a word, Emmerich Wagner continued to examine the leak in the tarpaulin. Lashley knew there was just no point in questioning him. The whole story was there on his *Fragebogen*. It might be kinder not to bother him. Before leaving, he made his way again to the smaller room and dropped two chocolate bars beside the children on the mattress. Out in the air again he breathed deeply. For a moment he stood still, looking at the wreckage of Thaelmannstrasse.

In Erie at this moment Ginny would probably be going to a Junior League meeting or a bridge party. He could see her getting into the tan sports roadster that her family had given her just before the war. She would be wearing her gray Persian lamb coat and probably no hat. Ginny's father was one of the big shots over at the ironworks and her mother was a Thurston from Chicago. Wonderful girl, Ginny—he wondered if she missed him.

He thought of Erika. She was nineteen. This was where she lived and this was how she lived. He thought too of Clay Hockland and the way he must have looked newly arrived from America, clear-eyed and long-limbed, swaggering a little in his uniform. He thought of the escape Erika had found in young Hockland's arms, an escape from the home he had just visited and the life that went with it. He knew now why she had fought not to let the boy go out of her life.

As he drove through the darkening streets he understood how right Marriner had been in giving him this new assignment. He was almost as worried now about young Hockland and Erika as he was about Thémis.

When he came to his office he found Nissen sitting on his desk. For once he wasn't smiling.

"For Christ's sake, Bob, I've been looking all over town for you. Marriner is chewing his fingernails to the elbow. Get over there fast. He's waiting."

VII

Outside the gate which closed off the corridor leading to the general's offices, the sergeant on guard examined Lashley's AGO card as leisurely as if he were reading a box score. Lashley stood impatiently, shifting his weight from one foot to the other. After the sergeant had glanced up two or three times to make certain the picture on the card was a true likeness, Lashley could no longer restrain himself. "The general is waiting for me," he said sharply.

"I'm only doing my duty, sir," the sergeant answered. His eyes narrowed and once again he looked from the card to Lashley. Then at last he handed it back decisively, clicked his heels, and saluted with excessive precision.

Lashley half ran to the door at the end of the corridor. With one hand on the knob, he paused to make sure his coat was properly buttoned. The general was a stickler for uniform regulations.

Parker was sitting at the only occupied desk in the outer office. The clock on the wall behind him showed a few minutes before six. Lashley had kept the general waiting beyond office hours. He could feel the sweat coming out on his forehead.

The lieutenant glanced up carelessly and said, "You may go in. The general is waiting."

Lashley went past Parker's desk to the door beyond. He knocked lightly and opened it.

The room was huge, thickly carpeted, and luxurious. The lighting was unusually good but not glaring, for it came from behind the rich mahogany paneling. The desk which commanded the room was neat, not a paper to be seen on it. Behind it two flags hung limply from standards. In front of it was the staff table, a long, narrow affair covered with green felt. On the table there were eight ash trays and eight blotting pads, and around it eight armchairs. The desk and the table were vacant.

Lashley looked about in confusion. He could see no one but Captain Gribemont leaning against a window sill at the far left-hand corner of the room and idly looking out into the night.

Then he heard Marriner's quiet, penetrating voice: "Come in, Lashley, and close the door," and he saw the general standing—grimly, he thought—before a map of the Eleventh Army area which covered almost the whole of the right wall. He came briefly to attention, closed the door, and walked into the room.

Marriner stepped away from the map and seated himself easily in one of the chairs at the green-covered table. The informality of his gesture was not lost on Lashley and he was relieved by it, for he had imagined Marriner waiting sternly behind his desk, ready to deliver judgment.

Lashley said, "I hope I haven't kept you waiting, sir."

The general leaned back wearily in his chair and pulled at the lobe of one ear.

He said, "You'd better take off your coat. You may be here a little while."

Lashley tossed his coat on a chair and sat facing the general across the green table. He was acutely aware that Gribemont had not moved from his position at the window. The serenity of the two men began to make him uneasy.

The general said suddenly, "I gave you a job to do today."

"Yes, sir," said Lashley.

"What have you done?"

Lashley studied Marriner a moment before replying. There was a magnetic quality about him. His head was the head of an intellectual, with its commanding brow and restless gray eyes. He had the quick, small body of a sprinter, but nothing about him suggested the soldier. He was waiting now for Lashley's reply and although his face was serious it was more the seriousness of the classroom than the parade ground.

"I saw both principals, sir," Lashley said.

Marriner frowned.

"I understand the man is dying." He spoke the words with reluctance.

Lashley said, "He has an outside chance, I'm told. We won't know till tomorrow. The girl is in pretty bad shape too."

Marriner leaned forward. "I'm not concerned with the girl. She's the responsibility of the German Reich, such as it was. We'll deal with her." He looked away, toward nothing. "I am concerned with the man. I'm responsible for him. He was sent from his home to serve under me, and our government had every right to expect that he'd be returned to his home a better citizen. Every man in this army is my responsibility, my personal responsibility. You understand that, Lashley."

"Yes, sir."

"Keep in touch with the hospital. If there's a doctor anywhere in Europe who'll give the man a better chance, let me know and I'll send a plane."

"Right, sir." Lashley was moved by the intensity of Marriner's concern. He began to understand why this singular man had been a legendary combat officer. Troops would fight for him and he would fight for them. There was no confusion in his mind. The division between his duty and his humanity was clearly defined. This was, Lashley realized, the essence of combat leadership.

Marriner settled back in his chair, but his eyes were still alert.

"Did it take you all day to see the principals?"

"I traced the girl's people—and saw them too," Lashley replied.

"Did *that* take you all day?"

Lashley said, "No, sir."

Marriner pulled at his ear again and now he seemed almost relaxed.

"You're still winding up the Steigmann case."

Lashley said, "I thought about it a good deal today, sir."

"So did I," said Marriner promptly. There was a trace of grim humor at the corners of his mouth.

Lashley said impulsively, "I issued an order to prevent the Delisle woman from leaving our jurisdiction." He looked away from the general's steady gaze.

Marriner said almost casually, "I know you did—about an hour after you left my house."

Lashley waited for one of those explosions for which Marriner was notorious. It didn't come. Instead the general leaned toward him and said with considerable candor: "All right, Lashley. What's on your mind?"

Lashley withheld his natural urge to speak freely. Experience had made him suspicious of men whose processes of thought had been molded at West Point, Fort Riley, and an army post in the Philippines. He had known too many younger career men whose training had blunted the sharp edge of their concern, who thought less about individuals and more about armies, less about pilots and more about air power, less about the feel of tragedy and more about the grasp of victory. This man seemed different. Perhaps he was merely cleverer.

Lashley said, "It's simply that I've come to the conclusion, sir, that the woman is withholding evidence of a pertinent nature."

"About Steigmann?" the general said sharply.

"Yes, sir."

"You mean you're not satisfied with the verdict?"

Lashley raised his eyebrows.

He said as tartly as he dared, "Not that, sir. I am naturally anxious to know everything about a case before I dismiss it from my mind. I don't like loose ends."

"What loose ends are there to worry about?" Marriner demanded.

Lashley felt his courage returning.

"For one thing, sir—I discovered last night that Rodal, my Czech witness, may not be reliable. He's the only witness I had against Steigmann. It set me to wondering whether I had a clean case. Frankly I still don't know———"

He looked unwaveringly into the general's eyes. "It's not that the man deserves consideration. I'm sure he deserves to die—but I'd like to prove it on the record, to *my* satisfaction. That's where the Delisle woman comes in. She has the information that would clinch it—at least, I think she has."

Marriner got up from his chair, walked over to the wall map, and then back to the table. His features were untroubled, his eyes distant.

Suddenly he faced Lashley. "That's nonsense and you know it. You knew yesterday that Steigmann was guilty as hell. You were convinced of it. I took the trouble to read your summation. I know men, Lashley. I know when they're faking—and when they're lying—and when they're evading the truth. You weren't doing any of those things yesterday. But now you're going soft. That's the trouble with war. It brings a lot of young fellows into the army and gives them dirty jobs to do before they're old enough to tackle dirty jobs. I know. When I had a division in the line, two of my regimental commanders went crazy. I had to send them back. They were under thirty-five. They were vulnerable because they thought they knew too much about life. That was nonsense. Sure they had guts. But they weren't old enough and they didn't know enough!"

He sat down abruptly and put on his horn-rimmed spectacles. He stared at Lashley a moment, then continued less heatedly.

"I wouldn't be giving you this talk, Lashley. I usually don't take the trouble. I haven't got the time. I have sixty thousand Americans under my command, and I police ten million Germans. I'm secretary of state when it comes to dealing with the French, the British, and the Russians. I have a hundred and forty thousand DPs here, and I've got to feed them and clothe them and maybe send them home. I have Frankfurt to answer to. And Berlin and Washington. And UNRRA. I'm trying to do a job, Lashley, and I do it the best way I know how, the only way it can be done—by drawing strong, hard lines and making them stick. This isn't America. This is Germany. It's a madhouse and I'm sitting on the lid. When a man is found guilty of murder he hangs. And I haven't got the time to find out whether his mother was once frightened by a zebra. He hangs."

Marriner leaned back in his chair and lighted a cigarette. He let the smoke out of his mouth slowly.

"I could bounce you out of this army tomorrow," he said, "but I won't. I won't because I know what's eating you—and what's eating you is a good old-fashioned American habit. I respect it. You don't like to see people pushed around—especially women. That's it, isn't it? Not Steigmann. The woman."

Lashley said, "That's one of the things, sir."

"All right," Marriner said. He called, "Gribemont!"

Lashley had forgotten the presence of the Frenchman, who came away now from the window and took a seat beside Marriner.

"Good evening, Major," Gribemont said in smooth, pleasant tones.

Lashley winced at the man's overbearing courtesy.

He mumbled something in reply and watched the Frenchman finger a role of yellow teleprinter paper.

The Frenchman said, "I am sorry if I am about to injure your sensibilities."

Marriner said, "Just read it, Captain."

Gribemont said, "It is in French. I shall translate as I go along."

He flattened the paper on the table. He said, "This was received this afternoon from the Deuxième Bureau in Paris. It was in reply to my urgent request for information about one Demoiselle Delisle. It is not a full dossier by any means." He nodded wisely. "But it is enough—quite enough."

"Just read it," Marriner said.

Gribemont read:

" 'Delisle—*fille majeure*, given name, Thémis. Born 1921 in village of Villeneuve, parish of Caen, province of Calvados, district of Normandy. Father, Thérrien Delisle, gentleman farmer, of the village of Villeneuve, deceased May 1945. Mother, Dame Alice Mongibault, deceased 1930. No other children. Thérrien Delisle was favorably known——' "

Gribemont cleared his throat and drew a long breath. He continued:

"There follows a description of the woman's height and weight and her general appearance. I will pass over this. We know she is most attractive." He glanced at Lashley. "Now——

"According to information we have been able to gather, Thémis Delisle came to Paris in 1938 and obtained a position as a mannequin in the establishment of Potvin, *haute couture* —that is a de luxe fashion salon—on Boulevard des Capucines. She displayed a very high intelligence and in 1939 she was promoted to the position of *chef de réception*—that is a sort of floor manager in charge of displaying the collection to clients——"

Gribemont commented, "You see, she is a very clever woman." He continued: " 'It was rumored at the time that Mlle. Delisle was friendly with one Pierre Flanders, a director of the establishment.' " Gribemont looked up. "The French word is *compagne*, which could mean much more than friendly."

He gave a small, affected cough and returned to the manuscript.

" 'After the enemy occupied Paris the establishment Potvin continued to function and indeed its business increased many fold. It became a favorite rendezvous for highly placed Germans. Goering, Abetz, and Von Faulkenhausen were known to have made purchases here of furs and clothes for their women. Delisle continued her post as *chef de réception* and she came into contact with many German officers of rank. Among these was Otto Steigmann, who entered Paris as chief of the *Sicherheitsdienst*—that is the police division of the Wehrmacht," Gribemont explained, " 'and later became deputy town commandant of Paris. It is worthy of note that Delisle was not impressed into foreign service by the enemy's labor organization although she was of the proper age——' "

The Frenchman's clearly enunciated words came to Lashley as the prologue to disastrous information. His fingers dug into the arms of his chair and his eyes were fixed steadily on the map against the opposite wall. He was aware that Marriner was regarding him with a benign expression. He should have expected something like this was in store for him when Marriner kept his temper during the early part of the interview. He wished the lights were dimmer. He did not relish the look of defeat that must be showing on his face.

" 'The recollection of one Marivette Bonhomme, *fille majeure*, a mannequin still working at Potvin, is that the German Steigmann called upon Delisle at her place of work several times during 1942 and 1943. Demoiselle Bonhomme herself saw Delisle enter Steigmann's automobile on at least two occasions. Further connection between Delisle and the German Steigmann is not yet established——' "

Gribemont paused to clear his throat. He laid the paper on the table before him, as an actor might do to increase the suspense. Then he picked it up again and went on with his reading.

" 'The actions of the woman's father, Thérrien Delisle, are especially illuminating. Despite his advanced age, Thérrien Delisle was a hero of the resistance in the province of Calvados. He was known in this district as a man of high resolve and exceptional pride in the glory of France. He used his advanced age and the isolated location of his *manoir* to the greatest advantage as camouflage, and in 1943 he became in fact *adjudant en chef* of the De Gaulle underground for the district between Isigny and Ouistreham. In this position he was of the greatest service in communicating to De Gaulle's headquarters information about the German coastal defenses and troop dispositions in the very area which was later to be the point of debarkation for the liberating troops of our Allies.

" 'It is noteworthy that on the 7th July 1944, in the *grand place* of the town of Bayeux, province of Calvados, General De Gaulle made his first return to the soil of France and publicly embraced Thérrien Delisle for his services to liberty.

" 'According to the recollection of the parish priest in the Church of St. Etienne in Caen, Thémis Delisle arrived in the city to visit her father at some date near the end of April or the beginning of May 1944. She met briefly with her father and then she disappeared. It was obvious to all who noted their reunion that a coldness existed between the father and the daughter.

" 'Shortly after the liberation, in the issue of *L'Echo de Calvados* published in Caen on the 15th August 1944, the following legal and notarized announcement appeared: "I, Thérrien Delisle, hereby publicly disown as my daughter and as claimant on my estate the Demoiselle Thémis Delisle, *fille majeure,* heretofore known as my daughter and my presumed heir, for good and sufficient reasons known to myself."

" 'Thérrien Delisle passed away in May 1945, leaving his entire estate to the parish of Bretteville-sur-Orne to be used for reconstruction of the church which was destroyed in the fighting. It is unfortunate that he did not confide to anyone the information pertaining to his daughter but he left no doubts as to his feeling toward her because on his deathbed he delegated the parish priest of Bretteville to make sure that no part of his estate be transferred to the woman.

" 'Although no direct proof has as yet been uncovered, it is presumed that the woman, Thémis Delisle, had relations with the enemy of a nature serious enough to impel her father to adopt this extreme course.' "

Gribemont's voice trailed off on the last phrase. His fingers lay motionless on the paper. After a moment he said, "This information was gathered in the four days since I submitted her name for inquiry. The investigation is continuing, but it is my opinion there is sufficient evidence to hold her for questioning under the laws of any nation including the United States."

He rolled up the paper and tossed it carelessly across the table to where Lashley was sitting.

Lashley picked it up and glanced over the first few paragraphs. The words made no impression on his mind. He felt like a boy who has been made to look foolish before his classmates. Out of the corner of his eye he saw Marriner sitting grimly far back in his chair.

Gribemont began, "My dear Major——"

He was interrupted by Marriner, who said brusquely, "Thank you, Captain, for bringing along this information. It was very good work."

Gribemont rose quickly to his feet. He bowed slightly and said, "Good evening, General. Good evening, Major."

Marriner watched him walk sedately from the room.

They sat opposite each other in the brilliantly lighted room as still as two men hunched over a chessboard. The clang of cleated heels hitting against pavement came through the open window. The night squad was marching to its guard posts and the staccato tone of a sergeant's commands could be heard at diminishing intervals until it was no more than a distant echo.

Marriner said quietly, "When a man disobeys a command in my army he is broken. When he ignores a suggestion by a superior officer he must be pretty sure of himself. But so must the superior officer. I didn't know anything about the woman when I spoke to you last night. I was guessing. No credit to me that I guessed right. You guessed wrong. We'll leave it at that."

Mechanically Lashley said, "Thank you, sir." He was thinking hard. "I suppose the woman's testimony is useless at this ——" he began after a moment.

"I certainly think so," said Marriner. "Just hand her over to Gribemont. Better still, have the provost marshal hand her over."

"I'll do another check on Rodal, for my own satisfaction."

"You're making it tough for yourself, Lashley, and that's a mistake. Don't go soft, because *I'm* not going to. The man is going to hang just as fast as it can be arranged."

"But, sir——"

"Let me tell you a story." The general pulled off his spectacles. He reached in his breast pocket for a cigarette and tapped it four times against the back of his left hand. He pulled a match from the stand in the center of the table, struck it, lighted his cigarette, and discarded the match.

"Look at this," he said, passing his hand over the six rows of decorations which covered the left breast of his blouse. "Ever since I was a shavetail I've wanted to see one decoration up here—the Silver Star. It may seem curious, but I still think the Silver Star is the best decoration in the army. It appeals to me. A man can have a dozen DSCs and Bronze Stars and Legions of Merit but they don't count as much with me as a Silver Star. It means the man went out there and won it— the hard way. You don't get it for being good at plans back in Washington, or for buttering up a politician. You get it for fighting. I like it. It's my kind of medal."

He paused to knock the ash from his cigarette.

"Once when I had a division back in North Africa I went out and did something that I thought deserved a Silver Star. So did my G-1 and he was the only officer on my staff who knew about it. He sent a note to the corps commander suggesting that I be awarded the Silver Star. Then I began to wonder whether what I had done was as good as I thought it was and I went soft. I thought the whole thing might look framed. I intercepted the note and destroyed it. I've been sorry ever since."

He smiled reminiscently at Lashley.

"I deserved that Silver Star. I would exchange it for all the salad dressing I've got up here—but now it's too late. I'll never get it." He shook his head slowly. "You've done an outstanding job on Steigmann. Don't do what I did. Don't go soft. Don't make it tough for yourself. And now let me get back to some of my other problems."

"Good night, sir," said Lashley, rising.

"Good night, Lashley, and good luck."

The rattle of his jeep was even and soothing. The hum of tires on cold pavement was a sound of power and purpose. The wheel was light to his touch and the night air was sharp against his face. He jammed down his foot impulsively. The drone of the motor rose to a higher pitch. Jagged walls appeared and fell away at either side like gray ghosts coming up out of the night and quickly vanishing. He leaned over the wheel and the muscles in his leg quivered, so he pushed his foot down harder. The wind whistled past his ears. The wheel vibrated in his hands like something desperately alive. The jeep rushed ahead, consuming the mists that swirled in the glare of the headlights.

The traffic circle in front of the courthouse came suddenly toward him. He pulled at the wheel and the tires screeched as he swung to his right and put on the brakes. A sentry pushed open the gates of the courtyard and waved him on. He rolled slowly inside, sorry that he had reached his destination so quickly, sorry that he couldn't drive on into the night. Only speed and distance could help him. Marriner had gone out of his way to be considerate, but the shock of Gribemont's report remained.

His office was lighted. The window was a yellow square against the darkness of the building. As he reached the head of the stairs he saw the shaft of light from his open door cutting across the corridor.

He went quickly toward the light, his heels ringing in the empty corridor. At the door he paused and peered cautiously into the room.

Thémis was seated in the chair in front of his desk, facing the door. She looked at him steadily through the smoke that curled from her cigarette.

VIII

HE STOOD QUIETLY IN THE DOORWAY, TRYING NOT TO SHOW HIS exasperation. He was in no mood to talk to Thémis Delisle, or even to see her. She had made a fool of him. Only the determined set of his jaw betrayed his feelings at this moment as he studied this contradictory woman.

He felt again the sting of Marriner's paternal thrashing and heard the sound of Gribemont's precious "Good evening, Major." He imagined the supreme satisfaction that had come to Parker. Even a clown like Kinsella had had brains enough to know that this woman was a cheap camp follower. His own lack of judgment appalled him.

She must have been waiting a long time. A tray on the desk was filled with her snuffed-out cigarettes and the narrow room smelled of stale smoke. But she had not taken off her coat. It was buttoned high at the neck as she had worn it constantly in the courtroom.

Her attitude was languid and maddeningly familiar. One elbow rested on the desk and in her other hand she held a cigarette with an insouciance that infuriated him. Beneath her small green beret her eyes at the same time looked at him and beyond him. Her full lips might or might not be on the point of trembling. Once more he noticed how delicately white her skin was against the dark fur collar. But the pose had lost its magic.

He told himself fiercely that a thousand show girls possessed the same delicate lines.

He pulled the door shut behind him and walked around her to his desk. There were messages awaiting his attention. He read them, trying to appear oblivious of her presence.

Nissen had scrawled on his scratch pad: "Cut and bleeding? Hope to see you at dinner—Excelsior." There was a typewritten message: "Call Captain Bossin at 135th Station Hospital. Urgent. 37-325."

He picked up the phone with studied detachment, dialed the number, and asked for Captain Bossin. While he waited with the phone to his ear he busied himself with various papers on his desk, pushing some under the flap of the blotter, crushing some into a ball and tossing them into the wastebasket. He avoided looking at the woman. He opened his overcoat, pushed back his overseas cap, and pretended intense preoccupation. He hoped he was being sufficiently rude.

At last Bossin came on the phone.

"This is Lashley. You called me."

The doctor's voice vibrated in Lashley's ear.

"Oh yes, Major, I'm glad you called. Been trying to reach you the last couple of hours. What do you think happened?"

Lashley waited.

Bossin's voice rose: "Hello, hello."

"Yes, Captain," Lashley said. "I'm waiting to hear what happened."

"Oh, okay. Well, we got a call from the stockade—about the girl. You know, Hockland's girl. I went over myself. The girl was running a temperature. Hundred and four. Now listen, Major, I'm no obstetrician, but I'm damn sure—— We've got to get her out of that stockade. She can't have a baby in that place——"

"Did you get her moved?" Lashley interrupted.

He looked quickly at the woman sitting across from him. She had turned her chair around and she appeared to be studying him closely, to be trying to understand the change in him.

She no longer mattered to him but he felt momentarily uncomfortable. He took off his cap and tossed it on the desk.

Bossin's voice came over the wire. "That's just it, Major. To move her they've got to get your okay."

"Where do you propose to take her?" Lashley said.

"Me!" exploded Bossin. "Hell, I don't propose to take her anywhere. Someone will have to see that she gets to a civvy hospital—there're a couple of broken-down places in this town. But the point is they can't move her without an order from you. That's why I called. Been trying to get you——"

"All right," said Lashley. "I'll get an order over. But she's to be kept under guard, remember." He thought a moment. "Send that Wac along with her."

The doctor groaned. "You lawyers. That girl couldn't escape from a paper bag. But have it your own way. Only get that order over there. And get it quick."

It sounded as if he were about to hang up. Lashley said, "Wait a minute, Captain. How is Hockland?"

Bossin's voice lowered.

"That's another thing. The kid's holding his own. You know, at nineteen you've got a lot of red corpuscles fighting for you. Temperature steady at a hundred and two. Respiration—not so bad. But it's got to come—the crisis, I mean. We'll know for sure tomorrow or day after."

Lashley said, "The general is concerned. He wants the boy to get every break. Can you use a specialist from Switzerland or England or somewhere?"

"Did the top brass suggest that?" Bossin asked sharply.

"Yes. Definitely."

"Well, tell him in this hospital every man gets the same break." The doctor snapped, "Him too, the old bastard, if he ever winds up here. Tell him that. And don't forget the order. Are you listening?"

Lashley was relieved when the phone clicked. His ear tingled.

He drew a sheet of paper from his desk and wrote the order.

He wondered whether Thémis was still studying him, but he refused to look up from his desk to see.

He addressed an envelope, sealed the order, and dialed a number on the telephone.

He said, "Major Lashley speaking. Courthouse Building. Send up a runner."

He turned the envelope in his fingers, staring at it. Putting it down, he reached into his inside pocket, found the dossier on Thémis Delisle, and ran his finger along the folded edge of the paper. At last he raised his head to look at her.

"What is it you want?" he asked coldly.

The harsh light revealed deep lines under her eyes. It made him wish that she had worn her brimmed hat with the flashing arrow through its crown. It would have shadowed her face and made it easier for him to do what he had to do. She put her forearms on the desk and clasped her hands.

"They took me from the train this morning," she began in a softly resonant voice. "Why do you keep me here in Reschweiler?"

He said, "I told you last night. I issued the order. This is a military zone and orders are carried out."

"Let me go," she implored. Her voice faltered. "There—there is nothing more I can tell you."

He felt strong now, strong and cruel. She had it coming to her.

He said, "I know there's nothing more you can tell me. Tomorrow you go. That's what you want, isn't it?"

She studied her clasped hands. "Yes," she murmured. "Tomorrow morning. Good."

"The French will pick you up at Mainz. You know that," he said, watching her closely.

"It doesn't matter." She shrugged her shoulders.

He said cruelly, "Nothing matters to you, does it? And what about last night? What about it?"

He leaned forward, trying to look into her eyes, but she turned her head away.

Her voice was low. "There is no explanation for last night.

It was a mistake, a terrible mistake. I shall regret it as long as I live—as long as I live——"

Now she looked at him. "You should have let me go today," she cried. "I wanted to leave here. I didn't want to see you again—ever again. For your sake as well as mine."

Yesterday he would have been sure she meant it. If it hadn't been for Gribemont's report, he would have sworn that she did today. The woman was a magnificent liar. He remembered something she had said last night: "More than anything else, the French love a spectacle." Apparently she was no exception.

There was a rapid knock on the door. With a quick glance at Thémis he caught up the envelope containing the order and went to the door.

A courier, red-cheeked from the night wind, saluted.

Lashley said, "For the officer on duty at Headquarters Stockade. It's urgent."

The courier took the envelope and saluted again. Lashley watched him hurry down the corridor, his cleated heels making a rat-tat-tat which in the deserted building was curiously welcome.

He returned to his desk with his mind made up. "There will be no scenes," he said incisively. "You are to take the train tomorrow morning. If you don't take it, you will be put on it. That's all."

She said slowly, "I came to ask one favor of you. I would like to visit Steigmann. Tonight—before I leave."

For a moment he was almost elated. "Why do you want to see him?"

"It is not much to ask," she parried.

This was the corroboration he wanted, he told himself. There was no mystery after all. The facts in the dossier explained what she had called her duty toward the Nazi. Duty!

He said, "It might be arranged—if you tell me why you want to see Steigmann."

"It is nothing you would understand," she said, and shrank from the sudden fury in Lashley's eyes.

"God damn it! You love the man. Why not admit it? You

are willing to go back and stand trial because of him. Why don't you admit it now and be done with it?"

"Please——"

"Admit it!"

Her mouth opened and closed convulsively before she found her voice. "Admit what? That I love him? Oh, I don't love him." Her voice was barely a whisper. "I detest him."

"Detest him?" he echoed savagely. "Yes, you detest him and you come here to save him. You detest him and you'll face prison for him. You detest him and you'll go to his death cell to say farewell to him. Do you expect me to believe that?"

"It is the truth."

"The truth! A woman like you doesn't know what truth is. If you don't love him, then why did you come here?"

"If I told you, you would not understand."

He said derisively, "There are some things I do understand. Tonight you won't see Steigmann. And tomorrow you go."

"It is a pity," she murmured as if to herself. "He will die with bitterness in his heart."

Lashley banged his fist on the desk. "With no more bitterness than the twenty thousand who died under his magnificent patronage. Have you seen the Lager Reschweiler? Go look at it. It's only six kilometers from here. Go look at it and then weep your tears for Steigmann. Climb to the top of the hill behind the bunkhouses. You'll find a stone building there. Go inside it. Look in the first room. Slabs—that's what you'll see—cement slabs. Not for those who died. For those who were murdered! Go along the passage and look in the second room. You'll see a shelf there. Oh, a neat shelf. Pick up the hammers and the chisels. Feel them. They're well balanced. They were for smashing teeth in case there was gold. Go to the end of the passage. You'll find a big, fat furnace there. Open it and roll out the iron stretcher. It rolls easily—on wheels. That's where they burned the murdered. Don't stop. Go to the door behind the furnace. Open it. There's a linden tree behind the building and an open grave big enough for five coffins. A tree and a grave. Don't be afraid. There are no coffins. Only a little white dust. It's very sanitary—the ashes of twenty thousand Czechs and Poles and Russians and Jews—yes, and Frenchmen! Twenty thousand! Then go back and sob over Steigmann because he's going to die bitterly!"

He stopped talking and glared at her.

"You do not understand," she said—and it seemed to Lashley she looked at him pityingly. "If he must die, let him die. I do not seek to save him. I did not come to save him, though you insist on thinking that I did. I told you I had a duty to perform, and that duty is done. If Steigmann must die, that is the nature of the world. He has killed and he must die——"

She raised her eyes to his. There were tears in them but the tears did not fall and her voice grew in depth and compassion.

"The twenty thousand died—yes. They died bitterly, helplessly, without hope. They died filled with hate and with fury, against man and against God. And they left to the world their hate and their fury. This was their legacy and we who remain are filled with it. The world is mad with it. They died bitterly and we live bitterly and kill bitterly and there is no end to it. Peace with honor! There is no peace and there is no honor. The weak have become strong, and the strong have become vengeful, and the vengeful have become greedy, and the greedy have become cruel. And there is no peace. The world has learned nothing."

Her voice became stronger.

"There must come a stop. When a man dies bitterly his bitterness lives and flourishes after him. I know. I have seen it. Europe is ravaged by bitterness. The French and the Slavs and the Russians and the Poles—they are ravaged by it. The Jews, they who have always died with faith, they too are ravaged by it. Peace? We do not seek peace. We seek retribution. That is what comes when a man dies bitterly."

She looked up at him and all the harshness had left her face. "It is a small thing I ask," she said quietly. "Let me go to Steigmann. Let me spend a few moments with him alone. Let a beginning be made. Let him die without bitterness."

He waited for a long time after she stopped speaking. And in the silence he fought a battle within himself. He wanted to believe in her because he wanted to believe in what she preached. Her words made sense, but at the same time he remembered the soldierly eloquence of Marriner. And the craftiness of Gribemont. And the dossier. The dossier!

His hand reached into his pocket and brought out the report. His fingers crumpled it.

He said slowly, "Is that the only reason you want to see Steigmann?"

Her eyes gave themselves to him completely. She said steadily, "Yes, that is the only reason."

"You do not love him?"

"I have told you I detest him. Why do you persist?"

"You were not his woman in Paris? You were not a collaborationist? You did not shame your own father and betray your own country?"

"No! No! No!"

There could be no question of the vehemence of her denial.

He said acidly, "You should not deny it. As long as you did not lie I had a certain respect and admiration for you. Your loyalty to Steigmann was at least honest. Now you are lying. And you lie very badly."

Then he tossed the dossier across the desk toward her.

"Read that!"

He stood up and turned his back on her and leaned on the window sill. The night was dark and misty. He could not see the river. Beyond the buildings across the street the gloom was impenetrable. In the courtyard below a guard, leaning against the sentry box, looked bored and chilly. It was getting colder. He pressed his cheek against the window and looked toward the far end of the courtyard. There was no light from the basement cells. He wondered whether Steigmann and the others had been removed to Bergsdorf Prison or whether it was merely time for lights out. He looked at his watch. It was eight o'clock. Nissen was probably waiting at the Excelsior.

He turned about reluctantly. She was reading the dossier. He could not see her face. She held the long sheet of paper so high that he guessed she was near the end of it. She had read it quickly. Why not? It held no news for her.

He sat down at the desk and idly turned a pencil in his fingers.

When he saw her fingers loosen and let the dossier fall to the desk, he hesitated to look at her face. Instead he studied the pencil turning in his hand and it might have been a work of art for the rapt attention he gave it.

She broke the silence gently, with a voice that contained neither hysteria nor venom.

"How strange," she said, "to read one's history on a single sheet of paper. It is like the moment when one is roused out of a dream and is not yet fully awake. There is neither dream nor reality."

He looked at her as she spoke. She might have been discussing a case history at a graduate seminar, so reflective was her manner.

"You are the person referred to?" he said, steadying himself upon legalities.

"There is no mistake," she answered, adding with the trace of a smile, "I am Thémis Delisle, *fille majeure.*"

"And you had relations with Steigmann in Paris and your father disowned you," he said persistently.

A sadness came into her voice.

"That is true," she said, and nodded. "Both facts are true."

He picked up the dossier and pointed it at her accusingly.

"Then this is an accurate statement of the facts," he said, his expression no longer angry but resigned.

He realized he had been clinging to the hope, obscure and forlorn, that his belief in her might be vindicated. And now that hope was leaving him.

She said almost to herself, "How quickly they seal the verdict. How quickly they condemn."

"Then it is accurate," he repeated. The words came from him slowly, reluctantly.

She seemed to sense what was going through his mind, for she smiled at him sadly.

It came to him that they were looking at each other for the first time as a man and a woman might look at one another if there were no outside problems to confuse them.

She did not look away.

She said, "You are a lawyer and I'm sure you are an honest one. You know that the truth is rarely found on the surface; it often lies deep buried."

She reached for the paper which he still held in his hand. He made no effort to keep it from her. He felt almost numb.

"In the courtroom yesterday you spoke some words I could not forget. About patriotism——"

Absently he recited the phrase: "The dark tragedy of patriotism is that men will fight for their country rather than for the principles that made their country beloved to them."

She said, "I believe you are honest. I trusted you because I believed it."

Holding the dossier in both hands, she glanced quickly over it, then back at him.

"When you spoke those words to the judges, you were speaking about Steigmann, but without knowing it you spoke also about my father. He too was a misguided patriot."

The room was silent. The harsh light beat down upon her white, somber face and it seemed to him that she was groping for the words that would make the past clear to him.

"My father was of the old Normans," she began slowly. "They are close to the land, the old Normans, and close to the church. They are born to their farms and they die on their farms, and the life between is as straight and as narrow as the furrows they plow in the spring. Neither war nor flood nor invasion can separate them from their land. That is why they are great patriots. They are the backbone of France. The Germans might conquer a thousand times and persist for a thousand years, but the old Normans would cling to their land and go to their church and they would remain French.

"My father was crafty, as the old Normans are crafty—and proud," she sighed. "Normans do not know France as the world knows it. They do not look beyond their farms. *They* are France. And when they are degraded, France is degraded. When their country's pride is ravished, their pride is ravished. They are the patriots.

"My father was one of them, perhaps the greatest. He despised the Germans because they committed an indignity upon his land, and therefore upon him. He was a brave man and high-spirited. They say he was the only Frenchman in Calvados who would face the Germans openly. I can well believe it, because he had no fear in him. No fear and no kindness.

"Oh, he was a great patriot, my father. A great Frenchman, a great Norman. *Holà!* They will build monuments to him in Calvados."

Again she ran her eyes over the dossier and she spoke quickly and excitedly.

"It's true! All true! I knew Steigmann in Paris—yes! My father was embraced by De Gaulle—yes! Even more. De Gaulle pinned on him the Medal of Liberation. He said to him, 'Thérrien Delisle, you have fought for liberty and justice. You have fought for France. I salute you!' My father disowned me—that is true too! On his deathbed he disowned me once more—yes, yes, yes!

"These are all the facts they had and so they conclude——

" '*Malgré qu'on n'en a pas encore trouvé de la preuve* . . . Although direct proof has not yet been uncovered, it is presumed that the woman Delisle had relations with the enemy of a nature serious enough to impel her father to adopt this extreme course.' "

She put down the paper and leaned across the desk. "Even on his deathbed my father would not admit his real reason. He was too ashamed. He really believed it was better to let people think I had betrayed my country. Because in his little world he considered my sin was far worse than treason."

Her voice dropped to a whisper.

"Not so long ago I was in love. Willfully and wonderfully in love, as only a young girl can be in love in Paris in the danger in the war. His name was Pierre Flanders. We were to be married. He was . . ." She paused. "How shall I tell you?

He was young—and strong—but kind and understanding. Perhaps my father might have liked him—except that he was a Jew."

She sank back into her chair and turned away her head. Lashley thought that perhaps she was crying. As he watched her the silence grew heavy in the room.

At last she looked at him. There were no tears in her eyes. "You do not understand," she said incredulously. "I have told you and you do not understand."

"I understand well enough, but I find it hard to believe that your father would disown you for that reason."

She looked at him sadly. "I am sorry you don't understand." Now bitterness gave her words an edge. "You cannot see the sins of any but the Germans. You can sit in judgment upon them and you can condemn them. That is easy for you. Victory has made you sure. You can see blood only on the hands of the Germans. I too hate the Germans for what they have done. I despise them! And yet——"

She laughed scornfully.

"People like you will build monuments in Calvados to my father. Children in the schools will hear legends about him. Thérrien Delisle, the old man of Villeneuve, who fought for freedom and for justice. For liberty, equality, and fraternity. Thérrien Delisle, whose love for his country was stronger than his love for his daughter. Thérrien Delisle, the patriot of France —a man who was consumed by a passion he shared with his enemies—he hated the Jews. He was a patriot and a fool. He worshiped his country but even more he worshiped his hatred. What kind of father is it who would rather have his daughter be called a traitor than have her marry a Jew?

"Even when he was dying he made sure they would believe I was a traitor. It was easier for him. Even at the end he still could not bear that anyone should know the truth. . . ." She paused. "And yet he *was* one of the patriots, one of the victors.

"You do not believe what I told you about my father. Yet you yourself have found words to describe him—better words than I can find.

" 'The dark tragedy of patriotism is that men will fight for their country rather than for the principles that made their country beloved to them.' " She gestured with the open palm of her hand. "You did not know you were speaking of my father."

She gathered up her purse and gloves and got slowly to her feet. Her face held a curious expression as she looked at him, one of kindness mingled with distaste, like a parent who has explained an ugly fact to a little boy.

"Where are you going?" he said.

"To my billet. Unless I may see Steigmann."

He said, "It can't be arranged tonight. It really can't."

"It is a pity," she murmured. "Tomorrow will be too late."

Without thinking about it, he buttoned his overcoat and picked up his service cap.

"Are you going to tell them in Paris—about your father?"

She shook her head.

"Have you seen a political trial in France since the victory? They spit at you from the jury boxes even before the case is heard."

He got up quickly and came around the desk to where she was standing. She turned her head away as he came close.

"Thémis," he said, "now that you have told me this, why don't you tell me the rest? What does Steigmann mean to you?"

She moved away from him toward the door and turned to face him. She shook her head slowly; there was nothing in her expression to tell him what she thought. She opened her lips as if to speak, then closed them.

"What is it, Thémis? Tell me."

"There is nothing I can say. You do not believe me. I should have known, that first day in the courtroom when I saw you . . . when our eyes met I thought—well, what does it matter what I thought? I knew then I would regret it."

He held out his hand to stop her, but she slipped by him and out the door.

In the light from the single naked bulb at the end of the

corridor he saw her go and, without pausing, turn and disappear down the stairs.

Perhaps it was just as well. Somewhere in his mind Marriner's voice was saying, "Don't go soft, Lashley." If she had hesitated he might have called her back.

The building was as silent as a ruin after she had gone. Lashley sat at his desk, lighting one cigarette from another. Reason told him that Thémis's dossier was true, and she herself had not denied it. But he was not satisfied. Something eluded him. His instinct about her rejected the facts, and the urges of his heart fought with the precise habits of his reasoning. Neither of them could he wholly accept, now that he had talked to her again.

When he finally looked at his watch it was nearly nine. All at once he felt hungry. In a few more minutes the dining room would be closing. Nissen would still be waiting for him if he hurried.

He would give himself the time it took to smoke one more cigarette to make his decisions. One cigarette. Seven or eight minutes.

After three deep draws he snuffed it out and, drawing paper from the top drawer, he wrote two orders. They reflected his confusion and he was not happy about them. The first was to the provost marshal confirming his verbal instruction to prevent Thémis Delisle from leaving Reschweiler. The second was to the security officer of Bergsdorf Prison, cautioning him to ensure that the prisoner Otto Steigmann was allowed no visitors unless such persons were in possession of a pass signed by JAG, War Crimes Branch, Eleventh Army detachment.

Then he snatched up his cap and went out.

WEDNESDAY

IX

Lashley rolled over sleepily and looked at his watch. It was a few minutes before seven and sunlight was striking the flowered wallpaper at the foot of his bed. The last time he had wakened it was dark and he had struck a match to see the time: five-thirty. He had slept badly, waking from nightmares to walk the room and smoke. He was hungry. He remembered that the officers' mess opened for breakfast at seven-thirty. He raised his head as if to get up and he fell back again on the pillow. He was hungry but he was also weary. He lay and blinked at the sunlight.

It made him think of the darkness in the cellar on Thaelmannstrasse and the children lying there on the straw mattress and coughing. At this hour Frau Wagner was probably bustling over the stove, and Emmerich Wagner no doubt was gazing at the tarpaulin on the ceiling and mumbling, "It must be a clear day. There's no water leaking down."

And then he thought of Erika Wagner and of the child she would bear, Hockland's child, and how curious are the accidents of birth that allowed a child to fall heir to a damp cellar in Thaelmannstrasse instead of a house on Elm Street in a town called Pleasantville somewhere in America. It wasn't the percept of God but the law of man which ordained that this child should die on Thaelmannstrasse and not live to grow up on Elm Street. He thought of his own father and mother and how lucky he had been to have been born to a sound middle-class family in Erie, Pennsylvania.

He wondered how much it mattered to a woman to understand her father, and he thought of Thémis and the father who had disowned her. In his mind he saw her clearly and all at once he felt elated that the day was just beginning and that he would see her again before its close. She wouldn't try to board the Paris train—not *this* morning. He was certain of it.

In spite of the finality with which she had left him the night before, something told him that he would see her again. It was right and it was inevitable.

He felt relaxed now, and happy. A train whistle died in the distance. A convoy of trucks passed on the street beneath and made his window vibrate. There were sounds of sweeping in the corridor. It was seven o'clock and the chambermaids had begun their day's work. He wondered what Thémis was doing. Then his mind tightened abruptly as he thought of Marriner. The general would be awake now, breakfasting in his mansion off Bismarck Allee, and soon he would be driven to the *Electrowerke* building, with Parker sitting smugly in the front seat next to the driver. And when the summaries of the night's reports were brought into the big office, Marriner would know that he had not sent Thémis away.

The thought brought him briskly out of bed. He would have to face up to explanations quickly demanded and quickly listened to.

He bathed and dressed quickly, the idea growing in his mind that he would be equal to whatever the day offered. Let Marriner do the worrying. He felt unexplicably serene. He even whistled as he went down the stairs to breakfast.

There were three officers in the dining room when he entered, all of them reading copies of the *Stars and Stripes*. One of them, a G-2 major, lifted his head and said, "G'morning, Lashley. French toast again. Stinks. They've got a great system in this mess. Whenever I don't get up for breakfast they serve ham and eggs. Whenever I do—French toast."

Lashley walked by him quickly and went to a corner table.

Blond Hedy brought him orange juice, French toast, coffee, and the *Stars and Stripes*. As she poured the coffee she brushed against his arm and said, "Herr Nissen wait for you yesterday *nacht*."

"Yes," he muttered, not looking up. A small item on the front page of the paper held his eyes.

It was datelined from Paris and it read:

The French Ministry of Justice stated today that an investigation was under way to determine the standing of the "mystery witness" who testified for the defense at the Reschweiler war crimes trial. The witness, Thémis Delisle, interceded unsuccessfully for Otto Steigmann, who last Monday evening was condemned to death. Reacting to sharp commentaries in the Paris press, a Ministry official remarked, "There is evidence that the woman was friendly with the enemy." She is believed to be en route to Paris in the custody of the French authorities.

As soon as he reached his office Lashley began to dial the number of 135th Station Hospital but he did not get beyond the third figure. His attention was arrested by the sight of Lance Nissen conducting a bearded man into his office.

They stood inside the doorway—stalwart, blond-haired Nissen, his young face, his broad shoulders, his uniform, in contrast to a very old, very frail man in a dark coat. It struck Lashley that this was the first time he had seen an aged Jew during the year he had spent in Germany.

He was almost as tall as Nissen, but his body was stooped with great weariness. The long black coat that hung loosely from his narrow body was thin material, patched in many places. His hand held his hat against his chest with trembling fingers, and his pale, almost transparent skin bespoke frailty and utter exhaustion. Yet there was an air of quiet strength about him, of dignity and peace.

Lashley said, "Please come in," and indicated a chair.

Nissen came to the side of the desk. "Listen to this man's story, will you?" There was a note of outrage in his voice.

"Who is he?" Lashley asked.

"Jakob Meyersohn." Nissen gave the name its German pronunciation. "He runs a tailor shop on Grenauerstrasse."

"What's it about?"

"Just listen. You'll hear. You'll hear plenty."

Both looked at Meyersohn. He passed his hand down the length of his beard, not nervously but with authority, as if he expected these young men to give him their respect, and he said, "Captain Nissen. May I ask to whom I am speaking?"

Nissen said in German, "I am sorry. We are so accustomed to speaking in English together——"

Meyersohn nodded. "I understand."

"This is Major Lashley. He was the prosecutor in the Steigmann trial."

"Major Lashley." The old Jew bowed briefly and sedately, and placed his hat on the side of the desk.

"Look, Bob," Nissen said in English, "I'll give it to you quick. As I get it, this man's lived here most of his life. Of course, not the last few years. The Nazis got his entire family, wife, sons, daughters, grandchildren, but somehow he's survived. He runs sort of a tailor shop—and, well——"

Lashley held up his hand. "Just a minute, Lance. I'd like to hear it from him."

He said in German, "Herr Meyersohn, would you please tell me what you have to say."

Meyersohn sighed. "I have come here," he said, "to plead for Frau Steigmann."

Lashley was puzzled. "But, Herr Meyersohn, no one has threatened Frau Steigmann in any way. Why should you plead for her?"

"Perhaps I must tell you from the beginning. Before the concentration camp I was a teacher of Hebrew here. When I was liberated I returned to Reschweiler in the vain hope that some one of my family had survived. Day after day I wandered through the streets, looking for a familiar face. One night, scanning the faces of those seeking shelter in the railroad station, I heard a voice say, 'Herr Meyersohn, I am Ilse Steigmann.'

"I looked around. It was a woman—a stranger. Poverty and hunger were written on her face, and on the face of her little son at her side. 'You knew me as Ilse Dostelberg,' she said. And then a whole world passed before my eyes. Ilse Dostelberg had been a friend of my daughter Ruth, and they were in school together. She came of a fine German family, and now—and now they had no place to live, and no food. I took her into my home. Through the kindness of your military government, I was provided with dwelling and rations, because I am a Jew and because I am very old."

Lashley interjected, "To recompense you in some small way for your sufferings—but not to share with the wife of a war criminal."

The old man shrugged his shoulders almost imperceptibly. "Perhaps. But *my* suffering was in the past. And it was an unexpected joy to be able to share. Besides, there is great goodness in Ilse. She is not her husband."

Herr Meyersohn paused, as if briefly fatigued, and shut his eyes.

Lashley said, "But I still don't see why you have to plead for Frau Steigmann."

Meyersohn looked from one man to the other, then addressed himself to Lashley:

"Last evening a man came to my house and demanded in a very loud voice to see Ilse. When Ilse appeared this man screamed that she must give him five hundred marks, otherwise she will be denounced to the Americans and thrown in prison. I pleaded with him but he shouted even louder."

"Who was the man?" Lashley demanded, though he had unhappily begun to suspect the answer.

"He did not tell me," Meyersohn replied. "He was a small man, and he spoke with a foreign accent and with great violence."

"Rodal, of course," muttered Nissen.

Lashley said, "Did you give him the money?"

The old man shook his head. "I have no money. Nor has Ilse. Ilse Steigmann has done no harm to a living soul all her life, Captain Lashley, believe me. Please do not arrest her!"

"Herr Meyersohn," Lashley said with feeling, "this man was not sent from here. It is not necessary to give him anything."

Meyersohn sighed. "I thought it was so. And yet he is in a position to denounce Ilse. It is done every day, often for dishonest purposes. I told him to come another time. He will return, so he said, at eleven o'clock this morning, and he warned me to have the money ready."

Lashley was no longer intent on Meyersohn's story. His mind was seized with the conviction that Rodal was insane and that whatever case he had against Otto Steigmann was foundering. Only a madman could carry bitterness so far as to threaten a harmless old man.

As though reading his thoughts, Nissen suddenly projected himself across the desk and shouted, "That's why I brought Meyersohn here. I want to do something about that son of a bitch—that cheap little blackmailer—that star witness of yours!"

Lashley turned on him furiously. "God damn it! I'll handle it in my own way—without your advice."

He looked at his watch. It was nine-forty. He said, "Will you leave Herr Meyersohn with me? Alone?"

Nissen opened his mouth to speak, then sighed. He picked up his cap from the desk and walked out.

The old man was fatigued, his head was nodding on his chest, and his thin, eloquent fingers were trembling. But his eyes were wonderfully alert and bright. Lashley thought he must be eighty at least, and wondered how he had survived Hitler's scourge.

"Where do you live, Herr Meyersohn?"

"Grenauerstrasse. Number 192. It is near Kaiser Allee."

Lashley had only a remote idea of the location, though he knew it was at least two miles away.

"You walked here? Up the hill?"

Meyersohn lifted his head. "A man does what he can; there was no one to send."

"Yes, Captain Nissen told me you had lost your entire family," Lashley said.

"Yes, my entire family. I prayed that I should die with them and not be left alone in the world. But God willed otherwise, and I survived. Sometimes I wonder why, for there were many, many more useful and more deserving of life than I, who died of gas, sickness, torture, and starvation."

The simple declaration of faith held Lashley silent for a moment. Then he said, "I still find it strange that you should harbor the wife and son of one who has done you so much injury. Is there no limit, Herr Meyersohn, to forgiveness?"

The reply was uttered gravely, and the old man's eyes shone. "In my loneliness and despair, I have cried out to God, 'Let me hate them with every bit of the life that is left in me'— but I knew God's answer before it was spoken. Hatred only begets hatred. It is evil and all the works of hatred are evil— slander, lying, wrath, war, and violence. Those who live in hate shall die of it. This is a simple truth and the sum of our Jewish teaching. See how we have survived, even though we are a scattered handful among the peoples of the earth. And should we ever forget this truth, and preach hatred and violence—on that day we shall be swept from the earth, as others have been before and since we came into being."

Lashley half turned to look at the window, which was streaming with sunlight. "I envy your faith, Herr Meyersohn. It seems to make everything so easy for you."

"Easy?"

"Yes, even unutterable suffering. It seems to be a constant and trustworthy guide in everything you do. I find that sometimes—sometimes it is not easy to know what is right and what is just."

He faced into the sun and listened for the reply.

"Faith is never easy. For faith, *true* faith, is always a constant, tortured, humble self-examination. It is a spur and a prod, not a mantle to muffle one's doubts and fears." He paused. "I can see that you are troubled. I can see that you seek justice in a spirit of humility. Out of the anguish of your heart, out of your humble searching justice will come."

And as Lashley turned from the window he looked at the old man's burning eyes and had the curious feeling that he had seen him somewhere before—and suddenly he knew he had seen him everywhere before, for this Jew had a light in his eyes, the light that shone in all of the learned and the humble everywhere in the world.

He looked down at his watch. Time was running short. It was already ten o'clock. He telephoned the motor pool and ordered a staff car. Then he rose and said, "When you go down to the courtyard you will find an automobile to drive you to your house. I will be there in an hour, and I will see this man who threatens Frau Steigmann."

Meyersohn placed his hat carefully on his head.

"I shall be indebted beyond my mean capacity to repay you."

Lashley said, "I think you have already repaid me, Herr Meyersohn."

Lashley dialed the number of 135th Station Hospital. When Captain Bossin came to the phone he didn't try to conceal his anxiety.

"I was just going to call you, Major. Better come over."

"You mean the boy is——"

"It's the crisis, Major. We've got him under oxygen. Temperature's way up. So's respiration. He's putting up a great fight but——" There was a pause. "I don't think he'll make it."

Lashley looked blankly into the telephone.

"Hello, hello," Bossin called.

Lashley said, "I'll be over, Captain," and put down the phone.

He wondered why the phone hadn't rung, why Parker's mannered voice wasn't summoning him to appear before the general.

Now would be a good time for the general to call. Now it wouldn't matter. The boy was dying, and in the light of this circumstance he and the general were insignificant. The general could break him; it didn't matter.

He got up quickly and pulled his coat off the hook as he went out of the office.

He stopped at the big room down the corridor facing the head of the stairs. Nissen was at his desk holding court over a War Crimes staff of Wacs and tech sergeants and Pfc. clerks.

Nissen looked up eagerly. "Want me to go along, Bob? We'll catch the bastard red-handed."

"I'd rather handle it alone, thanks," Lashley said. "But there's something else you can do for me. If a call comes from Marriner's office, tell them I'll be back in a couple of hours. And get hold of the provost marshal and find out if Thémis Delisle tried to leave town this morning."

"You mean she's still here?"

"I renewed the order last night."

Nissen gave a low whistle. "Okay, Napoleon." He made a gesture of polishing the double bar on his epaulette. "That extra grade is going to look damn nice on me when Marriner throws you out."

As Lashley turned to leave, Nissen called out, "Bet you a drink."

"What?"

"Bet you the little lady is on her way to Paris right now." Lashley scowled. "Bet," he said, and made for the stairs.

Crosby was singing "Easter Parade" over the radio in Ward 3. Most of the men dozed. Two were playing checkers on a small table between their beds. The patient nearest the door was reading *Western Stories*. The place smelled not unpleasantly of heat and rubbing alcohol.

At the far end of the ward extra screens had been placed around Hockland's bed. Two nurses came briskly and solemnly out of the enclosure and left the ward. A few moments later one of them returned, accompanied by an iron-gray major, and they went behind the screens.

Lashley heard one of the checker players say, "We got a croaker for sure." The other replied, "Them Fräuleins. They give yuh a dose or a bullet. Your move."

Bossin came out of the enclosure, saw Lashley, and hurried over to him. As he approached he removed the stethoscope from his ears and shook his head slowly.

"We've got a lounge out there," he said, and led the way past the reception desk and through a door marked "Officer Staff Only." Beyond was a cheerful room with comfortable chairs and magazines.

"Can you sit down for a minute?" said Bossin.

"I haven't got much time," Lashley replied. The clock on the wall showed twenty-five minutes past ten.

Bossin played nervously with his stethoscope.

"Same here, Major," he said. "I've got only a minute myself. We just decided to operate on the kid. We're going to remove the fluid from his good lung."

"What does that mean?"

"He'll breathe easier for a few hours, that's all."

Lashley said, "Is there a chance that he'll——"

"That he'll die on the table? No." Bossin pulled out a cigarette and lighted it. "He'll live a little longer. Maybe a couple of days. But he won't make it, not a chance."

Lashley frowned and said, "God damn it."

"Not God, Major. God didn't shoot him. God didn't arrange for the girl to shoot him. We did—all of us. It's funny how nice we can arrange these things. We're smart. We can arrange everything—washing machines and electric lights and radios. This shooting too. It's all our genius for arranging. God had nothing to do with it. All He did was give the kid a fine, strong body and an innocent mind. We did the rest."

Lashley said, "When can I see him?"

"We're going to operate in a few minutes. He'll come out of it tonight and he'll sleep fairly well. Tomorrow he'll feel stronger. Better see him tomorrow. It may be the last day. That's the way it is. You remove the fluid and they feel okay. And then they go fast."

They were silent after that. Bossin was smoking steadily, looking off into space. Finally he sat up with a start and said to Lashley, "I knew there was something I had to tell you. There was a Colonel Pike from G-1 here this morning. He asked about the kid and when we told him he said to keep the kid alive as long as we could. As if we wouldn't. Seems he's an only child, and the army is flying his parents from the States to see him——"

Lashley muttered, "That's big of the army."

"I think it is," said Bossin in a slightly offended tone. "It'll make it easier for the kid's people and it won't do the army any harm. It's good publicity for a change, after all the lousy publicity they've had about GIs and Fräuleins."

"When do they arrive?"

Bossin shrugged his shoulders. "Tomorrow, I guess." He took another long drag from his cigarette. "Remember what I told you about where the kid came from. I said it was Iowa or Kansas and I was right. His people are Mr. and Mrs. Elmer Hockland and they come from a place called Bensiman, Iowa. I can just picture the town."

Lashley was no longer listening carefully. He was thinking of Rodal and an idea began to take shape in his mind.

"Is there a psychiatrist attached to the staff?" he asked Bossin.

"We all take a stab at it," Bossin said. "I'm pretty good at the combat cases. After all, I was a battalion doc for two years. Why?"

"I'd like you to look over somebody for me—if I can arrange to get him here."

"Send him on."

Lashley thought hard a moment. "Look, Captain. This is a little tricky. I'm going to send a couple of refugees to see you —a girl and a man. I don't know what the pretext will be, but whatever it is, remember this: it's the man I want you to observe. His name is Rodal. Try to get a line on his mental condition, will you? You'll be doing me a great favor."

"What's the pitch?"

"He was a witness in a case of mine. I'd like to know how sane he is—or how mad."

"Good enough. I'll look him over."

On his way out of the hospital Lashley stopped at the reception desk phone to check with Nissen.

Nissen sounded breathless. "Bob—hello, hello—can you hear me? All hell's breaking loose and——"

"What's happening?" asked Lashley soberly. "Did Marriner call?"

"That's just it," yelled Nissen. "He didn't call here. But he did call the provost marshal."

"How do you know?" Lashley demanded.

"I spoke to the provost. At nine o'clock this morning Marriner phoned him himself. He ordered him to pick up the Delisle gal and deliver her by staff car to the French zone—get this—where there'd be an escort to meet her."

Lashley's fingers tightened on the phone. With his free hand he rummaged in his pocket for a cigarette. He fumbled frantically without success.

"Hello, Bob. That's not all."

"What else?" said Lashley grimly.

"They can't find the gal. She wasn't at her billet. She didn't go to the train. They're covering the town—and they can't find her. Are you in trouble, brother! What're you going to do?"

"I don't know. Right now I've got to see Herr Meyersohn," he said, and dropped the phone on its hook.

X

LASHLEY BRAKED HIS JEEP AT THE BIG TRAFFIC CIRCLE IN front of the *Bahnhof* and inquired of a German policeman the way to Grenauerstrasse. The policeman was young, perhaps twenty-four, and stolidly proud of his authority and of his deep blue uniform with the red piping. He halted traffic with a sharp note on his whistle and a commanding gesture of his arms—all preliminary to answering the major's inquiry.

While traffic piled up on the two streets which met at the circle, the policeman said, *"Grenauerstrasse, ja,"* and pointed generally in the direction in which Lashley was traveling. *"Grade aus bis zur Kaiser Allee, und dann nach rechts und links—zusammen eine Kilometer,"* he said, and returned unhurriedly to his post.

Lashley drove along Bahnhofstrasse until he came to the wide intersection of Kaiser Allee. Here a figure of Frederick the Great looked out on heaps of rubble which Lashley thought must have been the financial district of the city. The burned-out buildings around the park, not one of them habitable, had the solid architecture of banks and insurance head offices.

He turned right on Kaiser Allee. Except for some children playing hide-and-go-seek among the cones of rubble piled neatly along the curb, the street was deserted. Seeing his jeep, the children ran toward him shouting "Schocolate" and

"Chooeeng gom." They were sturdy children, with round rosy cheeks. It amazed Lashley as the contrasts in Reschweiler constantly amazed him.

But he did not slow down until the first cross street. It was Milchstrasse. The second street was Grenauerstrasse. Turning left into it, he parked his jeep close to the corner. He chained the steering wheel and walked along the street, watching the numbers.

It had been a lucky street. A stray fire bomb had dropped here and there, burning out a few scattered roofs, but obviously no blockbusters had come down. The street was lined on both sides with boardinghouses, festooned this morning with glaring red feather beds hanging from the windows for airing. The houses were nearly alike, each with a gate opening on a small discolored lawn in the center of which was a squat sign giving the name of the house; two steps leading up to a garishly curtained front door; and to the right of the door and below it, narrow cement steps leading down to the cellar door.

The first house was number 168 and the sign on the lawn read "*Ritterhaus.*" The second was "*Müllerhaus.*"

Lashley walked quickly until he came to number 192. It was a bigger house than most on the street and rather shabbier. Originally four stories, the roof had been burned and the red feather beds hung out only as high as the third story. The sign on the lawn read "*Bendlerhaus*" and beneath it, suspended on hooks, was a smaller sign—"*Meyersohn Schneiderei.*"

The gate creaked as Lashley pushed it open, and Meyersohn appeared at the door of the cellar apartment.

"You are a man of your word, Major Lashley. I beg you to come in."

He led the way along a passage so narrow Lashley had to twist his broad shoulders. They came into a small, oblong room sparsely lighted by a tiny window at the far end. Along one wall stood a pressing board, and along the other there was a table strewn with oddments of skirts and blouses and bits of cloth. Under the window there was space for two chairs and a tailor's dummy.

"Please be seated," Meyersohn said. "Would you like to see Frau Steigmann?"

Lashley said, "If I may."

"She is not well. She has been sick with worry since last night."

"Is she concerned also about her husband?"

Meyersohn shook his head. "She has cast him out of her mind, as one casts out evil thoughts."

"Then she believes he is guilty?" Lashley asked eagerly.

"She is a good woman. When they came to tell her of the verdict, she wept—as a good person must weep in the presence of death even for the most heinous of men—and she said, 'The Americans are a just people. If they have found him guilty, then surely he deserves to be punished.' "

Lashley stiffened in his chair.

The old man walked into the passage, pausing as he passed to pick up a remnant of cloth and toss it aside contemptuously. Lashley heard a sharp knocking and Meyersohn's voice saying, "Ilse, the American officer is here."

Lashley glanced about the little shop. A few GI jackets hung next to the pressing board, and piled in a corner of the table was their corollary—some bars of "Oh Henry" chocolate, three packs of chewing gum, a cake of soap, and a few loose cigarettes, the legal tender of the occupation zone. On a shelf beneath the window sill, in incongruous dignity, were several tomes, their leather covers so frayed with age that the Hebrew lettering was scarcely visible.

Meyersohn appeared out of the passage. "Frau Steigmann is coming down. Meanwhile, I will stand at the door to watch for the man."

Lashley heard a latch click and Ilse Steigmann came into the room.

She was a small woman, so thin that her heavy black dress hung on her like a kimono. When her face came out of the shadows Lashley felt a sense of shock, the same feeling of out-

rage he had felt when he first saw Rodal and Maria, and before
that, when his jeep rumbled to the crest of a French hill and
he saw the wreckage of St. Lô.

He could not imagine her ever having been a pretty woman,
although her grace and slightness indicated that she might have
been. Now her mouth was locked in a downward curve and
it seemed to pull all of her face into its ugliness. In the dimness
her eyes appeared of exaggerated size and curiously lifeless.
Her black hair was bundled at the back of her head. She was
a tragic figure and even knowing that she was the wife of a
ruthless man could not keep Lashley from pitying her.

She came forward timidly and extended her hand. *"Mein-
herr,"* she said in a dull voice.

Lashley stood up. "Frau Steigmann——"

There was no quickness in her blue eyes. He felt that he
might have said anything and they would have looked the
same. She continued to look at him for a few moments, then
her head sank and she wept.

Meyersohn came out of the passageway, saying, "He has not
come. Perhaps he has changed his mind——"

When he saw Frau Steigmann crying, he stopped short.
"Why do you cry, my child? It is not necessary."

Frau Steigmann did not raise her head and her quiet sobbing
filled the little room. The old man walked over and put his
hand on her shoulder.

Just then there was a thump at the outer door. Lashley
started forward, but Herr Meyersohn stopped him, saying, "I
will go alone. It is possible that he has changed his mind. I
have prayed that he be spared the commission of this evil." He
disappeared into the gloom of the passageway.

After a brief silence Lashley heard the sound of low conversation, then suddenly a raised voice harsh with the guttural
inflections of German argot.

He was starting for the door when Rodal plunged into the
room, shouting in German, "I want my money! Where is Frau
Steigmann——"

The Czech caught sight of Lashley and stopped short. He divided a quick, perplexed glance between the American and the woman, and his clenched hands came down to his side. He lowered his head, seeking to shield it from the light, turned abruptly, and ran back into the dark passageway.

Lashley caught up his cap and hurried after him. Meyersohn was still standing disconsolately at the foot of the basement steps.

"Herr Meyersohn——"

The old man looked up. His eyes were bright with tears. A large woman wearing a quilted red kimono, her gray hair done up in curlers, leaned from the stoop above and waved a dusting rag.

"*Dorten—dorten, Herr Offizier!*" she exclaimed.

Rodal and Maria were scuttling along the street, he bending low and she running with awkward little steps to keep up with him. They were nearing the intersection of Kaiser Allee.

Lashley jammed on his cap and went after them. He was fifty yards behind when they turned left into the big street and disappeared. He started to sprint, then slowed to a brisk walk. Windows on both sides of the street were suddenly filled with inquiring heads, mostly of housewives, and in this purely German neighborhood he was conscious of his dignity as an American officer.

By the time he reached the corner he was walking stiff-legged from the effort of trying to control his speed. Kaiser Allee was deserted. He turned slowly in the direction Rodal and Maria had taken.

As far as he could see there was not a habitable building on either side of the street, not even a catacomb where the fugitives might be lurking. Doors and windows were overflowing with rubble.

He walked about a hundred yards before he discovered his first frantic look was wrong. Two tiny places of business were wedged together in between the ghosts of the huge financial structures which had once lined the street. One displayed a sign, "*Kolonialwaren*," and a few dusty tins of food in its window. The other had no sign but he saw through its curtained door that it was a *Bierstube*.

He pushed at the door of the *Bierstube* and went in.

Three shabby men looked up furtively from one of the tables. The other half-dozen tables were empty. A single lamp glimmered dully behind a small bar and cast a sheen on the bald head of a huge man who stood with his hands motionless on the spigot of a wine barrel. A box radio on a shelf above the bar droned a Strauss waltz.

Lashley stood inside the door. "Did a man come in here?" he demanded.

"Man?" The bartender exchanged glances with the three men at the table.

"A man and a Fräulein," Lashley said sharply.

The bartender moved his head slowly from side to side. His shirt, open at the neck, had violent navy-blue stripes running vertically into his ample stomach. The shirt appeared to be of silk, and a bulky diamond flashed from a ring on his finger.

Lashley turned abruptly to the three men. They hastily picked up their steins, drained them, and shuffled to their feet.

"What do you want?" the bartender grunted, coming around from behind the bar.

Lashley glanced swiftly around the room. There was a door at the back, to the left of the bar. He started toward it. The bartender, moving rapidly for so big a man, intercepted him between two tables.

Their eyes met angrily across the inches that separated them. Lashley took a step forward. The German held his ground, his heavy breath striking unpleasantly across the American's face. They stood motionless, chin almost touching chin, and glared at each other like a pair of leashed dogs until Lashley could no longer stand the man's insolence. He shifted his right shoulder as if to thrust aside the fleshy face, and as he did the German turned his head slightly in a crafty gesture of non-belligerence, but did not move his bulky frame.

With his left hand Lashley felt for a grip on the beveled edge of one of the tables. Still looking into the man's face, he gradually raised one end of the table until its red-checked cloth slipped to the floor. The German's face was impassive. The table came higher. It teetered on two legs. Lashley watched his opponent and the man watched the table, grimly diverted.

With a sudden flip of his arm Lashley upended the table. It struck against a chair, spinning it out of the way, and fell upside down on the floor. The German looked at the upset table with a dull clownish curiosity. Lashley stepped around him, strode to the door near the bar, and pushed it open.

He was in a storeroom musty with the smell of spilled wine. An oil lamp flickered on a shelf. Sitting on stubby wine kegs in a corner were Rodal and Maria.

The Czech seemed only mildly concerned. He gaped at the figure of the American framed in the narrow doorway, then a look of injury mingled with defiance came into his cadaverous face. He leaned sideways and whispered into Maria's ear. His discolored lips moved but his voice was inaudible. The girl's eyes opened wide and a grin spread over her unwashed face. She tittered and pulled pleasurably at the ends of her scraggy blond hair.

Lashley stopped in the doorway. As it did every time he witnessed it, this strangely tender affinity between them intrigued and distracted him.

All at once the girl stopped tittering. She looked desolately into the Czech's face, extended her hands, and said in high-pitched German, "My hands are clean, are they not, Rodal?" And the reply came quickly: "*Ja*, Maria. They are clean. Fine and clean." He stroked her dirt-stained fingers.

Lashley heard the table in the *Bierstube* being righted and guttural whispers among the men. He closed the door behind him.

The Czech rose sullenly. The dull light made his face look deep yellow and, as though it were an X ray, it seemed to lay bare all the misery of his past. For a moment Lashley struggled again with the most familiar of all postwar dilemmas—the problem of judging between the tortured and the evil.

"I could arrest you, Rodal," he said.

"For why?" muttered the Czech.

"You know damn well why. You're a blackmailer, a filthy little blackmailer, and I could put you in jail for it. By God, I think I will!"

Maria began to whimper and Rodal reached over and stroked her hair. The whimpering subsided.

"You German?" Rodal said, looking unhappily into Lashley's face.

"You know I'm not!"

Rodal threw up one shoulder contemptuously.

"For why you protect German beasts?"

At that moment Lashley heard the stealthy brush of a body against the door behind him. He backed against it without taking his eyes off Rodal. "I don't protect the guilty. I punish them. I punished the seven in the *Gericht*." He stepped forward and grasped the man roughly by the shoulders. "My duty is to punish the guilty and protect the innocent. And I'll punish you, Rodal."

The Czech spat.

"You know nothing, my Major."

Lashley shook him angrily. "You're a devil, Rodal. You swore on the witness stand. I don't believe a word of what you swore. Do you hear that? Not a word!"

Maria squealed pitifully. The Czech shook himself loose from Lashley's grasp and sat beside her on the wine keg. He squeezed her hand spasmodically and whispered in her ear, before he looked up.

"You know nothing, my Major," he repeated.

Rodal made a sound as if he were spitting a cherry pit.

He said, "Frau Steigmann mus' give money. She beast. Mus' give money me *und* Maria. Not your bus'ness."

Lashley grabbed at the man's lapels and jerked him to his feet.

"You're mad, Rodal!"

Maria began to moan hysterically.

"You hear her, Rodal! She's crazy and so are you. You're a

blackmailing little devil. You don't belong in any case of mine, and by God——"

The air in the storeroom was foul. Sweat poured from his forehead into his eyes and made them smart. He glared at the Czech and he wondered how he had ever accepted him as his principal witness. Had he wanted so desperately to convict Steigmann? To score a personal triumph? The thought drained the anger from him and he dropped his hands from the Czech's coat.

He said roughly, "Tell me, Rodal, what were you before the war?"

"Student."

"What were you studying?"

"*Doktor—Medizin.*" The Czech's eyelids fluttered and his voice was morose.

Lashley said, "If you were studying medicine you must have wanted to help human beings."

Rodal spat into the corner.

"Why do you torture Frau Steigmann? Why, Rodal? She has done you no harm. She is a poor woman. She is suffering enough."

The man twisted his head until his chin touched his shoulder. He remained as if paralyzed in this position a few moments, moving his lips feverishly. Finally he turned to face his inquisitor and smiled with sudden and inexplicable ecstasy.

He lapsed into German. "Not everyone knows how to deal with these beasts—as I do. I know how to deal with them. They are afraid of me—all of them. I am the master now."

The last vestige of anger fell from Lashley's mind. He studied the Czech as a scientist might study an ailing guinea pig. The man was insane. Bossin would establish the fact. He must get the man to Bossin.

He said, "What about those out there?" indicating the *Bierstube*. "Your friends?"

Rodal tapped his chest significantly. "They suit my purpose. I do business with them. They are afraid of me—like all the others."

"They gave you the information about Frau Steigmann——"

Rodal scowled. "Who is she that she shouldn't pay?" he demanded. "She is no longer one of the master race. Let her not forget it. She has not even begun to pay. She has a body— let her sell herself." He panted with indignation.

Lashley said evenly, "You would send Frau Steigmann into the streets."

"Why not?" the Czech shouted. "The Americans pay. That's more than the Germans did, more than they did for Maria." He stroked the girl's head eagerly. "In the *Lager* on the hill they ravished her every day, five—ten times a day, whenever an SS beast wanted a woman he ravished Maria. Why should Frau Steigmann be spared? So she can be pure for another beast?

"You Americans are fools!" The Czech thrust forward his yellow face. "Your minds are stuffed like your stomachs—full of fats and good things. You hang one beast or a dozen, and you are satisfied. What good does that do me? Eh, what good? Who is going to pay me? At Bergen Belsen they locked me in a railway truck with ten others and threw in a stick of sausage. When we arrived in Nordhausen I was the one who was alive. I—Rodal. We fought for a stick of sausage. For six days and six nights we fought. We killed—and I survived. Who is going to pay me for that?"

His mouth, contorted in rage, suddenly broke into another terrifying smile. "They will pay me—all of them," he chuckled.

Lashley sought to humor the man. "We will discuss it. We will strike a bargain."

Maria was making little bleating noises. Rodal went to her side.

"Have you ever heard of Theresienstadt?" he shouted. "They brought her there when she was eleven. Eleven! They put a whip in her hand and they pushed her into the gas chamber. Her mother was there—in the gas chamber—naked —with all the others—all naked——"

The foul air in the storeroom was making Lashley queasy. He leaned against a wall and wiped sweat from his brow.

A wild grin lit the Czech's face. "It is difficult for you to listen. You will listen. Puh!" He spat.

"They pushed pins into her buttocks and she lashed the naked people—all the naked people and her mother among them. The beasts laughed. It was comical. Everybody danced under the whip. They danced until they could dance no longer. And when everybody lay exhausted from dancing, they took the girl from the chamber and they turned on the gas——"

The Czech's tongue moved on his lips and his eyes rolled as if they were loose in their sockets.

"Now you know why her hands are unclean." His head shook convulsively. "It was clever of them. They did not expend much gas because the people were already half dead. They saved money——"

He stamped his foot on the floor. He shouted crazily: "I want that money! I want it for me and Maria. Who will say we should not have it? Who will say Frau Steigmann should not pay it?"

Lashley waited until the man's panting subsided. Then he said, "Do you want to make a bargain with me?"

Rodal muttered suspiciously, "What is your proposition?"

"Do you want the girl to be well?"

Rodal looked at Maria. "She is not well. I would like her to be well."

"If you do not ask Frau Steigmann for money, I will arrange for Maria to see a good doctor."

Rodal sucked his lips. "I would like Maria to be well."

"Then you must promise you will not ask Frau Steigmann for money. If you break your word I will put you in prison."

The Czech pondered the matter and a devilish grin came into his face.

"How do I know you are not trying to fool me?"

Lashley said, "I will give you a note. You may go today to the American hospital and they will examine Maria and give you medicine."

Rodal nodded slowly and stroked Maria's hair.

"Give me the note."

Lashley wrote a note to Bossin and handed it over.

"But remember. If you trouble Frau Steigmann you will go to prison."

The Czech spat. And Maria uttered a series of little whines.

When Lashley came out into the street his eyes smarted with the glare of sunlight. He leaned against a pile of rubble and breathed deeply again and again.

He knew now that Rodal was a madman, that his testimony was worthless. If Bossin confirmed it he would act decisively. This much he promised himself.

He'd take care of that tomorrow. Right now he was going to get a quick cup of coffee and a sandwich and then get back to his telephone. Marriner would certainly be on his neck before long.

XI

At five o'clock he was still at his desk. The afternoon hours had gone slowly. He had spent them reading interrogation reports on a German butcher awaiting trial on charges of having incited a mob of townspeople to murder an American flier back in 1944. But his mind was only superficially concerned with the document. The telephone sat on his desk like a thing of menace. His eyes turned frequently to the clock on the wall. He was like a sentry at a front-line outpost, straining for an untoward sound but praying devoutly that he will be relieved before hell breaks loose.

Nissen had come in about three, pretending a heartiness which had failed to divert Lashley. He was a good friend, and his manner was refreshingly sincere, but his sympathy was better attuned to a crestfallen football hero than to matters of life and death. Lashley longed to see Thémis. All day long his thoughts had been returning to the evening before. Whatever the truth was about her, he knew he wanted to be near her. How bizarre that she should step into his life at this time. And how quickly she had come to mean so much. He admitted it now.

The mystery of her whereabouts persisted. The telephone had rung once during the afternoon. The bell made him jump as so often happens when one consciously awaits a sound. It

was the provost marshal reporting his failure to apprehend
Thémis. Lashley had dropped the phone quickly and tried to
concentrate on the document which lay before him. The case
of the German butcher was an interesting one, but the typewritten words danced on the page.

Now it was five o'clock. He gathered up his papers, shoved
them into a filing cabinet, banged the steel door shut, and
snapped the padlock. The office was officially closed for the
day. Let the phone ring now if it must—he wouldn't have to
answer it.

Curiously enough he was not anxious to leave the office. He
realized that he had been half expecting Thémis to come as
she had yesterday. Subconsciously he was listening for the
sound of her approaching footsteps, but the corridor was
empty and silent.

He wondered if she had been in hiding during the day.
Curious that she could have eluded capture so long, for she was
being sought as any suspected criminal is sought. The provost
marshal had carefully explained that Marriner had ordered the
woman expelled from the Eleventh Army area, which was his
prerogative, and he had specified the mode of transport and
the point of exit from the area. This was clever of Marriner,
Lashley thought, for it superseded his own authority to retain
Thémis on the pretext of further questioning.

He heard a step at the head of the staircase and a clatter of
heels on the corridor floor. He listened breathlessly. And then
he heard the insertion of a key in a door near by and he relaxed
in disappointment.

It began to worry him that Marriner had not summoned him.
The general was noted for his exacting discipline in matters
concerning his authority. And yet the day had passed and he
had not been called to explain his conduct. He was disturbed
by a sense of foreboding. Something was in the wind, something unpleasant and final, and he looked out on the cool, clean
night with troubled eyes.

Light footsteps came down the corridor. Someone was pausing at the head of the staircase as though undecided. Now the

footsteps came on once more, steadily and distinctly. He could not tell whether they were the steps of a man or a woman; they were at the door now. The handle squeaked and the door opened.

He swung his chair around. Standing in his office was Lieutenant Parker.

The lieutenant did not speak. Rummaging in his overcoat pocket, he brought out a brown envelope and, approaching the desk, held it out.

"The general would like you to read this, if you will, sir." The last words were uttered with a slight emphasis.

Lashley took the envelope.

"Is that all, Parker?" he said carelessly.

"The general gave me a message for you."

"Well?"

"After you read the communication."

Lashley glanced at him sharply. "Were those his orders?"

"Yes."

Lashley swiveled his chair around, turning his back on Parker. He tore open the envelope and read:

From: Gen J Marriner, CG 11th Army
To: Maj RM Lashley, AA-JAG
Subject: Execution of war criminals

1. On 8 April 46 US War Crimes tribunal under presidency of Col WH Macklin decreed sentence of death by hanging on six convicted criminals, after due legal processes entered into at Reschweiler.
2. The trial records were dispatched to JAG, USFET, and to CG, USFET, for review and possible approval and confirmation.
3. JAG, USFET, and CG, USFET, have approved the convictions and have confirmed death sentences of the six whose names and serial numbers may be found in Appendix A. The sentence of life imprisonment upon the seventh prisoner has also been confirmed.
4. I have this day commanded CO, Bergsdorf Prison, to proceed with the execution of the six condemned at dawn on the day of 13 April 46.
5. As permanent officer. JAG War Crimes Branch presently attached

for duty with the 11th Army, you are instructed to be present in the capacity of an official witness at the place of execution.

6. For your immediate attention and necessary action.

J MARRINER
CG 11th Army

Lashley turned about swiftly to face Parker.

"Is this a joke?" he demanded.

"It's official, if that's what you mean."

"Do you know what's in this?" Lashley said incredulously, holding up the communication.

Parker smiled discreetly. "I typed it out."

"What's got into the general? The men were only sentenced on Monday. The thirteenth is—let's see—Saturday. That's only five days from the day they were sentenced! What about their appeals?"

Parker said calmly, "They went forward with the trial records. They were rejected by Frankfurt."

Lashley made a fast calculation.

"But this is only Wednesday. Did Frankfurt look at the record?"

"If it'll make you feel any better," Parker said, "the JAG remained on duty nearly twenty hours to review the record. The general asked for all possible speed."

"For God's sake, why?"

Parker appeared to relish the major's consternation.

"It occurs to me," he said, "that the general explained that to you the other night—at his house. The public safety people——"

"God damn the public safety people!" Lashley exploded. "They didn't prosecute. They can go on sleeping with their frowzy Fräuleins. I've got to sleep with myself——"

"If I were you I'd take it easy on that subject," the lieutenant said.

Lashley came to his feet. "Don't talk to me like that, Parker. Don't you know how to address a superior officer?"

Parker mumbled, "Yes, sir," without changing the manner of his stance or the complacency of his expression.

Lashley sat down and eyed him belligerently.

"What's the message the general gave you?"

"It's about the Delisle woman—sir," Parker said cautiously.

"What about her?"

"The general is, shall I say, displeased—well, he's damned mad if you want to know."

Lashley said sharply, "Never mind your commentary, Parker. Give me the general's message."

The lieutenant hesitated. "The general wants you to surrender the woman to the French authorities without delay——"

"Wants *me* to surrender the woman?"

"He put it this way," said Parker. "If the woman is not surrendered to the French before the executions, he will have you up on charges."

For a moment Lashley was confounded. This was a turn he hadn't expected. But he might as well know the worst.

"Does the general think I'm sheltering the woman?"

Parker said, "I thought you didn't want my commentary, Major."

"Answer my question."

"As you wish." Parker appeared to have gained confidence. "We know the woman was here in this office last night—and"—he smiled—"and in your billet the night before—Monday. Does that answer your question?"

Lashley said nothing.

The lieutenant continued in a confidential tone: "You know, Major, you're the luckiest man in this army. The general has ruined officers for a lot less than you've done. But he doesn't like an army scandal. That's why he sent me to talk to you privately."

Lashley looked up angrily.

"Another thing, Major," Parker went on. "The general has called off the provost marshal—he called him off when the confirmations came through from Frankfurt. Nobody can prevent the executions now, but he wants the woman out of the area before it happens—and he doesn't want any open scandal about you and her. There's been enough bad publicity back home without prosecutors sleeping with trial witnesses. So just hand her over to Captain Gribemont by Friday night."

Lashley struggled to control himself. He said evenly: "Go back and tell the general I don't know where the woman is. I'll do what I can to find her."

Parker smiled knowingly. "Friday's two days off. It still gives you a couple of nights with her——"

Lashley jumped to his feet and started for Parker. In that instant he was ready to beat him up, and then his army training got the upper hand, and he stopped.

"Get the hell out of here," he cried. "Get out!"

The smile left Parker's lips. He backed toward the door and was gone.

At seven o'clock Lashley abandoned the hope that Thémis might appear at his office. Reluctantly he shut off the lights. He lingered a few moments outside the door, then turned his key in the lock and went downstairs.

At the front door Buckley, the guard, put down a picture magazine, saluted, and said, "Good night, sir."

Lashley paused. "By the way, Buckley. At about this time last night a woman came down from my office. Do you recall?"

"You mean the Frenchwoman—the one at the trial."

"That's the one."

"Yes, sir. She came through last night. I remember."

"Did you notice what direction she took when she left here?"

Buckley shook his head. "No, sir. Tell you the truth I didn't pay much attention, not after she went through the door. Say— Pepper might've noticed. He's the guard out by the gate."

Pepper leaned his rifle against the sentry box and scratched his head.

"I just can't rightly remember, sir," he said in response to the major's query. "Seems to me, though, she went this-a-way— down Mehlmannstrasse—sorta the way we go for the Red Cross Club."

"Thank you, Pepper."

Lashley noticed that he was a lanky youth with a shock of bushy black hair that lifted his overseas cap well off any part of his scalp.

"Swell night, isn't it, sir?" he said sadly.

Lashley nodded.

"Yessir, sorta smell the spring comin'," the youth drawled. He moved his head and looked off into the distance. "Spring-plowin' time back home now. The old man sure could use me. First time I ever missed spring plowin'."

"Well, next year . . ." Lashley's voice trailed off.

"Sure hope so, sir."

Lashley turned the jeep down Mehlmannstrasse. He asked himself why he had not found out earlier from Nissen or the provost marshal where Thémis was billeted. But the answer was too easy, for he knew how hard he had been resisting every impulse to go to her. He had no longer been able to excuse a visit on the grounds of his wish to prove Steigmann's guilt. And he must see her again. His desire to see her had expanded far beyond the matters of the mind. It was a matter also of the heart. Now that he had Marriner's orders he was torn between elation that he might even see her tonight and deep reluctance to go on such an errand.

He braked his jeep on the steep descent and put it into low gear. The gasp of the exhaust set his mind to thinking about young Hockland struggling fitfully behind the screens in Ward 3. He wondered about the Hockland parents flying over from Bensiman, Iowa, and how they would react to the ruined city and to the ruin also of their son's life.

At the bottom of the hill the street merged with Bahnhof-strasse. He slowed for the crossing. The brightness of the night, aided by a quarter-moon, made the dim street lamps seem superfluous. From all directions groups of GIs wandered toward the Red Cross Club, attracted by the beat of swing music.

It was unlikely that he would see Thémis, but still he looked for her as he drove along. He turned the jeep into Bahnhof-strasse and made for the parking lot in the rear of the Excelsior Hotel. From there it was a short walk to the place he associated with her and the moonlight. Americans capered past him, and snatches of their conversation came to him as he paused before the door of the hotel. Their gaiety was at complete variance with his mood. The bar was probably crowded and probably Nissen was waiting for him there as usual, but he did not want to talk to him about Thémis.

He crossed the street and took the pathway that wandered through the rubble-heaped Operaplatz. The gaunt, hatless German sat on the shadowed portico, as he had the other night, paring bricks with a pocket knife and dropping them into a wheelbarrow. Lashley noticed his energy and the devotion to his task. He thought of the victors cavorting in the Excelsior bar; and in the contrast tonight he saw something significant and foreboding.

He went on. The dust of pulverized stone lay like a fine carpet under the moonlight. The memory of another night was in his mind as he followed the pathway. In the unreality of the shadowy ruins he thought he saw the gleam of a bronze arrow moving beyond a pile of rubble. He passed his hand over his eyes and looked again. Now the arrow was gone. He started to walk faster, then slowed down again, fearing that what he had seen was only the product of his imagination. But this was no mirage. She stood before the bust of Schumann, looking up at the stone features, and her face was white and pensive and beautiful.

"Thémis," he called softly, afraid that the sound of his voice might cause her to vanish.

She looked around her and when she saw him she smiled. He had never seen her smile like that. It was a soft smile, and wonderfully tender.

He was aware that this was a moment of pure happiness. In the pale light, amid the silent ruins, finding her here as he had imagined she might be, he almost felt as though he were dreaming.

She held out her hands and moved toward him.

He murmured, "I wanted to find you," and he took her hands.

"And I you."

"All day, since this morning, I hated myself for letting you walk away last night."

"Since this morning," she echoed. "I too was sorry for last night."

Her eyes were wide and her voice was as soft as the night around them.

"When I was a little girl on my father's farm I used to watch the sun come up. And I used to make foolish little wishes——"

She sighed happily.

"This morning I made a foolish little wish." She closed her eyes to illustrate the act.

"And what happened?"

"*Voilà.*" Her hands closed tight around his. "And here you are."

"But you ran away," he said.

"Only across the river. Look." She lifted her foot and turned her muddy shoe to the light. "I walked up into the hills."

"You knew I wouldn't be there."

"No, my literal one, you weren't there. But it was beautiful in the hills. There was no war, nor the end of war, nor even a beginning of war. In the hills nothing was changed. It was spring quite as it used to be, and I could pretend there were no dark years between."

"You have a good imagination, my dear."

She laughed and she squeezed his fingers.

"You will hate me. When I was seven or eight I fell madly in love with my father's coachman—oh, madly in love. Today I pretended you were he."

"Why should I hate you for it?"

"Because he grew up to be fat and ugly, and he married Denise, who worked in the kitchen and was even fatter than he was. And he grew a beard and drank calvados like a fish. How would you like to be him?"

"It would be wonderful. With no worries, plenty of calvados —and a nice fat girl."

"Then I am jealous of Denise," she pouted.

The night wind carried sounds of revelry from the direction of the Excelsior. Lashley was suddenly back again in Reschweiler, holding hands with a girl who was wanted by the French authorities. It seemed that she too had come back to reality but she fought against it.

She said anxiously, "How did you think of me today?"

"I wanted to be with you."

"Then I shall not run away again," she said softly. "Except with you, Robert." She paused over the name. "*Robert* . . . It has a lovely sound in French."

He remembered watching her in the courtroom and wondering how she might look if she were happy. She was lovelier than he had imagined. Her eyes were dark and larger than he had ever seen them. He noticed again that her nose was slightly out of proportion to the rest of her face. But he wouldn't change that nose or anything else about her.

Touched by her sweetness and the happiness of her mood, he hated the task that lay ahead.

"Did you know they were looking for you today, Thémis?" he said.

"Who was looking for me?"

"The military police."

She laughed lightly. "As if I would run away from you. You must have known I wouldn't. You knew, *Robert.*"

He looked down into her face and its disarming quality kept him from telling her the unpleasant news which he had to tell her. Instead he said:

"Yesterday it didn't matter to you. Nothing mattered to you. And tonight——"

"Tonight I am happy, as if yesterday and all the other days and years never happened."

"Why, Thémis, what has changed since yesterday?"

She looked away and her face looked suddenly grave.

"Yesterday the world seemed to me huge and terribly overpowering, and it didn't matter whether I lived or died. And today, *Robert,* the world is suddenly small, and I have come alive again—oh, I can't explain it, but each breath I take is important to me, and I feel powerful, and I want to be bold and happy."

"What has happened, Thémis, between yesterday and to-day?"

She looked up into his eyes.

"If you do not know, Robert, I could not explain it to you."

A soldier and a Fräulein, their arms entwined, appeared around the bend of the path. Lashley watched in embarrassment as they approached, but they seemed to have no eyes for others and soon the path was once more deserted.

"I shouldn't have asked that," he said.

He bent his head and kissed her gently on the lips. Her arms came up and went around his neck, holding him close. He could feel her tremble.

"Robert," she murmured, and he kissed her again. Her eyes were closed now and her lips were very soft against his.

"Robert."

"Yes, Thémis."

"Schumann will never forgive us. He was so unhappy in his lifetime."

"Then we'll walk away from him."

"Yes, we will walk away—we will leave unhappiness behind." She opened her eyes and smiled.

They walked along the path. He felt the warmth of her against his arm as she clung close to him.

She said, "I pray someday——" but then her voice trailed off.

On the east bank of the Auer, across the river from the city's docks, a small park had been reclaimed from the forest. In Reschweiler's happier days it had been the scene of tombolas and picnics, for its escarpment provided a clear view of the river. A concrete parapet protected the merrymakers of another time from a sheer drop to the Auer's muddy banks, and there had been booths which sold *Wurstwaren*, a bandstand, and a merry-go-round.

Now the park had fallen into disuse except as a summer rendezvous for soldiers and their Fräuleins. The booths had long since been broken up for firewood and only their concrete foundations remained. The bandstand lay on its side, blown over by a bomb blast. The merry-go-round was twisted and rusted, its horses lying every which way. On the neck of a nymphlike metal figure hung a weather-beaten sign, *"Eingang 10 Pfennig."* A wag had scrawled on the sign, *"Eingang für Amerikanner, eine Stange Schokolade."* The parapet and a few park benches recalled better days, these and a breath-taking view of the night and the river.

Thémis leaned against the parapet, her back to the river below, and faced the bench on which Lashley sat. She spread out her arms as if to claim ownership of the park and the moon and the water.

"I discovered this all by myself when I came out of the hills. You see how grand it is, *Robert.*"

He didn't have the heart to spoil her pleasure and he was amazed at his own lack of courage. After all, he had gained a reputation in the army for making harsh decisions quickly on the evidence adduced. And now he was drifting. He could not bring himself to tell her the truth about her imminent arrest and about Steigmann's execution. He had tried. While they were walking to the foot of Bahnhofstrasse he had phrased the words that would plunge her into despondency, but at that moment she had squeezed his hand and the words would not come.

Now as he watched her slim figure silhouetted against the moonlit sky he was still putting off the evil moment and trying instead to find the answer to his strange behavior. He rejected the notion that he was in love with her, and he sought frantically to convince himself that this was something of the moment. He argued that the attraction was a matter of timing, a part of the greatest drama in which he had ever taken part. With the challenge of the trial, not only his mind but all his senses had become more acute. She was beautiful, she was unlike any other woman he had known, eluding his understanding, still remote. Besides, it was spring, and he was tired and lonely. These were sound reasons why he could not be genuinely in love with her, why this must be only an infatuation, however much he wanted her.

"Thémis," he said at last, "please listen carefully. The police were searching for you today to arrest you, to send you back to Paris."

At the sound of his voice she looked away from the river and the sky. "Why do you tease me so?" she said. "You wouldn't send me away, Robert."

Coming quickly from the parapet, she sat beside him and took his hands.

He said, "Try to understand. I wouldn't send you away, but the French government has demanded it. They insist."

"But you will not allow it," she said confidently.

He shook his head. "I am under orders from the general to hand you over to the French within forty-eight hours. Forty-eight hours, Thémis!"

He searched her face for the dismay he expected to find but her eyes continued to glow like a young girl's. He was annoyed by his failure to make her understand. She was making his task too difficult.

"Two days is a long time," she murmured. "Let's not worry about it until we have to."

"And when the time comes?"

"If you let them take me, I shall be content to go. Whether you send me to that nearest tree or to the guillotine, it makes no difference. If you send me away, Robert, nothing matters any more."

She said the words calmly, as if there were nothing more to discuss.

Even as he heard them Lashley knew that, whatever happened, he would remember her words as long as he lived.

She looked up at him and put her hand quietly into his. It was a gesture as simple and as trusting as a child's.

"Don't worry, my Robert. In the end it will be all right."

"In the end it *must* be all right."

"You won't try to send me away."

"Never."

Her head was on his shoulder and his arms were around her.

"Robert?"

"Yes, dearest."

"This isn't all."

"Yes, I know. I was dreaming, thinking of you and the sky and the stars. You and tomorrow, Thémis, when all the worries will be gone."

He sat for a long time holding her. Her eyes half closed, and she lay quiet in his arms.

Again and again he reasoned that there was neither logic nor wisdom nor even hope in the blind decision he was taking, but the unruly force that overwhelmed him was far too great and he could not deny it. He knew he loved her.

The night grew cold. They came down from the escarpment and crossed the bridge, clinging to each other as if to shut out even a gust of air which might separate them.

In this darkened, ruined city Lashley had a feeling of at last having found his life and a deep sense of belonging to someone and having someone belong to him.

He thought in amazement of Thémis and the night they had spent together. Monday seemed as unreal as something he might have dreamed. He had added scandal to her name and not once since had she reproached him. That embittered, reckless woman was no more this tenderly passionate Thémis than he was that man who had taken her with only a selfish thought for the moment's hunger. However they might achieve it, he was determined now that they must have a life together.

It was not until they were approaching the Red Cross Club on Bahnhofstrasse that Lashley remembered that an MP had been standing at his usual post on the city end of the bridge. He had been going to ask her up to his room. But the thought of the MP and the knowledge that everybody was watching them, reporting everything they did, stopped him. The thought made him mad—he'd be damned if he'd play right into their hands.

They passed the Red Cross Club, darkened, for it was nearly midnight, and walked silently up the Mehlmannstrasse hill until they reached a huge apartment block. Lashley remembered that it had been turned into a hostel for American women civilians. Outside number 29 she pressed his arm close against her.

"My billet is here," she said.

He surveyed the building suspiciously. The street was deserted except for a few darkened jeeps parked farther up the hill.

He said, "Who assigned you here?"

"Captain Nissen arranged it when I first arrived." She saw the anxious look on his face. "What is it, *Robert?* Will they —— No, no, don't let them!"

"No one will take you from me, Thémis."

She clung to him. "Until tomorrow, my darling."

"Anything can happen tomorrow," he replied. "Whatever happens, I'll find you."

He held her close a long time, and then he kissed her.

"Pray for us," she whispered.

She ran up the stairs and let herself into the building without looking back.

He walked thoughtfully down the hill, seeking to gain perspective for the tasks which lay ahead. But each time he thought of his many problems the memory of Thémis interposed itself and he was lost in the warmth of his love for her. Never before had he been unable to discipline his thoughts; it was a strange feeling and it troubled him now, when he needed to think most clearly.

He turned hastily into Bahnhofstrasse and stalked through the Operaplatz toward the marquee lights of the Excelsior. As he passed the monument of Schumann he paused briefly and remembered that he had meant to confess to Thémis his misgivings concerning the Steigmann verdict, to ask her what she knew about the man's guilt or innocence. He had even forgotten to tell her about the execution, and that omission truly disturbed him.

Still deep in his thoughts, he pushed through the doors of the Excelsior and went to the desk for his key.

"Hiya, Major. Had fun?"

The great bulk of Captain Kinsella loomed before him. The MP officer leaned carelessly against the counter, his boots crossed one over the other and his stubby hands folded on his stomach.

"Hello, Kinsella." Lashley felt a flush come into his face. He rapped on the counter until the sergeant came from behind the partition and gave him his key.

"What's your rush, Major?" Kinsella drawled with exaggerated friendliness.

Lashley turned on him fiercely. "What's on your mind?"

"Nothin' much." The captain smiled as if inwardly amused. He flicked the ashes from his cigarette with his little finger. "I see you unearthed the babe. Funny we couldn't grab 'er 'safternoon."

"What's funny about it, Kinsella?"

"Oh nothin'," the captain said languidly.

"Are you looking for the girl?" Lashley demanded.

"I was." Kinsella dropped his cigarette butt on the floor, stamped on it, and methodically drew another cigarette from his pocket. He lighted it and exhaled slowly. "I was—until the PM called us off the job."

Lashley had a sudden inspiration and snapped: "Then what were you doing watching her billet?"

"It just happened, Major," the captain drawled. "Funny how these things happen. I was just comin' down from the courthouse—we got a new batch o' krauts t'night—and there you was with the babe, standin' outside the house like you was scared to go in 'cause her old lady might be waitin' to bawl 'er out. Funny how it happens sometimes."

"You're lying, Kinsella. You were parked up the street watching her billet."

Kinsella looked grieved. "Now keep your shirt on, Major. Honest, I just stopped to light a butt."

"Well, what about it?"

"Oh nothin'. It ain't official. I just thought the PM might want to know why we didn't locate her 'safternoon."

"Why?"

"Hell, Major. You don't want me to answer that one, do you? Far's I'm concerned she's a sexy-lookin' dame and if you're havin' fun—hell, Major——"

"Is that all, Kinsella?" Lashley turned to go. He struggled to withhold the angry words that were on his tongue.

Kinsella shrugged his shoulders. "Just to show you I'm a right guy, I won't tell the PM—how's that? You don't like me, Major, but I'm not a bad guy. I always say a fella's gotta have laughs on the job or it ain't worth doin'. Now I couldn't make first base with the doll, but if you're scorin'—hell, keep at it. You got till Friday night anyway——"

Lashley looked at him furiously without speaking.

The captain continued: "Ever since you been here, you're makin' with the big brain and the big character. Okay with me, bub. Me, I'm just a bum with a couple of bars. I don't put on with the big brain. But I'll be God-damned if I could put a rope around a guy's neck and then go sleepin' with his dame even before they jerk him. I'm tough, Major, but not that tough. I gotta hand it to you."

Kinsella heaved his bulk into motion and walked clumsily to the door.

THURSDAY

XII

THE TELEPHONE PEALED IN THE DARKNESS; ONE LONG, URGENT note—then there was silence.

The sound reached into Lashley's consciousness as if it were an echo out of a bad dream. He pulled himself up on one elbow and wondered whether he had really heard it. He twisted around to the window and saw the stars shining in the sky, and the black outline of the distant hills.

The telephone pealed again, now in short, angry notes. Stupidly he lay on his elbow listening to it ring, trying to gather his wits together. Finally he reached out and grabbed the receiver.

"Hello."

He heard a man's voice say, "Hello. Is that you, Lashley?"

"Yes——"

"Sorry to get you up at this hour," the voice said with a briskness which belied its apology. "This is Colonel Pike, G-1."

"Yes, Colonel."

"You know this Hockland case. You're familiar with it——"

He sat up quickly. "Yes, Colonel."

"I've just had word from the hospital. The boy is going—pretty fast, they tell me." There was a brief silence. Then the colonel said: "Hello, can you hear me? Are you awake now?"

"Yes, sir," Lashley said, suddenly alert.

"Good. Better get down there and take a statement from him. With witnesses and all that sort of thing. You know what I mean."

Lashley said, "I got something from him the other day, Colonel——"

"Yes, I know. But you've got to get the thing absolutely firm. The general is personally interested. He wants a short trial for the girl and a perfectly foolproof one. No courtroom dramatics, you understand. Can you get a stenographer at this hour?"

"What time is it, Colonel?"

"It's nearly six. . . . Never mind about the stenographer. I'll get my own man—Master Sergeant Williamson. Very efficient. How soon can you get down to the hospital?"

"In about half an hour."

"Fine. I'll have Williamson meet you there—and, Lashley, I hate to tell you your business but—uh—get evidence that will make it a lead-pipe cinch. We've got to make an example of the girl. Damn it, we've got a job to do in this bloody country and we can't have these people shooting up our men."

"Yes—sir," Lashley said without enthusiasm.

"Go to it then." The telephone clicked.

In anticipation of death and the arrival of his parents, young Hockland had been moved to a private room on the second floor of the hospital's original building. The room was brilliantly lighted, although a purplish dawn was beginning to seep through the window and challenge the yellow gleam of the lamps.

Master Sergeant Williamson was already there. He was an extraordinarily neat young man who might have been a bookkeeper in civilian life. Pad and pencil in hand, he stood respectfully against the wall just inside the door.

Lashley closed the door gently and stood beside Williamson. He could not see Hockland, for there were three persons standing close to the bed and gazing through the transparent fabric of an oxygen tent. One was Captain Bossin. His thick black hair was disheveled and he wore a dressing gown over his pajamas. The second was apparently the night nurse, a tiny, wiry young woman who looked unusually efficient. The third was a full colonel who might be, Lashley judged, the medical head of the hospital. His silver hair shone more brightly than his colonel's eagles and his head inclined with the gentle inquisitiveness that comes from long bedside experience.

The three stood motionless as wax models. The only sound in the room was a hiss escaping from the oxygen containers. A cool, bracing smell filled the room. This was the smell of vigorous living, thought Lashley, not the smell of dying.

Finally Bossin glanced toward the door. Lashley nodded. The captain moved noiselessly behind the nurse and held a whispered conference with the colonel, then he went to the door, opened it, and motioned both Lashley and Williamson outside.

In the hall Bossin rubbed the back of his hair as if he were giving himself a shampoo.

"How're you, Major?" he said cheerfully. "Notice? It's going to be another great day. A few more days like this and they'll be opening the tennis courts. Haven't played in a hell of a time. Love it."

Lashley was taken aback. He said, "What about Hockland?"

"The kid? He's got a few hours. We figure he'll go sometime around noon." He glanced at the sergeant. "Your undercover man?"

"He's a stenographer," Lashley said, frowning. "We're going to take a statement."

Bossin said, "Won't be long. The kid's just fallen asleep. Let's go have coffee. They'll call us when he comes to."

They walked along the hall, Williamson trailing dutifully behind them. In an alcove near the head of the stairs a blond, middle-aged nurse was scrutinizing a pile of medical charts.

Bossin said to her, "Garbo honey, can you fix the sergeant up with a chair and a cup of coffee? He's an FBI man disguised as a sergeant impersonating a college professor. Here's your chance, honey, to get that man before you go home. The major and I are going down to the lounge."

As they continued down the stairs Bossin said, "You know, any single girl who didn't join up as a nurse is nuts. Greatest opportunity for spinsters since the California bride ships——"

The captain chatted on inconsequentially while he conducted Lashley into the lounge. On a small table in a corner of the room a coffee urn steamed over a flickering oil fire. Bossin filled two cups from it.

"When did Hockland take the bad turn?" Lashley said.

"It was tough getting up, eh?" Bossin chuckled. "Well, now you know why my wife always says she should have married an insurance salesman. The nurse got scared when his respiration took a dip about an hour ago. She called everybody except the general. Silly girl."

"I'm glad they called me," Lashley said sharply.

"Well, gives you a chance to look at a pretty day being born." He turned to the window and his eyes blinked against the brilliance of the early sun. "Know what that means to me? Tennis. Get some good clean air in my lungs. Feel my muscles again."

Lashley said impulsively, "What's wrong with you, Captain? You're taking this a little lightly—compared to the other day."

Bossin halted his cup in mid-air. "You mean the boy upstairs?"

Lashley nodded.

"Look, Major. You can't go on worrying about death. Anybody worth his salt worries about the living. When a man's gone, he's gone—and believe me, Hockland's gone. Not a thing anybody can do for him."

"That's no reason for being lighthearted," Lashley said.

Bossin gulped at his coffee. "A doctor develops a philosophy about death. I've learned enough about it so I know I won't be afraid when my time comes. It's something chemical. Nature administers her own anesthesia. I never saw a patient 'die that I didn't get the impression he was meeting it half-way."

"What about planned death—like an execution?"

"Only saw one like that, during the Ardennes battle. Remember we grabbed a bunch of Germans who were posing as Americans and we shot 'em? They called me in because they figured one of the prisoners was malingering paralysis. Wouldn't walk to the stake. Funny thing about him. He had a stroke all right, a form of shock fright. Kept screaming he wasn't afraid to die, but he wanted to walk to the stake like a man. And he couldn't. I believed him. That man was meeting death halfway too. You know why? Because he knew he had laid his life on the line when he got into an American uniform. If a man knows he deserves to die he meets it half-way."

"What happened?"

"I gave him a heavy shot of morphine. He managed to walk to the stake. Died like a man."

Lashley looked uneasily at Bossin. He said, "Captain, did those refugees come to see you yesterday?"

"Oh sure—sure," Bossin said airily. "Glad you sent them. I had a field day. Kept them here most of the evening—so everybody could have a look at them. What a pair! One's got a paranoia I wouldn't wish on my worst enemy and the other's a dementia praecox they'd give a thousand dollars at Johns Hopkins just to examine."

"You mean the girl——"

"The girl's hopeless. No one can do a thing for her. All I did was give her a bottle of mild laxative. Her breath smelled like the stockyards."

Lashley said, "What about the man?"

"He's paranoiac. The embittered kind."

"Would you consider him sane?"

"That's hard to say, Major. I'd have to keep him a couple of days to be sure. If you want a snap judgment, I would say he's insane most of the time—at least, as long as he's around here."

Lashley caught his breath. "Why around here, Captain?"

Bossin mused over his coffee. "Well, he's an embittered paranoiac. It's not uncommon. His mind gravitates between delusions of persecution and suspicion of the outside world. As long as it's only suspicion of the outside world, he's fairly harmless. There's a million of them walking the streets back home. But when it comes to delusions of persecution, he's dangerous because his persecution complex is centered on Germans. Whenever he comes in contact with practically any German, he goes off. At least that's my guess. He's got to get back home—to his own surroundings—to better memories. As long as he's around here he'll blow higher than a kite."

"Would you consider him a trustworthy witness against a German?"

Bossin shook his head decisively. "Not on your life."

"Would you give me a certificate to that effect?"

"Not inside of a week. I'd have to keep him under observation at least that long."

Lashley stared momentarily into the sunlight streaming through the window. He was seeing Steigmann in a cell at Bergsdorf. This was Thursday. Another dawn and another, and they would lead Steigmann into the courtyard to hang him. He cursed Marriner for the order requiring him to be present. He shrank from that duty. And he made up his mind that the hanging must not take place. Not on Saturday. He would wash out the conviction and move for a new trial. Not because Steigmann might be innocent, but because he had not proved his guilt.

He turned to the captain. "Have you ever noticed, Bossin, that few Americans are serene about death? It's an Old World custom. I sometimes envy the Europeans for it. For them death is a link with a great past. For us it's an unforgivable break with the future. I suppose they can apply themselves to death better than we can."

Bossin laughed without humor. "That's what I'm trying to tell you, Major. Don't cry for the dead, cry for the living. I've crossed young Hockland out of my mind. I'm worrying about

another kid now, down in Ward 2. Got a dose of syphilis—
first time he ever touched a girl. What will that do to his life?
There's something to worry about——"

He sidled to the coffee urn, still looking at Lashley. "And
another thing. What about the girl? She's having a baby any
day now. If you want to worry, worry about the baby—a new
life."

There was a knock on the door and the thin, wiry nurse
put her head in.

"The patient is awake now, Captain," she said.

On their way upstairs Lashley said, "What about Hockland's parents?"

"Doubt if they'll make it," Bossin replied. "Their plane's
due in Paris this morning. The army's got a C-47 waiting to
fly them here. How long does it take—two and a half hours?
That means around noon. Touch and go."

They reached the door of the room. Lashley put his hand on
the doorknob and paused. "Does Hockland know he's going
to die?"

Bossin said, "Nobody's told him, if that's what you mean.
I think you'll find that he knows. He's that close to it."

They went in.

The nurse and the white-haired colonel were looking down
through the transparent curtain and smiling dimly, as though
Hockland had just said something amusing. Williamson stood
nervously against the wall inside the door.

Bossin motioned Lashley forward. "Okay, do your stuff,"
he whispered.

Lashley peered through the fabric of the tent. The young
soldier's eyes were open. His face was peculiarly colored, as
though white enamel were painted on a dark yellow base, and
his lips were pale and slightly parted. His breath came in short
gasps.

He looked dully at the newcomer for a few moments, and
then he mumbled something which Lashley could not hear
over the hiss from the oxygen containers.

Lashley said to Bossin: "Is it possible to turn this thing off for a few minutes?"

Bossin looked at the colonel. The latter said, "It will probably be easier if we remove the tent. Not more than five minutes though."

While the nurse made some adjustments with the fabric at the foot of the bed, Bossin said, "By the way—Major Lashley, Colonel Ericson. The colonel is chief of medicine here."

They nodded briefly and solemnly.

With a few quick moves the nurse detached the tubes running out of the base of the containers and pulled the tent away on its casters.

Lashley motioned to Williamson to come forward.

They leaned over the dying boy. He looked at them with the sleepy curiosity of a baby who has not yet learned to talk. His eyes were placid; they revealed neither fear nor sadness, although his mouth quivered as he breathed with incredibly quick gasps.

Lashley said gently, "Can you hear me, Hockland?"

The youth nodded almost imperceptibly.

"Then try to remember. Did Erika Wagner shoot you?"

Hockland's eyelids fluttered and his lips moved, but if they formed words Lashley was unable to hear them.

Lashley caught himself breathing quickly in involuntary mimicry.

"Can you speak a little louder?" he said.

Hockland's face contorted. "I'd like—to see—Erika," he gasped.

Lashley glanced helplessly at Bossin.

"Did you see her take the gun in her hand and shoot you?" he said with an immense effort to enunciate his words clearly yet quietly.

Hockland listened patiently. Then he wrinkled his nose. He seemed puzzled.

"Erika," he mumbled. "Erika—good kid." He lost his voice for a moment and his lips struggled silently. He closed his eyes, and then his mouth opened wide as if to cry. At last his fitful breath made sudden contact with his vocal cords.

"Good kid—not her fault," he cried sharply. "Not her fault!"

He sank back and the struggle of his breathing filled the room.

Lashley wiped the perspiration from his forehead and came away from the bed. He looked appealingly at Bossin and at the colonel.

Bossin said in a low voice, "He's had morphia, you know. Try it again. He'll understand you after a while."

Lashley rubbed his damp hand across his tunic and swore under his breath. He made himself walk back to the bed, and again leaned close to young Hockland.

"Take it easy, son, and listen carefully. I know you're tired. You don't have to think much. Just answer yes or no. That's all. Just yes or no. This one more question and then you'll go back to sleep again. Now remember, son. Just yes or no. Did —Erika—shoot—you? Yes or no . . . yes or no . . . yes or no."

He looked imploringly into the boy's eyes.

Hockland's chin quivered. He mumbled, "Good kid—loved me."

Without an instant's delay Lashley said, "Think hard— think hard. Listen to the question. Think hard, Hockland. Listen to the question—now listen. Answer yes or no, yes or no. Did—Erika—shoot—you? Yes or no."

The youngster's mouth, still open, sagged at the corners. His eyes seemed to swell. He was making a tremendous effort to remain conscious. His breath came even faster, as though a tiny electric motor were now operating at the back of his throat.

Lashley brought his head still lower. He felt the boy's hot breath on the side of his cheek. He swallowed hard.

"Come on, Hockland. Yes or no, yes or no. Did—Erika— shoot—you? Yes or no. No or yes."

Hockland's eyes closed. For a moment his breath was a trifle more measured. Then it increased to a runaway tempo. It was hot. Lashley again felt the sweat on his forehead. A tiny rivulet started down his cheek. He saw it splash on the lobe of the boy's ear.

"Don't stall, Hockland," he said sharply. "Don't stall, damn it. Yes or no, yes or no. You're in the army, Hockland. Do you hear me? This is an order, soldier. Yes or no, yes or no. Did —Erika—shoot—you? Out with it!"

The youngster's head shook in a spasm of agony. His closed eyelids quivered. He was barely conscious.

"Pull yourself together, Hockland. Don't stall. Answer the question. Did—Erika—shoot—you? Yes or no. Quick now!"

Hockland's chin shuddered. He opened his mouth wide as if to shout, and then closed it.

"Y-y-yes," he mumbled, and his chin jerked to one side.

Lashley straightened up and stepped back from the bed. He clapped both hands over his face.

Bossin came forward, took one look at the boy, and turned to the nurse. "Oxygen."

Lashley wiped his eyes and glanced at Williamson. "Did you get it?"

The master sergeant nodded.

Lashley said, "Type out the report and get Captain Bossin and Colonel Ericson to witness it. Then send it to me."

He looked once more at the dying boy, then hurried from the room. The blood was pounding in his temples. He felt as an executioner might feel after a job. He fled along the hall, down the stairs, and out into the air. He cursed Marriner, and the army, and his job, and the war, and Hitler, and the whole God-damned world.

The jeep darted swiftly away from the hospital and hummed along a deserted street. Lashley hugged the steering wheel as though he might keel over without its support. He had done his duty. Marriner would be happy. Pike would be happy. The Hockland parents would be happy. Justice would be happy. He had been the butcher for them all. He had thrashed the boy into signing the girl's death warrant. He had reached into Hockland's helpless mind and torn from it the dream the youth struggled to keep, to carry into his last sleep. Kinsella had been right. He was tough, tough, tough.

The clarity of the morning air brought the streets of Reschweiler into sharp relief even to the laths which jutted from the frames of broken dwellings. He braked his jeep. He had come to a footbridge across the Auer. There on the opposite shore he saw a low parapet, a withered merry-go-round, an overturned bandstand.

Looking angrily ahead of him, he raced up the incline of Bahnhofstrasse. He swung around the corner of the Operaplatz to a stop before the Excelsior.

Nissen was having breakfast.

"Been out?" the captain said, looking up from a copy of the *Stars and Stripes*.

"Hockland's going," Lashley said. "I took a statement."

"Oh. Thought you were someplace else."

Lashley said brusquely, "Where else?"

Nissen grinned.

"Don't get touchy with me, Bob. The whole town knows it."

"For God's sake, knows what?"

The captain tossed his paper across the table. "It's even official." He put his finger on an article. "Read the last paragraph."

Lashley scanned the page. The principal item was a local story headlined:

SIX, INCLUDING STEIGMANN,
TO BE HANGED SATURDAY

The last paragraph was datelined from Paris:

The confusion regarding the whereabouts of Thémis Delisle, French "mystery witness" in the war crimes trial of Otto Steigmann, was cleared up last night. The woman is under surveillance in Reschweiler and is expected to arrive in Paris within forty-eight hours. According to word received here from the office of General Joshua Marriner, commander of the Eleventh Army, the woman is being temporarily detained for questioning at the request of Major R. M. Lashley, army prosecutor in the Reschweiler trial. It is believed the woman has additional information to offer.

Lashley flung the paper aside.

"That Marriner's smart as a whip," said Nissen.

"I don't see it," Lashley replied heatedly.

"You haven't seen him in action long enough. He——"

Nissen's voice trailed off. He eyed Hedy as she swayed up to the table. She poured Lashley's coffee.

"Herr Nissen?" she said, holding the pot with a practiced hand.

Nissen looked at her with amusement. *"Nein, Liebling."*

"Dankeschön," she said haughtily and scurried away.

"Wonderful gals, these Germans," Nissen mused. "The life-blood of the Greater Reich. Bitchery, bed, and babies—in that order."

Lashley had retrieved the newspaper. He was studying it intently.

"That's a hell of a way to put it."

"You don't know Marriner, Bob. He's as honest as you are, and about four times as clever. He's the smartest man I've ever met anywhere."

"What's smart about this?"

"There's one thing about Marriner you'll get to know—if you're here long enough. He can't abide a public scandal in his command. He's never had one, and he never will. Anybody who points a finger at his command gets it burned—whether it's Ike or a congressional committee. When you hid the girl——"

"I didn't hide her."

"Whatever you did with her, they couldn't find her. So Marriner covered up for you—for himself. Just like that." Nissen snapped his fingers.

"Wait till the hangings are over," Nissen continued, "and the girl is back in Paris—then duck, brother. What a job he'll do on you."

Lashley shrugged and went on drinking his coffee.

Shortly after eleven o'clock the office telephone rang. Lashley swiveled his chair around to answer it. Colonel Pike was on the line.

"Well, Lashley did you get it?" the colonel asked.

"Get what, Colonel?"

"Snap out of it," the colonel bellowed. "You know what I mean. The statement from what'sizname—the soldier—Hockland."

"Yes—yes, sir," Lashley said quickly.

"Did he name the girl? Witnesses and all? I mean it's all wrapped up, isn't it?"

"Yes, Colonel. It's all wrapped up all right."

The colonel's voice crackled with enthusiasm. "Say, that's swell. The general will be tickled. Good work, Lashley. Sorry I had to get you up."

Lashley looked distastefully at the telephone.

"Hello there," the colonel called. "Hockland's gone. You know that, don't you?"

Lashley breathed heavily. "When did it happen?"

"About ten minutes ago. They called me."

"I'm sorry." Lashley could think of nothing else to say.

"It's bad enough. But as long as we've got the statement, we're geared for a fast job on the girl. Say, Lashley——"

"Yes, sir."

"I've got another little job for you. Hockland's parents, you know. Their plane is late. They won't get into Paris for a half hour or so. Means they'll get here around three. I think it'd be nice if you went out to meet them. I mean you could tell them how quick we got the murderess and all that. It might help."

"If you like, Colonel."

"Yes, I definitely think it's an idea. You won't have to tell them about their son. I've already signaled to Orly Field. They'll tell them there."

"All right, sir."

"One more thing, Lashley. The PR in Washington tipped

us off. Camilla Cameron is in the plane with the Hocklands. You know her, don't you?"

Lashley said, "I've heard of her."

"Well, I don't like it. These God-damned sob sisters can make a Greek tragedy out of a crap game. She's liable to write this thing up to make it read that the army is making a whorehouse out of Germany. So be careful. You know. Efficient, sympathetic. And don't say a word you don't have to. Remember, everybody reads her stuff, especially in Washington."

"I'll do my best, Colonel."

"Good enough for me, Lashley. The general tells me you're one of the best men we've got. Says you're doing a hell of a job on this French girl. Okay, go to it."

Lashley's hand lingered on the telephone a long time after the colonel had hung up.

It struck him the general was playing him for an idiot, as an expert fisherman plays a marlin—so much line, so much struggle, so much sport, and the result never in doubt.

His hand tightened on the telephone. He lifted it, then in helpless fury flung it back on the desk. He grabbed his cap and coat and walked out of the office. The hell with Marriner, he thought, I must see Thémis now.

At number 29 Mehlmannstrasse three girls stood conversing on the outside steps. They wore WAC uniforms without insignia except for a brassard bearing in six-inch letters the initials "U.S." One of them was gesturing as though describing a dress for the edification of the other two.

Lashley parked across the street and kept the motor of his jeep turning over. He watched the girls impatiently. Another girl had now taken over the conversation and was apparently trying to demonstrate a hair style.

Finally one of the girls went inside the apartment house, and the other two walked down the hill. Lashley turned off the motor and hurried across the street and into the vestibule.

The inner door was locked. He pushed at it angrily and peered through the glass into a dim corridor. He saw a tired-looking woman carrying a mop and a pail emerge from a doorway. He rapped sharply on the glass.

When the woman opened the door, he said, "I want Miss Delisle."

"Delisle? *Das fransösiche Fräulein?*"

"*Ja.*"

The woman pointed her broom upstairs. "*Zimmer fünf,*" she said lifelessly.

He took the stairs two at a time and found himself in a hall that was almost completely dark. He lighted a match. The door in front of him was number 7. He moved farther down the hall, passed another door, and tossed away the match as he came to number 5.

He knocked lightly.

"*Oui.*"

"Thémis, open up," he whispered.

He heard her cry, "*Robert!*" and then there was a rush of slippered feet. The door swung open. The light from her room burst into the hall and blinded him for a second.

He saw first the trim outline of her shoulders and the long sweep of her dressing gown; and her hands held out to him; and her face, unsmiling but flushed with emotion. Her brown hair, shining in the light was caught back from her face with a pale green ribbon. Now his eyes, accustomed to the light, were dazzled again by her freshness and her beauty.

He kicked the door shut and caught her in his arms.

"Robert," she laughed, "why didn't you give me warning? Look at this room—look at me."

"I'm looking at you," he said, and kissed her first tenderly and then passionately.

"*Robert,*" she murmured, "you Americans . . ."

He held her close. "You don't know how good it is to see you," he said.

She led him over to a window seat and they sat half turned to face each other.

They were silent for a moment. He squeezed her hand, and

she looked up quickly, as if she felt a foreboding in his touch.

He said, "You must listen carefully, Thémis."

"What is it, Robert? What has happened?"

He studied her as he might study a key witness.

"Steigmann is to die tomorrow night—early Saturday morning."

Her face was impassive and her eyes were unwavering. She got up and turned toward the window. Her hair fell lower on her shoulders as she raised her head. He could no longer see her face. The arch of her shoulders told him nothing of what she was feeling.

When she finally turned he saw that her eyes were still clear.

"There is nothing I can say, Robert. If I said I was desolate, I would be lying. If I said I was content, it would also be a lie. After all, I knew the man."

She was very serious now. The dark shadow of the trial lay on them both.

He said, "You don't want to visit the prison? To see him?"

She shook her head slowly but resolutely.

He wanted her to decline. He was in love with her and he sought jealously for every facet of her heart. And yet he wished he might hear a faint protest from her—something—anything that might shed light on what had happened between them in Paris.

"Why have you changed your mind? The other day you wanted to see him."

"What is past is forgotten," she said. "It has nothing to do with us—with you and me."

He looked at her appealingly. "Thémis, please listen. Rodal has failed me. His evidence isn't worth a damn—he's crazy. I've been trying to decide whether I should ask to have the execution canceled."

"But why?"

"Rodal's evidence is really all I had against Steigmann. Perhaps you can help me. I know you can——"

"No, Robert," she said quickly. "I won't talk about it."

He pleaded, "If you love me, you must tell me."

She broke away from him and threw herself on the bed, and her muffled sobs filled the room.

He said, "I am troubled, Thémis. I am killing Steigmann. I am killing him. And I don't know whether it is right and just. I don't know, Thémis. And only you can help me. Can't you see, Thémis? You must help me. You must!"

She half raised her head. "In Paris I did something I had to do and for a reason of which I am not ashamed. But I will not talk about it. Not even to you. Never."

She dropped her head into her arms. He sat helplessly on the bed beside her.

"Let me be alone, Robert," she sobbed. "Let me be alone."

He put his hands on her shoulders and kissed the back of her neck.

"I must go now, darling. Until tonight."

He went out quickly and closed the door.

XIII

BERNHAUSEN FIELD, THE PRINCIPAL AIRPORT SERVING RESCH-weiler, was situated twelve kilometers from the outskirts of the city. It lay on the west side of the Auer, where the valley was wide and flat, and it took its name from the town of Bernhausen, which included a railway switching yard, a few dwellings, and a fifteenth-century church teetering on the banks of the river.

A gravel drive edged with whitewashed stones swung off the main highway and led directly to the passengers' lounge, a low frame building.

Three German war prisoners squatted near the entrance to the lounge. They were dressed in black fatigues which had "PW" stenciled on the pants and sleeves. One of them ran forward as Lashley parked his jeep.

"Baggage, *Herr Offizier?*"

Lashley grunted, *"Nein,"* and went into the building.

The lounge was crowded and noisy. Soldiers dozed in chairs, sprawled on kitbags, or clustered three deep around a Red Cross doughnut bar which occupied a corner of the room opposite the dispatcher's desk. The windows looking out on the airfield were open and the sound of airplane engines warming up in various keys reverberated in the smoky atmosphere and almost drowned out a voice singing "Don't Fence Me In" over the loud-speakers.

Lashley joined a queue in front of the dispatcher's desk.

"Hey there, Major!"

It was Gubbins of the United Press. The tall, cadaverous newspaperman was waving a doughnut from the Red Cross bar. He struggled free of the soldiers about him and came forward.

"She'll be in in a couple of minutes, if that's what you're worrying about. The Hockland plane, isn't it?"

"Thanks, Gubbins."

"Nothing, Major. She'll be unloading at Gate 3. Say, I got a bone to pick with you."

"Oh."

"Yep. What's this about Camilla Cameron? Since when is the army giving free rides to trained seals so they can scoop us right on our home territory?"

"Honestly, Gubbins, I don't know anything about it—except that she's on the plane."

"Well, it's a God-damned outrage. We get paid for sticking around this dump, and every time a story breaks the army brings in somebody to take the cream off it. Why, Camilla's got the old lady sewed up tighter'n a drum even before I can get at her——"

"Come now, it's not that big a story."

"That's just it. Before Camilla gets through with it, she'll have Truman leading the parade to Arlington and she'll sell it to the movies for nine billion dollars. Say, what's the Frenchman doing here? You know, the fellow at the trial—Gribemont."

"Is he here?"

"Right out there, mooching around Gate 3. What is it, Major?"

Lashley glanced through the open window. Captain Gribemont was pacing the landing apron at Gate 3.

"You've got me, Gubbins. Why don't you ask him?"

"I did. He's one of those guys—ask him a question and right away he becomes a diplomat. You know—ice and Emily Post. Gives out with the my-dear-fellow routine. 'My dear fellow,' he says——"

Lashley mumbled, "See you later," and pushed out into the warm sunshine that beat down on the field. Hurrying through Gate 3 he caught up with the Frenchman.

"Are you waiting for the Hockland plane?" he called out before Gribemont was aware of his approach.

The Frenchman turned about. If he was surprised he did not show it. "Major Lashley," he said stiffly. "How do you do."

The motors of a stationary plane near by roared suddenly. Both men held their caps on their heads against the force of the slipstream.

Lashley put his lips close to the Frenchman's ear and shouted, "I'm all right. What are you doing here?"

Gribemont stood patiently until the roar receded. Then he said, "I'm waiting for the special plane from Paris."

"Does the Hockland affair concern you too?" Lashley barked with as much belligerence as he could convey in the simple query.

"My dear fellow," Gribemont said with an injured air, "the plane happens to be carrying two men I wish to meet."

"What have they got to do with the Hocklands?"

The Frenchman shook his head slowly. "They have nothing to do with the Hocklands. If it interests you—and I believe it does—the men are Lieutenant Pierrard and Sergeant Greviers of the Deuxième Bureau." He said, "They are arriving in order to escort the Delisle person back to Paris. I believe she will be—uh—available tomorrow night."

"Why are they on this plane?" Lashley demanded.

"It was convenient. We French have no priorities on your scheduled flights, you know. General Marriner arranged it. Very thoughtful of him. The general is quite a remarkable man. He thinks of everything."

Lashley turned away and strode to the edge of the concrete apron. He was conscious of a web tightening around him no less than around Thémis, for the suspicion grew in him that he had been enticed to the airfield primarily to witness the arrival of the French guards. He cursed Marriner's cleverness.

The general was manipulating every stray incident to force him voluntarily to surrender Thémis, as a battle tactician employs every contour of terrain to confound his adversary into submission.

Gubbins came running up to him. "What's the angle on Gribemont, Major?"

Lashley muttered, "Nothing to do with the Hocklands," and he continued to walk with quick, angry steps.

The silver plane came down out of a faultless sky. It bounced twice on the runway before rolling to a halt at the far end of the field, swung off the concrete, and rumbled across the discolored terrain toward the apron of Gate 3. Its motors roared, each in quick succession like two violently argumentative mates, as it pivoted on its undercarriage. The moment the engines died the plane's door opened. Three prisoners of war pushed a landing platform into place.

A flight sergeant appeared on the platform, looked around, and stepped back into the plane. Then a tall, middle-aged man in a gray overcoat came out carrying a suitcase.

Lashley guessed he was Elmer Hockland. He called up from the foot of the landing stage: "Mr. Hockland?" The man looked down at him. "Be with you in a minute," he said. He stuck his head into the plane. Lashley heard him say: "Ready, Edna? This is it. Steady over the bumps now."

He stepped back, straightening his broad shoulders. It was easy to see where the boy got his height and his rawboned lankiness. Thirty years from now young Hockland would have looked like this.

Two women came out. Lashley recognized Camilla Cameron immediately, although she was not nearly so pretty as the picture which was printed at the head of her dispatches. She was blond and better than forty if one judged by the sag of her jaw, and her mouth was loose as though made so by years of constant chatter. She wore what looked like a custom-made trench coat—very pert—and something which simulated an overseas cap.

The woman whose arm she held—though one glance showed this precaution to be unnecessary—was obviously Mrs. Hockland. She was short, inclined to be stout, and capable-looking in a neat navy-blue suit and a well-worn muskrat coat. Her face under her simple navy hat was pale and strained with fatigue and grief. But it was calm. Her eyes were dry and resigned. She tried to extricate herself from Camilla's clutch and glanced at her husband.

"I'm right here, Dad," she said quietly. Lashley thought she might have been silently adding "ready for anything."

She looked like home to Lashley, like many other American women scattered on farms and in small towns from Maine to southern California: steady, not very articulate, but intelligent about the business of everyday living. Women who did their own housework, and did it well, and who, when that work was done, had time for their church Ladies' Aids, Parent-Teachers Associations, Red Cross chapters, and local garden clubs. Women like that had bred and reared a million or so kids like Hockland, never thinking that those kids would be fitted out with uniforms and guns and sent to Leyte and Saigon and Sicily and Germany to do the foul business of war.

Mr. Hockland said gruffly, "Well, come along then. Let's get going."

"Have you got the suitcase?" his wife inquired.

"Of course I have."

Camilla squeezed her arm. "Now there, you poor darling, don't worry about a thing. It will all be taken care of."

They came down the steps together. Lashley went to the big man's side and said, "I'm Major Lashley. If there's anything I can do, any questions I can answer——"

"There's plenty I'd like to know," Hockland said bitterly. "But I want to get my wife settled first. We just heard about Clay back there in Paris." He choked.

"Mr. Hockland?"

Gubbins inserted himself between Lashley and Hockland, and began asking questions about the trip.

Lashley heard Camilla saying, "Now, my poor darling, just say something to me while they take the picture——"

A correspondent-photographer had arrived inexplicably and was aiming his Speed Graphic at the group.

"Not everybody, you dumb cluck—just the two of us," Camilla shouted. "Now"—turning to Mrs. Hockland—"just say anything, anything at all—to me."

Lashley suddenly remembered Gribemont. He looked about and caught sight of the Frenchman walking toward the passengers' lounge with a fellow officer. They were followed at a discreet distance by a French enlisted man. A revolver butt stuck out of his open holster.

Gubbins was saying, ". . . so it's your opinion, Mr. Hockland, that we should withdraw our troops from Germany. Do you mean immediately or after——"

Lashley's attention was diverted by a large pea-green automobile coming around the corner of the lounge. It was Marriner's Cadillac. It stopped at the edge of the apron, and Lieutenant Parker hopped out and walked briskly toward the group. He saluted Lashley but addressed himself to Hockland.

"Lieutenant Parker, sir. General Marriner asked me to see that you and Mrs. Hockland are comfortably settled. I've already arranged your entry with the security officer. The general's car is here—any time you're ready."

The man from Iowa shook Parker's hand. "That's mighty good of the general." He turned to his wife. "Look, Edna, the general sent his own car for us."

Mrs. Hockland had managed to break free of Camilla's hold. Gubbins was talking to her and writing down her replies to his questions. Her husband cut in on them. "We can't keep the general's car waiting. What are you telling him?"

Lashley said, "Would you like to go to the hotel first—or the hospital?"

Mrs. Hockland laid a hand on her husband's arm. She spoke to Lashley. "To the hotel, please. Dad and I'd like to be alone a bit before—the other thing."

They walked toward the automobile, Camilla following close at their heels.

Hockland said to Lashley in a low voice: "Are you the man who knows all about—what happened?"

Lashley nodded.

Hockland said, "Suppose I see you at the hospital in about an hour. I'll be alone. That's no place for Edna."

A driver held the door open for them. As Mrs. Hockland bent to step into the automobile Camilla Cameron suddenly threw an arm around her and cradled her head against her shoulder. The newspaperwoman gesticulated madly with her free arm.

"Get it! Get it!" she whispered hoarsely to the photographer. He pulled his camera into position, but as he was adjusting the lens Mrs. Hockland broke away and climbed into the automobile. Hockland followed her.

Camilla looked murderously at the photographer.

"Dumb bastard," she muttered.

She got into the automobile and slammed the door.

Parker hopped in beside the driver. The car slid away.

Lashley was standing in the corridor when Hockland came out of the room where his son's body lay.

There was something sturdy and courageous about the big man's grief. His eyes were dry and a look of stark indignation covered his hard, outdoor face. He closed the door gently, and as he lingered with his hand still on the knob his shoulders sagged as though the muscles that held his huge frame erect had suddenly become atrophied. To Lashley it was an eloquent and tragic gesture. Hockland was a man of the land, and his joy in life was his land and the strength he gave to it. Now the one to whom he would have given his land was gone.

He turned upon Lashley.

"I want to know just what happened to my boy," he said gruffly.

"We'll go downstairs," Lashley said. "Captain Bossin—he's

the doctor who treated your son—will let you have his office for a while. We'll be alone."

At the head of the stairs Hockland paused. "Did they do everything they could for Clay?"

Lashley said, "Everything."

The man nodded. "I'm sure they did."

Bossin's office was small. It contained a desk and two chairs and some shelves piled with medical books and clinical equipment. Its single window was huge and looked out on a lawn that fronted the building. Lashley saw that the sun was moving along the eaves on the dwelling across the street. It was approaching dusk.

Hockland seated himself on a small chair which was hidden by his bulk. He bent forward, his elbows on his knees, his jaw resting on his clenched hands.

"He was a good boy—my only boy," he muttered. "We'll be alone now, Edna and me. I don't know who'll have the farm."

He looked up from under his unruly hair and said harshly, "I want to know what happened to him."

Lashley said gently, "I don't know where to begin, Mr. Hockland. How much do you already know?"

"Just what was in the telegram and the papers. Some German girl waited for him and shot him in cold blood. What else is there, Major? You'd better tell me from start to finish. I want the facts. All of them."

Lashley leaned on the edge of Bossin's desk and looked into the man's face. "All right, Mr. Hockland. There's nothing to hide. But I'm glad your wife isn't here. It's not a pleasant story—for a mother."

"Let me be the judge of that," Hockland grunted.

"Your son was having an affair with this German girl."

"What do you mean—an affair?"

"A love affair."

Hockland began shaking his head. "If you mean he was carrying on with her, I say it ain't true. I'm saying right here

and now, it ain't true. Why, the boy was just out of high
school. He was going around with the Borglum girl, Gwennie.
Seeing her all the time. He treated a girl right. We live clean
where I come from. Clay wouldn't know a loose woman if he
saw one——"

"I'm not saying this German girl was a loose woman. She's
only nineteen."

"Nineteen? Old enough to shoot my boy. And break his
mother's heart. What kind of a story does she tell? Where is
she? You've got her, haven't you?"

"She's in the hospital." Lashley studied the Iowan moodily.
"She's going to have a child—any day now."

Hockland burst out: "Hospital! You mean here?"

"No. She's at a German hospital, a civilian place."

"Look here, Major! My boy is lying up there cold. He's
dead. And you stand there and tell me the woman who killed
him is in a hospital having a baby like nothing happened.
What kind of Americans are you around here? That woman
deserves to hang, baby and all!"

"You don't mean that, Mr. Hockland. Americans don't hang
anybody without a trial. Not even in Germany."

"Let me tell you. I'm staying right here on the spot until
I see that woman hang with my own eyes. Somebody's got
to pay for this——"

"Revenge and justice are not the same thing, Mr. Hockland.
They only sound like the same thing. As far as the girl is
concerned, she shot your son, without a doubt. She will be
put on trial as soon as her child has been born."

"Damn her and her child."

Lashley braced himself against the desk.

"It's—very possible that it's your son's child, Mr. Hockland."

"That's a lie!" The Iowan sprang to his feet. His face was
suddenly dark red with anger, and his tightly compressed
mouth was outlined in ugly lines. His huge body was taut
with the tension of wrath.

Lashley watched him impassively.

Hockland relaxed slowly. He pushed gnarled fingers through his hair and turned his face away. "I didn't mean to call you a liar, Major. It's just that I know my boy better than you do. Funny," he muttered, "how I talk like he's still alive. It'll take a lot of getting used to."

Lashley said, "Maybe we can talk tomorrow."

"Yes, tomorrow. Guess I'm tuckered out." Hockland took up his hat and moved toward the door.

They walked together to the front hall.

Lashley said, "By the way, Mr. Hockland. Where did they put you up?"

"At that big place. The Excelsior Hotel."

"I'll take you. I'm driving there now."

"I guess not, Major. Got to see General Marriner. He asked me, you know. He must be a fine man, the general."

"Yes." Lashley sighed. "He's a fine man."

Dust weaved across the city's jagged rooftops. It seemed to Lashley as he watched from his window that this night was party to the tragedy it covered. He was repelled by its spurious comfort. Somewhere out there was Clay Hockland lying stiff and wasted beneath a white sheet. And the elder Hockland blindly searching for retribution as a shaggy animal might seek it. And the undernourished body of Erika struggling to bring new life into the world.

There was Rodal trying to make "the beasts" pay for the suffering he had endured. And his Maria whimpering for want of memories her empty mind could not hold. There was Marriner desperately ruling the morbid empire to which he had fallen unwilling heir. And Steigmann concerned no longer with days but with hours. And there was Thémis.

He too was not excluded. He was a part of the ugly drama. He too was fumbling with life and death, and doing nothing to resolve the dilemma into which he had fallen. He knew why this night was repellent to him. It was the last full night for Steigmann. It might also be in another way for Thémis, for him. Tomorrow night would be too late. The hours between were precious as no hours had been before in his life. All afternoon he had put off thinking about Steigmann and the worthlessness of Rodal's testimony. Now he could no longer avoid doing something about it. He came quickly away from the window, caught up his cap and coat, and made for the door.

The telephone jingled. His hand remained on the doorknob and he looked at the instrument as though it were human. It jingled once more. He hated to answer it, for it seemed to him in his keyed-up state that there was something ominous in its sound. It was probably Marriner trying to forestall him. The man was telepathic. Each time he moved toward decisive action Marriner was one step ahead.

He cursed under his breath and lifted the receiver.

"Major Lashley?"

"Yes."

"This is Camilla Cameron." The voice was utterly charming.

"Yes, Miss Cameron."

"Strange I should find you in the hotel. I've been tracing you all over town and here you were in this very hotel all the time——"

Lashley fidgeted at the phone. "What is it, Miss Cameron?"

"I wonder, Major, if you know that you've made a terribly big reputation for yourself back home. The papers were full of the Steigmann trial——"

"Miss Cameron, would you excuse me now——"

"I'll state my business very quickly, Major. I'm phoning for Mrs. Hockland. She's here beside me. . . ." There was a pause. "Can you see her for a minute or so—now?"

Lashley gazed helplessly into the mouthpiece.

"Is it important?"

"It's terribly important."

"Where is Mrs. Hockland?"

"On the second floor—206."

"I'll drop by on my way down."

He found Mrs. Hockland in a large, twin-bedded room. She sat uncomfortably on the edge of a chair. Though she had taken off her hat and coat, she looked as transient and alien to her surroundings as a robin in a city street. She sat very still and stiffly braced. Only her clasped fingers worked convulsively.

Camilla Cameron lounged spaciously on one of the beds. She was eying him as a tipsy male might eye a checkroom girl in a night club. She crossed her legs and said in a desultory voice: "It was good of you to come down, Major."

Deliberately ignoring her, he said, "Is there anything I can do for you, Mrs. Hockland?"

She looked up at him and he read purpose in her gray eyes. "Is Elmer—Mr. Hockland—still—at—the hospital?"

"I believe he's with General Marriner now."

Camilla said huskily, "The poor sweet! So brave. I've told her it would be better if she would break down and cry."

She glanced at Lashley, then at Mrs. Hockland. "Come now —tell the major what you'd like him to do."

"I want to ask a favor." A tremor passed over the woman's face, but she spoke with great calm. "It means so much to me."

"What is it, Mrs. Hockland?"

"Would you—take me to see—the girl?"

He looked reflectively at the woman, then at Camilla.

Mrs. Hockland said, "You know, the girl—who did it. She's in a hospital. I want to see her."

"Don't you think you should wait until your husband is with you?"

"Oh no," she replied quickly. "Elmer—Mr. Hockland— wouldn't want me to go."

Camilla said, "You see, Major, he's terribly, terribly bitter."

Lashley's shoes moved impatiently on the carpet. He glanced at his watch. It was after six o'clock.

"Please," Mrs. Hockland urged. "Please take me."

Lashley breathed hard. "All right. We can go right now."

"Thank you, I felt sure you would. We'll start before Elmer gets back. I'll—I'll just wash my face." She got up and walked in quick, short steps to the bathroom.

Lashley turned furiously on Camilla. "Did you promote this?"

"Well," said the newspaperwoman languidly, "not exactly. I found out about the girl being pregnant and I thought she should know. After all——"

"After all, nothing! You missed out on a deathbed scene this afternoon so you went ahead and promoted something else to make copy for your column. Why couldn't you wait a day or two——"

"Now wait a minute——"

"You don't give a damn for Mrs. Hockland—you and your phony darlings. You want to splash some tears all over the papers tomorrow. You make me sick."

Camilla leaped from the bed.

"Look here, Lashley. I don't have to take this from you or anybody else. If you want to be ruined, I'm just the little lady who can do it. Just like that!" She snapped her fingers.

Before he had time to reply Mrs. Hockland came out of the bathroom and they both turned around. Mrs. Hockland was wearing her hat. She took her coat from the rack and said steadily: "I'm ready now."

Camilla went to her, patted her on the cheek, and took down her own coat.

Lashley said, "Where are *you* going?"

"Where do you *think* I'm going?" she answered viciously.

"Not with us."

"Oh yes, I am, big boy."

Mrs. Hockland said: "If the major doesn't think you should come, Miss Cameron——"

"He can't prevent me," she said with feeling.

Lashley said quietly, "The girl is a prisoner, Miss Cameron. If you want to see her, you'll have to make application to the JAG of this area."

She ran to the phone. "You son of a bitch," she said to him under her breath, "you can't get away with this. What's his name?"

"Lashley," he said, mimicking her tone. He turned to the older woman, who stood bewildered.

"Come along, Mrs. Hockland."

The little woman was silent during the journey to the outskirts of the city. She looked straight ahead into the bright night. Neither the ruins nor the huge reservoir over which they passed by viaduct appeared to divert her from the weight of her thoughts or from her purpose.

Lashley did not know how to open a conversation with her. He felt awkward and abashed by her composure.

Suddenly she said with mournful sweetness: "Did you know Clay?"

"Not until the very last," he said gently.

She was silent again.

They came within sight of the hospital. It was a modern structure four stories high and it had five wings radiating from a center block. In its isolated location on flat, open ground it gleamed under the moonlight like an apparition of wholeness in a land of bits and pieces. The Americans had requisitioned it when Reschweiler was occupied, but it had been returned to civilian use when the battle wounded were sent back to the United States.

As they swung into the driveway Mrs. Hockland said, "He was just an average boy. He wasn't ever very smart in school. Sometimes he was quite lazy around the farm. But he was a good boy, Major. A good boy. I loved him." She bowed her head.

"Riding along, I've been thinking. I'm glad I'm here in Germany—and not back home. Everything is strange here. Sad and broken, everything—so I feel as if I belonged. It's like the place is made for dying and feeling sad. It's easier being away over here. But I don't know what I'll do when I go home—I declare I don't." Tears ran out the corners of her eyes and down her cheeks. She turned her head from Lashley and unobtrusively wiped them away.

She was quite calm when they entered the hospital rotunda.

Lashley spoke to a tall, angular nurse whose mouth was twisted to one side as if by a paralytic stroke.

"*Wo ist das Fräulein Erika Wagner?*"

She surveyed the two of them with unhappy eyes. Then she said, "*Kommen sie bitte mit mir.*"

They followed her up a staircase and into a corridor which Lashley judged to be at least seventy-five yards long. The whole of it was lighted by a single electric bulb. The gloom and the emptiness made the inside of the hospital a caricature of its gleaming exterior.

With a weariness bordering on insolence the nurse pointed down the hall and said, "*Die letzte tür.*"

Lashley could see a Wac leaning against a window frame at the end of the corridor. She was smoking. As they approached he recognized her as the same girl who had looked after Erika at the stockade. On a nearby door a cardboard sign read: "No admittance. U. S. Military Police."

The Wac stamped out her cigarette. "Oh, it's you, Major," she said. "Gee, I'm certainly glad to see somebody come. Somebody with authority. Those MPs up at the stockade don't pay any attention to my phone calls. What happens— what do I do if she dies?" She gestured with her thumb toward the room.

Lashley turned to Mrs. Hockland. "You'd better sit down for a minute." He took the Wac down the hall a short way. "What's the matter?"

She pursed her lips and shook her head. "Major, I can't take it much longer. I can't even stay in the room. The labor pains got started today. It's horrible."

"It isn't pleasant, I suppose, having a baby."

"Oh no, Major, it's not that. Ma had eight after me. I remember the last three like it was yesterday, and it wasn't anything like this. You ought to talk to the doctor. Even he says there's nothing he can do. You watch. She's going to die."

Lashley suddenly felt relieved—it might be a good thing if the girl died. Better for everybody.

"Call the doctor," he said. "Tell him I want to see him."

"Anything you say, sir." She walked rapidly down the hall.

He turned back to Mrs. Hockland. She sat on a bench, staring straight ahead at a blank wall.

"Would you like to see her now?" he asked.

"If you please."

They went in. A single lamp hung from the ceiling and illuminated gray streaks of corrosion on the plaster walls. The room was bare except for a washbasin and a bed, but it was vibrant with the moaning of the girl. She lay on her back, her eyes closed and her mouth open, and her face looked horrible. She might have been six or sixty, for her suffering seemed ageless. Her skin glowed greenish gray under the light and her black hair was stringy and unkempt. There were no sheets on the bed. She lay on a discolored mattress and her only covering was a dark brown blanket. Lashley saw that she was wearing a nightgown with a pattern of red roses, a relic of some happier past.

Mrs. Hockland tiptoed to the edge of the bed. She looked down on the girl's face. It was an empty look, bereft of emotion, as though she were looking at a piece of mechanism of which she had not the faintest understanding. The girl seemed scarcely to be breathing. She opened her eyes wide and moaned louder than she had before. Neither the moan nor the girl's open eyes appeared to change the expression on Mrs. Hockland's face.

She looked a long time. Then she moved her head from side to side as if measuring the pitiful length of the girl. Her eyes came to rest at the base of the bed. The blanket was pulled out and one of the girl's feet protruded. Quickly and with a practiced hand the woman took hold of the blanket and tucked the edge of it neatly under the mattress.

She turned to Lashley and said in a lifeless voice, "It's Clay's baby."

He said, "You can't be sure——"

"It's Clay's baby," she muttered as if to herself. "She wouldn't have done it if it wasn't Clay's baby. It's Clay's baby." Emotion came into her face. She closed her eyes hard and her mouth quivered as she fought for self-control. "Clay's baby," she whispered.

The girl let out a horrible groan, raised her arms from under the blanket, and clasped her hands together.

Mrs. Hockland looked at the bed and her face twisted as though she too was struck by a sudden pain. She stood motionless and Lashley could not tell whether it was hate or pity that struggled inside her.

The door behind them opened, and a man in a long white surgeon's overall came in.

Lashley touched Mrs. Hockland on the arm. "Come outside for a minute."

She reacted obediently. He led her from the room and placed her on the bench in the hall. He returned to the room.

The doctor was surveying his patient. He was young, perhaps thirty, and his face was peculiarly expressionless. He must have been in the army, for he pulled himself into a position of attention as Lashley approached.

Lashley said in German, "When do you think she will have the baby?"

Erika began another series of deep groans. The doctor eyed her coldly and beckoned Lashley to a corner of the room.

"It is difficult to say," he replied in low tones. "She is very seriously ill."

"But after all, she's in labor, *Herr Doktor*," Lashley said.

The man nodded glumly and knowingly. "We found an abscess on her right lung. It is a common thing. We have five or six cases like it upstairs. Girls should not have babies when they are undernourished. The baby saps all the strength they have. There is nothing left with which to fight——"

He looked over at the bed as though to sharpen his memory of the case.

"It is a question," he continued casually. "The abscess possibly will subside and she will be well. Or it may burst and become gangrenous. Then she will die. It is a question. But I think she will have the baby."

Lashley was affronted by the man's casualness.

"*Herr Doktor*, there must be a treatment. What do you do with the others?"

"With the others?" the German echoed. "Surgery. But not with this one. She is too weak. As you see, she is in labor."

"There is nothing else that can be done?" Lashley said sharply.

The doctor shook his head thoughtfully. "Nothing—nothing." He raised his eyebrows slightly. "Is it important that she live?"

Lashley frowned. "What do you mean by that?"

The German lifted his hand apologetically. "I meant nothing impertinent, *Herr Commandant*. It is just that if the American authorities are interested they have the germicide required to treat her condition. I refer to penicillin. It is very useful in such a case."

"You have no penicillin?"

"We have never had any."

The thought came to Lashley that he could obtain penicillin from Colonel Ericson at the station hospital. If he did, the girl might recover—only to stand trial. He pondered the alternative. Suddenly he was sickened by his power over life and death. It was too close to that of God.

He said, "Do what you can for her."

The German clicked his heels and inclined his head slightly. The gesture made Lashley uncomfortable. It was as if the doctor had read his thoughts and was making obeisance to the all-powerful.

In the hall Mrs. Hockland was weeping softly. Lashley put on his cap, studied her a moment, and reluctantly touched her shoulder.

He said, "We'd better go now. Your husband will be getting back to the hotel."

She removed the handkerchief from her face and looked at him with moist eyes. Her voice was surprisingly steady.

"I'm not going," she said. "I'm not leaving here. It's no use to talk to me, Major. That's Clay's baby being born in there and I'm going to wait here for it. It's like—like—if Clay was married and his wife was having a baby—I wouldn't be leaving her, would I? Well, I'm not leaving. And that's that."

She settled herself more firmly on the bench, as though she feared he might try to pull her off.

"Mrs. Hockland," Lashley said, "think what you're doing. Think of it. This girl killed your son. He told me so on his deathbed. She shot him. We don't even know it is Clay's baby. There may have been others. Think it over, Mrs. Hockland."

"There's nothing to think over," she said stoutly. "My boy sinned. But the baby hasn't sinned, and neither have I. I don't care if they say there was a hundred others. It could be Clay's baby, and what's Clay's is mine. I'm not going back home to be alone in that house all the rest of my life. I've thought it all out, sitting here. I'm not leaving without that baby. That baby's my grandchild, and here I stay until I get it."

The doctor came from the room, and the sound of the girl's agony came with him.

Mrs. Hockland got to her feet. She brushed off the front of her skirt with capable fingers. Her shoulders straightened. She dismissed Lashley with a nod, turned, and walked into the room. The door softly but firmly closed behind her.

For a moment Lashley contemplated the door's white frame. Then he went quickly down the hall and out of the building.

XIV

A CUTTING WIND BLEW IN GUSTS AGAINST THE WINDSHIELD OF the jeep, retarding its speed and causing the motor to roar with an almost human frustration. It seemed to Lashley as if Nature were conspiring with everyone else to keep him away from Thémis. He pushed his foot hard on the accelerator. The jeep shuddered, raced along the viaduct, and turned swiftly up Bismarck Allee.

Free at last of the Hockland affair, a panic of impatience seized him. This was Thursday night, and time was already running out. Friday was the last day. The French guards would be waiting for Thémis, while in the prison yard at Bergsdorf they would be hammering together portable sections of a scaffold.

He passed the gates of the courthouse, swung recklessly into the descent of Mehlmanstrasse, and pulled up at number 29. As he dashed into the gloomy vestibule two khaki-clad figures hurriedly disengaged themselves from a rapt embrace. The inner door was locked. He shook the handle angrily.

The girl beside him said, "Just a minute, hot pants. Don't break it down. We need it." She took a key from her bag and opened the door for him. He was on the staircase before he paused to yell thanks.

The first-floor corridor was lighted. In a few strides he was at the door of number 5, knocking hard on the thin panel and listening for her footsteps. He knocked again, violently now, and rattled the handle.

The door of number 6 opened. A woman wearing a dressing gown scowled at him. "Are you drunk or something?"

He said, "Miss Delisle—where is she?"

The woman glanced at the bronze medallion on his epaulette. She said, "Maybe downstairs in the canteen." Her door slammed and the bolt lock clicked decisively.

He tore down the stairs to the front hall. There was another staircase in the back, and at the bottom of it he found himself in a modest dining room. The supper hour was apparently over. German girls were clearing the tables, talking animatedly to one another. Thémis was not there.

He came up the stairs slowly, wondering where she might be. A dozen possibilities passed through his mind, and suddenly they were dispelled by the terrifying thought that she might have been arrested already. He had almost forgotten about the two French soldiers who had arrived with the Hocklands, and Gribemont's smugness at the airport.

The wind outside had become bitterly cold. He drove slowly down the hill, scanning both sides of the street. At the corner of Bahnhofstrasse he braked his jeep as a dark figure emerged from the direction of the Excelsior. It was not Thémis. He increased his speed again and drove to the parking lot behind the Excelsior.

Another idea made him pause at the door of the hotel. He dashed across the street and along the pathway which traversed the Operaplatz. The statue of Schumann stood in lonely splendor amid the waste and destruction. There was no sound except the whine of the wind, and no life beyond the stubborn industry of the gaunt German who sat in the ruins of the portico and pared bricks with a pocket knife.

He turned back to the hotel. The lobby was oppressive with lights and the conversation of idleness. A full colonel was exacting roars of laughter from a group of junior officers. Lashley blinked and surveyed the room carefully. Suddenly he started.

Thémis was sitting in a deeply upholstered chair facing a far corner, half hidden by a potted palm. She was holding her chin very high and taking quick nervous puffs from a cigarette. A dozen paces away Captain Kinsella leaned against the wall and chatted with a French soldier. It was the soldier who had arrived with the Hocklands, the one who carried a revolver.

Lashley doubled his fists and strode over to Kinsella. Before he could utter a word the bulky captain raised a hand in front of his face with mock timidity.

"Orders, Major," he said jocosely. "This time it's orders."

"Whose orders?" Lashley demanded.

"Hell, I don't know," Kinsella said. "I'm a captain. Get my orders from a major. Christ knows where he gets 'em from——"

"What's the order?"

The captain screwed up his face and glanced at the Frenchman beside him. "Oh, sort of keep an eye on the gal—see she don't pop off somewheres before we pick 'er up tomorrow night. Savvy?"

"All right, Kinsella. Show me the order."

The bulky man shifted from one foot to the other. "I got 'em verbal, Major——"

Lashley said, "You're a damned liar."

The captain's eyes flashed with anger. He shoved his chin close to Lashley's scowling face. "You're pretty safe, ain'tcha, Major, calling me a——"

"You're a God-damned liar, Kinsella. You've got no orders."

"Well, this French fella's got orders."

"His orders don't mean a thing around here and you know it. He's not going to take the girl—not tonight or tomorrow or any other night. Now get out! Go on, get out!"

Kinsella held his ground a moment, then buttoned his coat with easy deliberation, set his cap at a jaunty angle over his right eye, and walked slowly to the door. The Frenchman followed him gingerly. They conversed briefly at the door and pushed out into the night. Lashley watched them go. He felt no satisfaction in this victory, for he told himself it was only temporary.

An inordinately pale Thémis was observing him tensely. She half smiled as he approached, and shook her head as if to chide him gently.

He said, "Thémis, will you come with me?"

"Wherever you go, Robert," she replied quietly.

They dodged through the crowded lobby toward the elevator. As the gate closed he caught a flash of Nissen gaping at them, and he was at a loss to judge whether the man's handsome face was stricken with horror or astonishment.

Thémis was trembling. He poured a drink of straight whisky and when he brought it to her he leaned down and kissed her gently on the lips. Her fingers linked behind his neck, and she murmured, "Again. Kiss me again." She was warm and all he could think of was how vital she was to him. He held her away and looked into her face. Her eyes were soft and wide, her lips relaxed. He kissed her hard.

"Feel better, darling?" he asked, and smiled pensively.

"Oh, Robert, I am happy now, to be with you, completely happy."

He sighed. "Oh, Thémis, this isn't any good. This furtive sort of thing isn't for us." She dropped her arms in astonishment.

"Happiness for the moment only doesn't count, Thémis." He went on, "It's only war happiness, it isn't really happiness at all. It's misery."

She murmured, "Is there any other kind for us?"

"Of course there is. There's the kind that goes on and on —into the future."

She looked away and her words came slowly. "Then we shall be unhappy. We can count on no future."

"You've been pessimistic, Thémis, you . . . Surely you know for those who want it badly enough there is a future. The secret, darling, is to go about getting it bravely."

"I used to be brave," she said. "I know now it's easy for the lonely to be terribly brave. It is easy when one has nothing to lose. But you see I have something to lose now, and I am a coward."

He crossed to the window, watching her as he walked. "Long before I knew you I fell in love with your courage, the courage that made you come to Reschweiler to testify, when there was no need for it."

"Then you have robbed me of it, Robert. All day I have been afraid."

"Of what?"

She looked at him with a great tenderness. "That I will lose you."

"You will never lose me. Nor I you."

Her smile was sad. "You saw the men tonight. They have been following me everywhere—all day."

"You saw how quickly they disappeared."

"No, Robert. It was like brushing flies from fruit. They will be back."

He looked out into the night. The waning moon hung over the horizon, and it seemed to him that it no longer held either romance or mystery. It was like a clock's face, a symbol of the hours that were passing recklessly as the scudding clouds.

He turned to her and said, "Thémis darling, please don't be afraid. We won't lose each other. I know it."

"I wish I could believe that too, Robert. But there is no way we can be together after this. The men are waiting for me. They will take me back to France."

He looked away from her. "I fell in love with the Thémis in the courtroom, the Thémis on the witness stand, the Thémis who had her little gesture to make, who stood up and fought the world to make it——" He turned his eyes sternly upon her. "She was neither loving nor fearful. Only brave. What has happened to that Thémis?"

She did not reply at once. Her eyes, deeply green beneath the light, were wide with contemplation. Then she said, "Falling in love, Robert, has little to do with courage or goodness. Love makes life precious, and when life is precious even the bravest are afraid."

Her face became gravely troubled and she was silent. He moved quickly from the window and sat beside her. He took her hands.

"Thémis, do you love me?"

She murmured desolately, "It is so small a word."

"There is no other."

"Oh, my darling——" Her voice was breathlessly quiet. "I love you with all my heart and soul and mind and body. I love you more dearly than life is dear, because even that is yours. You have made me feel alive again. You have made me forget all the dark yesterdays. Perhaps without them I should never have met you, never have known and loved you today."

She turned her face and pressed it hard against his shoulder.

"And tomorrow?" he murmured.

"I cannot think of tomorrow. It doesn't exist—as yesterday no longer exists."

He held her close, determined to overcome her despondency. "Listen, Thémis. Please listen. Really it isn't hopeless—I've thought of a way. There is a train tomorrow—at noon. It goes north to Luxembourg and Belgium. You will be on it—and you will wait for me in Belgium——"

She shook her head but said nothing.

"I have a plan." He was talking louder now, and more slowly, as if force and emphasis would convince her. "The train makes a stop at Bernhausen. I will drive you out and you will board it there," he said patiently. "I can arrange it. Why, you'll be in Belgium before they discover you're gone."

She stared at him almost incredulously. Color was coming into her skin and her eyes were brightening.

"Oh, *Robert*, can it be done?"

"I'm sure of it. I'll meet you there—as soon as I've finished what I have to do here, when I am free of the army."

"When will that be?"

"Soon, my darling. Only a few weeks. But first I've got to clear my conscience. I've decided to ask for a retrial. Steigmann——"

"But why—why—why?" She was agitated now and she

walked back and forth in the little room. When she stopped and stood before him, her face was set in anger. "I hate him. He is not innocent. As God is my judge, he is not innocent. Let him die now and be forgotten."

"Then why did you sacrifice yourself in a hopeless cause for a man you say you hate?" Lashley was angry too, exasperated by her contradictoriness.

"I was not trying to save him," she answered with cold patience. "It was something I believed I had to do, I had a feeling of obligation. . . ."

"I still don't understand why you refuse to tell me about it," Lashley snapped at her.

"I tried to explain once, that evening in your office, but I saw then that you would not understand. There are some things that are logical only in the heart and futile in one's conscious mind. Steigmann was evil, and I believed the world judging him was also evil—just as evil—I was trying to find goodness at least in myself."

"Thémis, will you tell me this: do you believe he should die?"

She pressed her hands together and looked at him intently, "Yes, oh yes. He deserves to die and with no more thought on your part."

"You don't understand either," he said. "My conscience won't allow me to let him die tomorrow, without——"

She interrupted him vehemently. "What is this conscience of yours that you have to fight with it night and day? First you want Steigmann to hang, then you want to put it off. You cannot believe him innocent. Surely you are certain of his guilt. But you worry it around like a bone——"

"But the law——" Lashley broke in.

She picked up the word and threw it back at him.

"The law—is that what you want, or is it justice? You lawyers with your mealymouthed words and your precious integrity, chasing down side streets after the law, while the truth, the beautiful truth, is staring you right in the face. You and your law."

She paused in the tirade long enough to catch her breath. Her eyes were blazing. "You talk of justice, but you do not recognize it." She walked over to the window and stood there with her back to him. When she continued it was with an air of resignation.

"But I know you, my *Robert*. You will never be happy if he dies unless it's legal beyond a shadow of a question." She turned now and looked at him, and once more her eyes were soft. "You're like that, my dear, wanting everything the way it should be, and perhaps that's one reason I love you. If I could only make you see, *Robert* . . ."

Lashley looked away from her and stared unseeingly at the bust of Hitler on his bureau.

"I can't see, Thémis. I'm confused by it all."

"Maybe it would help if you went and talked to Steigmann. He knows he deserves to die. Perhaps talking to him will put your mind at rest. Why don't you go? Promise me you will, *Robert*."

"I was thinking of seeing him—as a last resort. Dearest, it isn't just the trial that worries me now about Steigmann. If we had never met, I might not be worrying about him tonight. It was you who unintentionally brought the first doubt into my mind. And whatever it was you meant to him, I have taken that away. I stole it from him. We stole it from him. That has not changed him, or his crimes. It has not changed him; it has changed me. It has not made him less guilty, but me less worthy."

She came to him quickly and put her fingers on his lips.

"*Robert*, don't torture yourself. I am not the jury. This is not a courtroom. This——" Her arms swept the room. "This is ours tonight, and we are together in it."

He held her close and kissed her, then, picking her up in his arms, he carried her across the room and put her down on the ugly narrow bed.

Her head dug into the pillow, and as she turned momentarily away from him he thought she quivered. He bent down and kissed her neck and his lips lingered where he kissed her.

Somewhere beneath, in the dark shelter of her brown tousled hair, her fingers reached for his and drew them to her mouth and she kissed them.

He inclined his head on the pillow beside her. She lay still. Her breath came softly on his fingers and slowly she turned to him.

As he took her in his arms he knew that he was not the Lashley of Monday night, who knew only desire. Now he was with the woman he loved.

Tonight he was the driven and the driver, the seeker and the sought, the one who knows the sweet ache of competition.

FRIDAY

XV

THE DAWN WAS GRAY. IT CAME HESITANTLY OVER THE ROOF-
tops, gathered courage, and peered in through the curtained
windows. Lashley sat, fully dressed, in front of his writing
table. A small lamp cast its yellow light on the paper in front
of him.

Now he put the lamp out and applied himself once more to
the document on which he had been working. He struck out a
word and inserted another. He put a line through a redundant
paragraph. He read the document again and again. Frequently
he glanced at the bed and the slim figure that lay there. The
calm of her breathing gave him singular pleasure. She lay on
her side, the dark tangle of her hair almost obscuring her face,
one arm outstretched as if it waited for him. She looked as
sweet and defenseless as a child.

This was Friday and he wondered who else, besides Steigmann, might be studying this sullen dawn. Perhaps Mrs. Hockland, sitting vigil over the new life that was struggling within
the womb of the German girl. And Mr. Hockland, voicing his
grief in short incoherent syllables. General Marriner would be
awake now. The general would soon know what was in the
document that he had just finished.

He reread the sheet before him. It was properly addressed
to the Judge Advocate General, USFET, Frankfurt-am-Main.
It seemed complete and reasonable. All that remained was to
have it typed in three copies—one for his file, one for the gen-

eral, and one to be put on the Frankfurt teleprinter. This simple petition would save Steigmann.

He stretched his arms lazily and looked at Thémis once more. In spite of her arguments last night, he had waked himself early in order to work on the petition. Perhaps she was right. Perhaps he would never send it. But anyway it was ready.

Light, quick footsteps sounded in the hall. It seemed early for the maid to begin work and he glanced at his watch. It was not so early. It was nearly seven. The overcast must have delayed the dawn.

A timid knock sounded on the door. He got up from his chair and tiptoed across the room. He paused. Perhaps it was the maid with her pail and broom. He listened for the familiar clatter but there was none. Now there were two timid knocks. He heard a voice whisper, "Major Lashley."

He knew at once it was Mrs. Hockland.

Lashley stepped to the door quietly. He glanced at the bed and was relieved to see that Thémis had not been aroused by the knocking. Then he opened the door a few inches, took care to insert himself in the aperture and slipped out into the hall. He closed the door behind him but did not click the snap lock lest Thémis might awaken and call to him.

Mrs. Hockland apparently had not slept. She wore the same neat navy-blue suit, and her face was gray and pinched. She looked years older.

"I'm sorry to disturb you," she said.

He said softly, "It's all right, Mrs. Hockland——"

"I've been sitting up, waiting for it to be light. I kept thinking Dad might wake up—Mr. Hockland. I don't want him to know about anything. Not yet."

"I wasn't asleep. What is it?"

Her eyes held his.

"It's the girl—she's—she's——" She swallowed convulsively. "She's not going to come through. Her face is yellowing. It's been yellowing worse and worse. Even that German doctor says she is going to die. The Wac told me. She told me what the doctor said—we'll lose the baby."

Lashley shook his head futilely. "I'm sorry."

She brushed aside his pity and came directly to the point. "Major Lashley, I've got to have Clay's baby."

He said, "I know, Mrs. Hockland, but what is there to do?"

He felt ashamed now that he had ever thought that it might be better for the girl to die in childbirth than to be condemned by a military court. He had not considered that the baby might also die. Now he knew that the prerogatives of God were not for him. It was enough that he must cope with the prerogatives of man.

The woman was saying, "Can't you get her over to another hospital? To an American one? They've got everything in those other hospitals. The doctor said so. He said they've got everything there to fight with. Can't you, Major?" Her eyes held his.

A stoop-shouldered German girl clumped down the hall, lugging a pail of water and a mop. She came on, not bothering to conceal the righteous pleasure she obviously felt over catching a man and a woman conversing outside a bedroom at seven in the morning.

He waited until she passed. Then he said, "Is she worse than she was last night?"

"Much worse," Mrs. Hockland replied. "Her fever's up. And you can see the doctor over there has given her up. I came back here and I've been waiting to ask you if—maybe——"

He said, "I'll run up to the hospital and ask the colonel, if you like, but I'm sure he won't do it. They don't take Germans, Mrs. Hockland."

The woman looked up incredulously. "It's not the girl, it's the baby. Don't you understand? It's the baby—Clay's baby." Her face worked with pain and puzzlement. "The baby is American."

The remark touched him. A few seconds later he realized it was an unwitting expression of all the cruelty practiced by a precocious humanity in the name of civilization. "The baby is American." This woman didn't know what she had said. She couldn't know, in the isolation of her Iowa home, how cruel it was that the world was neatly packeted into groups of people and how unjust that the unborn were marked for evil or for good, as though they had sinned or were sanctified within the womb.

He said, "I'll see what I can do."

"Please, Major! Right away?"

He nodded. "Right away."

"And if they don't—if they can't take her, ask them for some penicillin? That's what the doctor says she needs, penicillin. I'll pay for it. Whatever it costs."

He said, "We don't need money. They'll give it to us, or they won't."

"You'll ask them though—hard. Won't you, Major?"

"I'll ask them—hard."

She pressed the palms of her hands against her forehead and closed her eyes and murmured, "Oh, I'm glad. Thank you." She looked up at him and repeated, "Thank you. I've got to go back now." He felt awkward and turned his face away until he heard the retreat of her quick footsteps.

He went back into his room and closed the door gently so that the snap lock didn't click.

Thémis had turned in her sleep. Now she lay on her back and her hair fell away from her sleeping face. The feather bed had slipped to the side, exposing the front of her pink slip. He looked hard at the slip where it covered her breasts and thought to himself, My God, it's lucky she isn't awake; if she just looked at me, I'd stay with her all day. Virtuously he pulled the feather bed up to her chin and tiptoed away from the bed.

The paper he had prepared lay on the table and he glanced over it as he buttoned his jacket. He threw his coat over his arm, devoted one more moment to looking at Thémis, and walked softly out of the room.

The officers' mess was empty. It lacked twenty minutes before the breakfast hour. Lashley rapped on the kitchen door and yelled, "*Kaffee, bitte, kaffee.*" A wizened little pantryman came out, surveyed him morosely, and said, "*Ja wohl, mein-herr. Eine Minute,*" and disappeared.

A bundle of *Stars and Stripes* lay on the floor beneath the mess sergeant's desk. Lashley ripped off the cord and took a copy. He glanced through it and saw only two items which were of interest to him. One was a brief account of the death of young Hockland and the arrival of his parents. The other was a story about the multiple hanging that was to take place in the prison yard at Bergsdorf. There was nothing, locally or from Paris, about Thémis.

The pantryman placed a cup of coffee on the table. Lashley gulped it, burning his tongue in his haste. Then he lighted a cigarette and went out to the parking lot.

Colonel Ericson had not yet arrived at the hospital. Neither had Captain Bossin. A sleepy-eyed night nurse who seemed to appreciate that Lashley's mission was urgent directed him to a dwelling immediately behind the hospital, saying, "The colonel should be up now. He usually arrives here promptly at eight."

He found the house easily enough and was admitted by a primly aproned German girl who explained to him that the colonel had not yet come down. He asked when she expected the colonel to come down, and in the midst of her diffident reply he heard someone, apparently the colonel himself, shout from the head of the stairs, "Whoever it is, come on up."

He found the colonel shaving, and he stood at the bathroom door and explained as persuasively as he knew how the problem of Mrs. Hockland and the girl, and the need for penicillin.

Ericson shaved carefully and listened, and Lashley could not tell whether the peculiar twists of his mouth presaged a negative reply or were made necessary by certain mechanical difficulties in scraping the stubble from his pointed chin. When he was finished he put his razor under the faucet, dried it carefully, then washed his face with what seemed to be unnecessary thoroughness.

Finally he sat on the edge of the bathtub and said, "How long have you been in the army?"

"Four years, sir."

He smiled pleasantly. "I've got twenty-three years behind me, and if there's one thing I've learned, it's this: the army can do practically anything—from governing a country to making diapers out of gun cotton. I've seen both done. The army can do anything if it's directed to do it. But if it isn't laid down in orders, it couldn't provide a match to light a candle in a stygian darkness. I used to scream bloody murder once too, but I've learned, Lashley. It's the only possible way to run an army."

Lashley said, "But there are certain circumstances in this case——"

The colonel shook his head. "Look. There's stark tragedy in every house in Germany and in about half the houses in France, Belgium, Holland, and Italy. If we do anything beyond orders, the smallest thing, we're swamped, done, finished. This is a machine, Lashley, and thank God it's a machine. Otherwise— we'd be worthless."

"It seems to me that something could be done," Lashley persisted.

The colonel pushed his hands through his gray-white hair. He said, "I wish to God there was something I could do. There isn't a regulation under which I could do a thing—unless I wanted to risk court-martial. And in the last year I've run across maybe five hundred cases where I was tempted to risk court-martial. That's the way it is."

"What about penicillin?"

"I couldn't give you a unit."

Lashley said angrily, "Colonel, I've seen fifty men lined up in the VD ward waiting to be shot with penicillin. I suppose you'll have twenty or thirty out there today. Suppose for the record you had thirty-one. Or suppose one of the men only thought he had gonorrhea and didn't. You'd have some penicillin left over, wouldn't you?"

The colonel said glumly, "It's a good try, Major, but it won't work. I can't dispose of army property and you know it."

Lashley grumbled, "I think I understand, sir," and turned to go.

"Just a minute." The colonel got up and examined his chin in the mirror. He said, "There was a case a couple of weeks ago. A corporal—one of my own orderlies—came to me for penicillin. Seems he had a German girl friend who contracted lobar pneumonia. I couldn't supply it to him, but he got it all the same."

"How?"

"I don't exactly know. He didn't get it from here. We lock our penicillin in the same cabinet with our morphia. Both have too great a black market value——"

He looked at Lashley. "Perhaps you didn't hear me. I said both have too great a black market value. For God's sake, wake up!"

Lashley said with surprise, "You think it can be bought on the black market."

"That's not what I said, but it's what I mean," Ericson snapped. "They've got tons of the stuff. They hijack our trucks, they steal from our bulk stores, they have it shipped from America—they've got it, I tell you. It's a bigger racket than cigarettes, and it makes me mad enough to tell Germans to go to their own black market to get the stuff and not come whining to me. Now let me get dressed, Major, and good luck to you."

Lashley said, "Thank you, Colonel," and walked thoughtfully toward the stairs.

"Another thing, Major," Ericson called out to him. "Better get out of the army before it breaks your heart or sews it up tighter than mine."

It began to rain as Lashley drove back to the Excelsior. Clouds which had been forming since daybreak moved over the rim of the hills in great black masses. Thunder rumbled in the distance and when the rumbling ceased the rains swept down in violent gusts. The city, its ruins agape, lay naked and defenseless beneath the downpour.

Lashley pulled up in front of the hotel and dashed inside, shaking the water from his coat as he walked to the desk.

He asked the sergeant on duty, "Has Captain Nissen come down?"

"Yes, sir," was the reply. "He's having breakfast."

Nissen viewed him with amusement as Lashley came over to where he sat.

"My dear Dr. Watson," Nissen said as he munched on a slice of toast. "I note three things. Your coat is wet, you have neglected to shave, and you look tired—from which I deduce you have had a most satisfactory night and you have just returned from conducting your fair mistress to her manse. Elementary, my dear fellow."

Lashley scarcely heard him. He said, "Lance, what do you know about the black market in town?"

Munching contentedly, Nissen said, "Cigarettes are eleven hundred marks the carton, up a hundred from last week."

"I don't mean that. Where do they hang out? How do you get in touch with them?"

Nissen said, "Just go outside and buttonhole the first civilian you meet and zip, you're in the black market."

Blond Hedy and her coffeepot materialized at the table. Nissen eyed her with good-humored appraisal as she poured a cup for Lashley. She gave a poor exhibition of appearing not to notice and wiggled her behind as she flounced away—a matter which Nissen did not fail to observe.

Lashley said, "I've got to buy some penicillin. Don't ask me why—just tell me where I can get it."

Nissen whistled. "That's high finance, Bob. There's a lot of the stuff around but I'll be damned if I know how to put my finger on it. Did you try the hospital?"

"There's nothing doing at the hospital."

"I mean the civilians working around the hospital."

"Let's leave the hospital out of it."

"Well then, let me see," Nissen mused. "What first-class crooks do I know? Hedy's kid brother? No. He's only in the chocolate and chewing-gum racket——" He snapped his fingers. "What about that precious witness of yours—you know, the Czech—Rodal? There's a character who could probably sell you the Krupp works, cheap. He's your man, Bob."

Lashley nodded thoughtfully. "I'll try him, if I can find him. How many cigarettes have you got?"

"Help yourself." Nissen tossed over an opened package. "I mean how many cartons have you got upstairs?"

Nissen whooped, "Oh no, mister, not my stock in trade. I'm saving up for a Leica. They want twenty-four cartons for a secondhand job, the crooks."

"I need about five cartons, Lance."

"Now look, you're breaking my heart——" Nissen paused as he caught the deadly serious manner of his friend. He rose from his chair and said, "All right, I'll get you five."

They proceeded to the first floor, where Nissen occupied a room similar to Lashley's. The captain unlocked a wardrobe cabinet and extracted five cartons of cigarettes. He said, "There's fifty-five hundred marks' worth. Personally, I'd rather give you my blood."

Lashley said absently, "I think this should be enough."

"Enough!" boomed Nissen. "That's five hundred and fifty bucks in our money. What does penicillin cost back home— two bucks a throw?"

Lashley packeted the cigarettes under his arm. He proceeded to the door, then turned about impulsively and said, "Lance, I'm thinking of petitioning Frankfurt to set aside the Steigmann verdict."

Nissen said archly, "Fine. Just fine. And you've been hiding Hitler under your bed these last ten, eleven months." He locked the cabinet and reached for his cap and coat.

"I mean it, Lance. I have the petition all ready to send now —as soon as the teleprinter opens."

Nissen put on his coat. He said, "I wouldn't kid about a thing like that. Somebody might hear you. Remember, you were the prosecutor."

Lashley said, "God damn it, I know that. I'm doing it."

The captain stood paralyzed, his arms halfway into the sleeves of his coat. He gasped, "Don't do it, Bob, because you don't know what it will mean."

Lashley said, "I've thought it out, Lance, and I'm prepared to go through with it."

"For God's sake, man, they'll ruin you. I can't let you do it, Bob."

"You can't prevent me. Neither can they. What's more, they can't ignore the petition. They've got to act. I built the case against Steigmann and I can smash it."

Nissen slumped into a chair. He said, "It's not the army. Hell, you're getting out anyway in a couple of months. It's what'll happen to you at home. They just put you up on a pedestal and they'll pull you down. They'll mark you yellow, a backslider, a Nazi lover—you know how they are back home; they like nothing better than to tear down a hero. You might as well throw your career out the window, right out into that rain."

Lashley said, "I'm afraid that's the way it's got to be, Bob. If I let them go through with this I'll be no good to myself. I'll never be able to handle another case as long as I live."

Nissen squirmed with exasperation. "What for, Bob? What for? It's not as if you were saving the man's life. He's going to hang anyway—if not tomorrow night, then they'll get him in a new trial. And if that doesn't work, the French will get him—you know that."

Lashley said, "He's not going to hang on the unadorned testimony of a madman. That was my fault, and I've got to make it right. Rodal is a madman, a hopeless maniac. His evidence wouldn't sustain a traffic charge."

"I don't get it, Bob. Honestly, I don't get it. It's not as if Steigmann were a Dreyfus, or a Sacco or a Vanzetti. He's a Nazi down to his toes. There isn't a person in the world with a good word to say for him—except that woman. Don't tell me she's behind this."

"She's got nothing to do with it; in fact she doesn't like it any better than you do."

"Then for God's sake, exactly what are you accomplishing?"

"It's this, Lance. Let's take for granted the man is guilty. Then there's no miscarriage of justice if he dies tonight or six months from tonight—there's no miscarriage of justice *as far as he's concerned*. But what about us? Does it make any differ-

ence to *us* whether he dies after a fair trial or on a hodgepodge
of inadmissible evidence? You bet it does! We're the conquerors, Lance. We're sitting in judgment on the whole world—we
and the Russians and the British. But most of all it's us—the
Americans. We're hoping to bring peace and sanity and justice
into the new pattern of life. We can't deal in retribution and we
can't cater to hysteria. We've got to come into court with clean
hands and hard, honest minds. We're really the ones who are
on trial—and God help us if we're found wanting——"

He looked with tortured affection upon his distraught friend,
and he said, "I've got to get that penicillin, Lance. Thanks for
the cigarettes."

When he came to the head of the staircase he paused a moment, wondering whether he should go up to see Thémis. Then
he thought of the girl screaming in her bed at the hospital, and
of her baby, and he plunged down the stairs and out into the
driving rain.

The engine coughed and sputtered as he drove to the turn-
around in front of the *Bahnhof*, and the rain swept into the
open sides of his jeep. The streets were deserted except for
rubber-coated *Polizei*, but through the arches of the *Bahnhof*
he saw a vast conglomeration of men and women and bundles
and children and suitcases waiting out the rain.

Lashley was thinking how extraordinary it was that here he
was plunging into more trouble, without even worrying about
the legalities involved. Just because he felt sorry for Mrs.
Hockland and an unborn baby. If Thémis could see him now
she'd realize he wasn't always hampered by the letter of the
law. Remembering that, he thought of the petition in his pocket.
In spite of Thémis, in spite of Nissen, he was stubbornly determined to send it. But perhaps it might be better to wait until
he had seen Steigmann.

He urged his jeep along the wide street until he came to the
Kaiserplatz. The statue of Frederick the Great was obscured
by the density of the rain. He leaned forward over the steering
wheel, straining his eyes to see through the spattered wind-

shield, and turned right on Kaiser Allee. At the third block he swung around and came to a halt in front of the little *Bierstube*.

The door was open. Someone he had never seen before, a paunchy little man with a withered right arm, thin lips, and squinty, colorless eyes, put down a copy of the Reschweiler *Rundschau* and looked at him with furtive suspicion. Without a word the man hobbled to the door of the storeroom, pounded on it, and shouted, "Gottfried!"

The bartender emerged, wiping his hands on a rag. He wore the same shirt he had worn before, a dark blue one with vertical stripes which accentuated the bulge of his stomach. He scowled when he saw Lashley, and looked down at the floor where the water which ran off Lashley's coat was forming into dark puddles.

He said in German, "What do you want?"

Lashley said, "I want to see Rodal."

The bartender shrugged his shoulders. "He sometimes comes here."

Lashley placed his five cartons of cigarettes on a table. He said, "I want to do business with Rodal."

The big man was surprised and his eyes showed it. He pushed his tongue against his upper lip and appeared to be counting the cartons.

Lashley said, "There are fifty packets here."

"I'll give you ninety marks each." The man was lost for a moment in mental calculation. "Forty-five hundred marks for the lot."

"Get Rodal for me. I'll do my business with him."

The bartender turned to his crippled companion. "Go and fetch Rodal," he commanded.

The cripple did not budge. He said unpleasantly, "Why should I go in the rain? There's time enough."

The bartender moved with amazing lightness of foot. He slapped the flat of his hand against the cripple's head, knocking him against a table. "Fetch Rodal," he shouted.

The cripple got up, scowling and rubbing his face. He turned up his coat collar and scurried out into the downpour.

Lashley sat down. He and the bartender eyed each other sullenly and did not speak.

After five minutes Lashley said, "How long before Rodal gets here? I'm in a great hurry."

"One or two minutes more. He was probably asleep."

They fell into another silence. Then the bartender said, "Why do you do business with Rodal? He is a cheat. And he is crazy. I'm offering full value."

Lashley said, "You're a liar and a fool. You've already tried to cheat me. The market is a hundred and ten marks a packet."

The German did not appear to take offense. He said, "I offered you yesterday's price. Today's may be higher—I do not know."

"You are lying again. Yesterday's price was a hundred and ten."

The man smiled in an ugly manner. "I want to be friends with you. I do a big business in cigarettes. In the future I can buy all you have to offer."

Lashley said, "I do not do business with liars."

The man grunted. "I was only doing my best. You are a good fellow. I will not try to cheat you any more."

The door opened and a gust of rain heralded the arrival of Rodal, accompanied by the cripple. Both men were drenched. They shook themselves like shaggy dogs and wiped the rain from their eyes.

The Czech's face fell when he saw Lashley. He looked suspiciously at the others as if he had been fooled, and he grumbled in German, "What kind of trick is this? He is not the man."

The bartender said, "What do you care? He wants to do business with you."

Rodal snarled, "I want my *laissez-passer*."

"What are you talking about?" Lashley said impatiently.

Rodal turned on him viciously and spilled out a torrent of words. "They know what I am talking about. They know well enough—may they be consigned to hell—they know all right. The *laissez-passer*, that's what I want. The lieutenant on the first floor of the courthouse promised I would have it today."

A wild look came into his round little eyes, and he clasped and unclasped his hands. "For me and Maria to see the beasts killed, that's what I want, and it's not your business."

The bartender said, "You're crazy, Rodal. This man has fifty packets of American cigarettes. Fifty packets, you fool."

The Czech's eyes fell on the cartons and without changing the manner of his talk or the displeasure on his face he said, "How much do you want for them?"

Lashley beckoned him into a corner and whispered in his ear that he wanted to exchange the cigarettes for penicillin. Rodal listened sullenly and pulled at his lower lip. Finally he said, "Fifty packets—it is possible. I have friends."

"What is the price?" Lashley demanded.

The man blinked his eyes, thinking.

"A small bottle for ten packets." Rodal indicated the size between his thumb and middle fingers. "Five bottles altogether."

Lashley said, "But I must have it immediately."

Rodal jumped up with alacrity. "Come with me. Take the cigarettes." He looked at the two Germans in sardonic triumph and pulled up his coat collar before opening the door upon the swirling rainstorm.

They drove to the Kaiserplatz and swung left toward the *Bahnhof*. At the first corner before the traffic circle Rodal told him to turn right. They were on a short street in the heart of the city, and it contained the curious collection of loft buildings, shabby shops, and ancient dwellings characteristic of the area around any central railway station. They stopped at a narrow lane cutting between two drab buildings of red brick.

"Wait here," Rodal muttered. He gathered up the cartons, shoved them under his coat, and jumped down from the jeep. He kept close to the side of a building to avoid the rain, bending almost double to protect the cigarettes under his coat. Lashley kept looking after him, for he did not trust the Czech, nor could he withhold a professional urge to know and remember the location of a black market operator.

He caught glimpses of Rodal dodging from stoop to stoop

but the man was hardly discernible through the driving rain, and when he finally disappeared into a doorway Lashley knew he would not be able to identify the exact location. He sat back in the jeep and waited.

There was an insistent rapping on a window of the red brick building before which he was parked. A curtain was drawn aside and a red-cheeked harridan wearing a soiled negligee beckoned to him with her fingers. He ignored her. She rapped again and nodded her head insistently. After another attempt to entice his interest she gave up and let the curtain drop.

He looked at his watch. It was twenty minutes past nine. He was cold and wet. His fingers drummed impatiently on the steering wheel. He cursed his naïveté in trusting Rodal to go by himself. God knew when the man would return—if he did return. Perhaps the rascal had already sold the cigarettes and made his way out by another route. Fifty-five hundred marks was a lot of money to trust to a calculating madman.

He looked at his watch again. It was nine twenty-three. If Rodal returned quickly he could deliver the penicillin to the hospital in twenty minutes. Would that be in time?

A gust of wind swept rain into the jeep. He turned off the motor and was about to go seeking Rodal when he saw the man fighting his way back down the lane.

The Czech was drenched. His teeth chattered as he climbed into the jeep. He sat smugly, as if deliberately waiting for Lashley to ask him whether he had achieved success.

"Did you get it?" Lashley said.

Rodal smirked, nodded his head, and pulled from his pocket three tiny bottles, each containing about two fluid ounces of a yellowish liquid. Lashley examined the seals and the labels. They seemed authentic, for they bore the name of a well-known American firm and were stamped: "United States Army Medical Stores."

Lashley said, "Where are the other two bottles?"

The Czech grinned maliciously. "The price of the medicine is very high, and cigarettes have gone down," he said.

Lashley turned on him violently.

"You're an accursed liar. Give me the other bottles." He grasped the man's lapels. Water trickled through his fingers as he squeezed the cloth. It ran down his wrists and inside his sleeves.

Rodal said guardedly, "It is very hard to do business with this man. I have no other bottles. Look in my pockets."

Lashley pushed him away with a hard shove. He knew it was useless to argue with the man, and he contented himself with saying, "You put the rest of the money in your pocket. You're a thief."

Rodal looked reproachful. "I made a small profit—just enough. What did you expect? Did you imagine I would do this for nothing? All you Americans are the same. You think the whole world should serve you."

Lashley stepped on the starter. "You are an ingrate as well as a thief. The Americans liberated you."

"Pfui!" the man muttered. "You talk like all the rest. You treat us like we were slaves from birth until you came to Europe. Pfui!"

Lashley backed out of the street. At the corner Rodal jumped nimbly from the jeep. He stood leaning against the driving rain, his hands holding the ends of his coat collar together. "If you have more business," he shouted through the downpour, "I am always at the *Bierstube.*" He scurried away and finally disappeared behind the obscurity of the solid sheets of rain which lashed against the naked ruins.

The full violence of the storm struck as Lashley headed for the hospital. He could hardly see ten feet ahead of him as he emerged from the last buildings of the city and drove onto the open viaduct. The wind, like an angry juggler, caught up great gusts of rain and spun them across the flat ground.

By the time he reached the hospital he was soaked through. He stopped the jeep, got down stiffly, and stumbled into the vestibule. The nurse with the twisted mouth eyed him with an empty venom which he had come to recognize as the standard expression of the conquered in the presence of the victors. He walked hastily to the staircase.

He was halfway down the hall when he spied Mr. Hockland. The big farmer sat on the bench outside Erika's room, and he was obviously in deep thought, for he gave no sign that he was aware of anyone's approach until Lashley stood over him. When he looked up his face was blank like the face of a man who is beyond all emotion. In a low voice he said, "Good morning, Major. It was good of you to come."

Lashley said, "Where is Mrs. Hockland?"

"In there." He jerked his thumb toward the room and smiled gravely. "You know how the womenfolks are at a time like this. Mom's set her heart on having that baby, taking it home with us. She talked me round to it. That's Edna."

"What does the doctor say?"

"He's in there now with her and the Wac." He fingered the brim of his hat disconsolately. "I don't know, Major. It looks bad. I don't think—there's any use."

Lashley said, "I've got some penicillin."

The big Iowan nodded his head without enthusiasm. "It's mighty nice of you, traipsing around in this weather. We appreciate it, Mom and I do. Better tell them inside."

Lashley rapped lightly on the door and went in. The doctor was leaning over the bed. He had lifted one of the girl's eyelids and was looking at her in a manner which indicated deep concern. On the other side of the bed and at the head of it stood Mrs. Hockland, her lips tightly drawn, her eyes fixed on the girl's forehead. The Wac stood stiffly against the far wall.

For an instant Lashley thought that Erika was dead. Her face had turned a deep yellow and seemed to have shrunk since last night, and he could hear no sound from her lips. But when he tiptoed closer to the bed he saw that she was comatose, breathing fitfully through open lips, the quick murmur of her breath all but drowned out by the sound of rain against the window.

Mrs. Hockland's eyes turned to him but she did not move. "Have you brought it, Major?" she whispered.

"I've got it, Mrs. Hockland."

"Thank God," she breathed, and some of the tenseness left her face.

The doctor came away from the bedside. He drew Lashley into a corner and said in German, "The abscess has burst. It is very bad."

"I have brought penicillin, *Herr Doktor*," Lashley said. He produced the three bottles.

The German took one and weighed it in his hand, then went to the window and held it up against the light. He examined the yellow liquid from several angles and his young, serious face was filled with deep emotion. It struck Lashley that in medicine or war or industry the Germans reserved their most fervent emotions for new and wondrous scientific discoveries.

The doctor returned to where Lashley was standing and he said almost joyously, "This is the first penicillin I have ever had in my hand." He looked at the bottle and his eyes were bright.

"Will it help the girl?" Lashley interjected in order to bring the man out of the spell the tiny bottle seemed to cast on him.

The doctor shook his head decisively. "Not at all. There has been a tremendous absorption of toxin into her system in the last hour. By now it would be like pouring water on a phosphorous fire."

Lashley said, "Then there is no hope?"

The doctor extended his underlip. "There is always hope. A miracle might happen. One never knows in childbirth—sometimes it is a struggle between the baby and the mother. One absorbs all the life and repels the poison and only death is left to the other——" He paused. "In this case we will know in a few hours. The baby cannot be long delayed."

Lashley said, "What happens if she dies before the baby is born?"

"We are prepared for a caesarean." He handed back the bottle with reluctance.

Lashley ignored his hand. He reached into his pocket, took out the other two bottles, and placed them on the table beside the window. He said gruffly, "If it is no use to the girl, use it on another case."

The doctor lifted his eyebrows and shot a quick, curious glance at the American. "Thank you, *Herr Major,*" he said curtly, and returned to the bedside.

There was silence in the room. Only the labored breathing of the girl and the sound of rain beating against the window gave the scene reality. Mrs. Hockland's face showed her desperate anxiety. The doctor held the girl's wrist with one hand and in the other he still held the bottle of penicillin, which he contemplated with passionate interest. The Wac stood motionless against the wall, like the unwilling policewoman she was.

Lashley looked at his watch. It was half past ten. He turned about quickly and tiptoed from the room.

Mr. Hockland hadn't changed his position. He sat dejected, his face framed by his big, purposeful hands. Without looking up, he said in a low voice, "What do you think, Major?"

Lashley said, "There's still hope. She's got a chance."

"It'll about kill Edna if she doesn't get that baby," the big man murmured.

Lashley walked indecisively along the corridor. There he realized that his mission was completed. There was nothing more he could do here. Now he was free to return to Thémis. He would have to look up the train schedule from Bernhausen, get her some kind of travel orders, and drive her to the station. After that he'd see Steigmann. But first he'd have to get her out of the hotel and over to her room. He buttoned up his coat and dashed out of the hospital.

The storm had abated somewhat, and now the rain came down steadily as through a finely meshed sieve. Lashley urged his jeep across the viaduct. A convoy of military trucks blocked the road at the far end. One truck was stuck in the mud just off the shoulder of the highway, other trucks had moved up in front of it, and men were slouching about in the rain, adjusting tow chains.

He waited a minute or two, then he rolled cautiously off the viaduct to where the first truck straddled the road, and he examined the terrain beside the pavement. A shallow ditch overflowed with water and beyond it was a wire fence. There appeared to be just enough space for him to pass between the first truck and the fence. He shifted into the auxiliary gear and rolled down into the ditch. The wheels of his jeep slithered in the ooze, the motor roared with its exertions, and Lashley held his breath. Slowly the jeep swung around the truck and mounted the shoulder of the road. The motor screamed as if in triumph and he was once more on the pavement and racing toward the heart of the city.

At last he came to a stop in front of the Excelsior and dashed in through the revolving doors, almost upsetting a colonel who was coming out without looking. Too impatient to wait for the elevator, he took the stairs two at a time and burst into the room.

The bed was rumpled and empty. He called out, "Thémis!" There was no answer. He looked on the bureau and on the desk to see if she had written him a note. He found nothing. Possibly she'd gone back to her room, but still he couldn't understand why she'd gone away so mysteriously. The only thing to do was to hurry over to Mehlmannstrasse. Surely she'd be there.

XVI

As he ran down the stairs to the lobby of the Excelsior Lashley's hand wandered to his chin and he remembered he hadn't shaved. He hesitated an instant to look into a mirror on the first-floor landing. His black stubble made him look like a caricature of a combat soldier.

The jeep was slow in starting. He pulled out the choke and pushed his foot viciously on the button, and was rewarded with a series of sputters. He gaped helplessly at the rain coming down in leisurely grandeur, then tried the starter again. This time the engine roared into life. He swung around the Opera-platz and into Bahnhofstrasse. The jeep slithered dangerously as he turned up Mehlmannstrasse. He stopped at number 29.

The vestibule door was open. He raced through, almost stumbling over a pail of water which held it open, and scrambled up the stairs. The moment he came into the upper hall he saw that her door was ajar and he suspected that she was not there. He pushed into the room. It was deserted, and only the casing of a lipstick lying discarded on the dresser gave evidence that it had been lately vacated.

As he stalked about the room in angry frustration the slight scent of her familiar perfume came to him. She must have been there very recently. He looked at his watch and saw that it was half past eleven.

The door creaked. He turned about. A chambermaid had

thrust her head into the room and was watching him, her young face screwed up in inquiry.

He said in German, "The woman who lived here—when did she leave?"

The girl put down her mop and pail. "Oh, it must be an hour, *Meinherr*. Maybe more."

"Did you see her go?"

The girl seemed indignant. She said, "I helped her pack her belongings. Oh, she was a fine lady. She gave me fifty marks. Fifty marks! And not because she didn't have change. Three bills she gave me, two twenties and a ten——"

Lashley said, "Do you know where she went?"

"That I don't know," the girl mumbled with excruciating matter-of-factness. "There were people in the room watching her pack—they were foreigners, I would say—Frenchmen. They drove away in an automobile."

Lashley brushed past her and clattered down the stairs, muttering, "Gribemont, Gribemont," over and over again by way of concentrating his frantic mind on the problem of where the Frenchman might be likely to take her. After all, she was only technically detained as long as they remained in the American zone. Damn clever of Gribemont to get Thémis out of the Excelsior and over to her own rooms, without giving her a chance to leave him a note. Or was this Marriner's fine hand at work again? Anyway, he decided, the only thing to do was to find Gribemont—if that was possible.

He drove through the center of town to the eastern outskirts, where the *Electrowerke* building stood in dripping solitude in its little park. He left his jeep in a space which was reserved for the chief of staff and went into headquarters. A guard saluted him briskly and continued to study him. Self-consciously Lashley rubbed at the stubble on his chin.

He said, "Where is the Allied Contact Section?"

"South wing, second floor, sir."

Lashley mounted a wide staircase and walked quickly along a corridor. He watched the signs on the doors as he passed: British liaison, Czechoslovakian liaison, Belgian, Russian, French——

He went in without knocking. A dark frizzy-haired girl wearing the uniform of a French lieutenant greeted him with a cheerful, "Good morning, Major." She was chubby and rather pretty and there was a coquettish inflection in her voice.

He said, "Where can I find Captain Gribemont?"

She replied, "He left some time ago. I couldn't say where he is at this moment."

"Did he say where he was going?" His voice was heavy with anxiety and he leaned eagerly over her desk.

The girl seemed intimidated by the urgency of his question, perhaps by his shaggy, sleepless appearance. She stammered, "I—I—really don't know. He—I—think I remember he was talking on the telephone with the airport—about some plane. I really can't say."

Lashley went over to the window and looked up at the sky. The wind had died down but the rain was still heavy. The dwellings on the fringes of the park, scarcely three hundred yards distant, were ghostly outlines against a murky horizon. He surveyed the dismal scene with pleasure, as though he felt pride of ownership in the wretched weather. He called back at the girl, "They can't take off in this visibility. Nothing can take off, absolutely nothing."

She said vaguely, "I don't know what you mean, sir."

"It's all right, miss, it's all right," he muttered, and as he moved across to the door he saw her staring at him with genuine alarm.

He did not realize how fast he was traveling on the slippery pavement. The gas pedal was pressed down to the floor board, and his mind was leaping far beyond the downpour that slithered off the hood of his jeep. He was thinking of what he would tell Gribemont, how the girl had escaped his jurisdiction, how she was required to remain pending further developments in the Steigmann case, anything to hold her. And he was thinking of Thémis, how he would hold onto her when they were alone, and never let her go.

Never.

At a fork in the road less than a mile from the airport

entrance a truck with a trailer suddenly loomed out of the mist. It was traveling fast toward him and as it swung into the main highway the trailer skidded crazily into the center of the road. Lashley let up on the gas pedal. There was no time to use his brakes. The trailer teetered in front of him like a dancer off balance. Lashley flung his wheel hard to the right. The tires of his jeep screeched in agony, and as they hit a shallow ditch a great sheet of water flew upon the windshield, blinding him temporarily. The trailer was past him now and he pulled hard to get back on the road, though he could not see where it was. He prayed that no car would be approaching in the opposite direction, for he was without vision.

His aim was truer than he knew. Before the windshield cleared a car fled past his shoulder. He strained his eyes, and finally he could see the road stretching safely ahead. He turned into the airport entrance.

The passengers' lounge was empty. A Red Cross girl sat behind the doughnut bar desolately munching one of her prodigious stock of doughnuts. Across the lounge a flight clerk sat at his counter reading a book. He was also nibbling at a doughnut. On a blackboard behind him the flight schedules were superimposed by huge white lettering: "All flights canceled. Field closed."

Lashley stepped up to the counter. "Did a flight take off for Paris?" he asked.

"All flights canceled," the clerk droned. "Nothing till tomorrow morning. Field's closed."

"Was there a special flight scheduled for Paris?"

"All flights canceled," the clerk said again. "They just closed the field."

Lashley shouted, "Wake up, man, and answer my question. Was there a special flight scheduled for Paris?"

The voice of authority brought the clerk quietly to life. "Yes, sir," he said. "We washed it out with the rest."

"Was the party here? Some French officers and a woman ____"

The clerk nodded. "Just left, not three minutes ago."

Lashley felt suddenly numb. The tension fell away from his mind, and he was momentarily logey. He echoed aimlessly, "Not three minutes ago——"

"Sure," the clerk said. "You must've passed them coming up."

Lashley nodded thanks and stepped back from the counter. He walked a little uncertainly across the lounge, out into the rain, and paused on the gravel walk. The downpour hit his face, and it seemed to him refreshing, for inside of him he was feverish with the thought of Thémis under arrest, Thémis in the custody of Gribemont and his satellites, who were determined to make an example of her.

He couldn't imagine where they'd taken her, but it occurred to him that Gribemont might have gone back to his office. Anyway, he'd find out.

He climbed angrily into the jeep. The engine started and the tires spun over the brimming pavement. The pleasant rippling monotone they made seemed to mock his anxiety. Thémis was somewhere in the gray, rain-swept city, somewhere within the walls that rose up before him out of the murk. She was sitting quietly, her white face immobile like a doll's, her mouth without passion, her purse swinging in a short arc from her arm. He would find her, and make her laugh again, as she had laughed only with him.

Again the jeep swung into the driveway of the *Electrowerke* building. Under the canopy of the entrance he saw the general's big Cadillac and Parker standing at its open door. He pulled up abruptly and waited. He did not want to meet the general. He did not trust himself to say anything to the general. To hell with the general. He peered through the rain until he saw the guard at the door straighten up, and then Marriner came out briskly and stepped into the Cadillac. Parker shut the door just as briskly, hopped into the front seat, and the car rolled away. It was all done in a staccato manner which seemed to Lashley bizarre and rather comical.

The entrance was clear now. He pulled his jeep close to the curbstone and chained the wheel. Inside the building the main hall was liberally populated by officers standing about in groups, smoking and talking noisily. The unusual accumulation caused him some wonderment. He looked at his watch and he understood. It was one forty-five, and these men were killing the remainder of their lunch hour. Suddenly conscious of his stubble, he lowered his head and edged over to the stairs. An unruly excitement was rising inside him. He ran along the second-floor corridor, watching the door plates, until he found what he was seeking. He paused a moment to remove his sodden cap and push his hair carelessly into place. Then he turned the handle viciously and went in.

Captain Gribemont was alone in the office. He sat on the edge of a desk, one leg swinging thoughtfully, and he appeared to be immersed in a document. At the sound of Lashley's sudden entrance he raised his eyes from the paper he was studying. His finely chiseled face, with its gray mustache and lean pallor, maintained a stony aplomb.

He said gently, "You are wet, Major. Do give me your coat. You know—this is a very bad time of year in which to take cold."

His mannered voice made Lashley twitch with anger.

"Where is the girl? Where is she, Gribemont?"

The captain studied his fingers. "You mean the Delisle person?"

"Yes, the Delisle person," Lashley exploded. "Now don't tell me you haven't got her because I know you have. You're holding her here—in town. Where is she?" He stood threateningly, his back against the door, and glared at the Frenchman.

"My dear fellow——"

"God damn it, Gribemont, don't give me any of your fancy language. Tell me where she is."

Gribemont said archly, "I was about to suggest, Major, that you come away from the door. Someone might push it open and bowl you over."

Lashley took a step forward, muttering against his teeth, "I'll come a lot closer than you'd care to have me come——"

"Really, Major, we're not children," the captain said in an

aggrieved manner. But despite his poise he moved from the edge of the desk to a chair behind it, and from his new position he regarded Lashley unhappily.

"Please sit down," he entreated.

Lashley said, "I have no time to sit down." He paced to the window and turned abruptly. "I'm warning you, Gribemont— you're not an enforcement officer here, you're an observer. I demand you tell me where you're keeping the girl. What's more, I'm going to take her."

"I'm afraid that's impossible," the captain said in a low voice.

Lashley swung his body across the desk and thrust out his stubbled face. "Just who in hell do you think you are? You can't arrest people in this zone. You're a visitor here—by courtesy of the United States Army. Do you understand that? You couldn't arrest *Hitler* if you found him. Now where is the girl? I'm in a hurry——"

Gribemont shook his head in a manner so leisurely as to indicate the hopelessness of Lashley's position. "You will have to ask General Marriner."

"What's he got to do with it?"

"He asked to have her brought to his office only a little while ago."

"Why?" Lashley said uneasily, moving back from the desk.

"He was interested," Gribemont said amiably. "He knew of course that we were taking her into custody—for questioning —and when the plane failed to take off he asked to see her. Quite simple."

"That doesn't alter your jurisdiction. She's still my witness——"

The captain raised his eyebrows. "Ah, but it does. The general ordered her to be placed in *our* custody. Do you question the general's authority?"

Lashley retorted, "I'd question the President's authority over a witness in any case of mine. There's such a thing, Gribemont, as American justice—and nobody tampers with it."

Gribemont commented bitterly, "But it is permissible to tamper with justice in—shall we say?—a romantic way."

Lashley tightened his grip on the beveled edge of the desk. He scowled at the captain. Then slowly he became aware of the sincerity in Gribemont's face and his muscles relaxed.

"I do not wish to be unpleasant," the Frenchman said, "but you will understand I am bound by a certain duty to my country——"

"You refuse to tell me," Lashley said more calmly.

"I refuse."

Lashley breathed deeply. "Then I will find her without you."

Gribemont said, "It is really of no importance whether you do or not." He added quickly, "But I am sure you won't."

"That's my affair." Lashley turned toward the door. He knew just as well as the Frenchman that he couldn't bulldoze Marriner into giving her up. He was suddenly and desperately weary.

He heard Gribemont say in an exasperated tone: "My dear fellow, you treat me as though I were a bully and a scoundrel. It is something I highly resent."

Lashley glanced at him scornfully as if to say, "Who cares?"

The Frenchman continued in the same incredulous voice: "Have you any real idea of the relationship between this woman and Steigmann? You obviously haven't."

Lashley's hand faltered on the doorknob. It was the one mystery that prodded incessantly at his subconscious mind. And though he discounted in advance anything the Frenchman might say, he was willing to listen. He turned about sullenly.

"*You* tell me," he rasped.

Gribemont's face assumed a grave and judicial air. "Because, my dear fellow, she was Steigmann's mistress. Quite an ordinary case, Major. The same old sordid story——"

Lashley was no longer listening. This was too obvious an explanation. He had thought of it too long ago and had discarded it. It failed to explain the enigma of the girl. It fell short of clarifying why a common mistress should sacrifice her liberty in a hopeless attempt to save a guilty criminal.

He said, "Have it your way, Gribemont." He was too weary to argue.

The Frenchman said, "You don't believe me."

"No."

"You see, Major," Gribemont said not unpleasantly, "you have built up some curious conceptions about this girl. I am too much of a Frenchman not to recognize the signs of romantic fancy—for which, mind you, I do not blame you. Some cocottes are the most ravishingly romantic persons in the world." His voice took on a stern quality. "But facts are facts, and I have the proof."

"You have the proof," Lashley echoed sourly.

Gribemont said, "But certainly. With all the furor in the Paris papers the Deuxième Bureau has not been idle. Would you like to read the latest report?"

"I don't want to read anything. I've had experience with your dossiers."

The Frenchman allowed himself to smile. "It's all here—everything. The woman lived in an apartment on the Rue du Bac. We have the depositions of the concierge, the charwoman, her own maid, two mannequins who were her closest friends—even, my dear fellow, the deposition she herself signed this morning. Quite simply, she was Steigmann's mistress. Here, look at it." He threw a document across the desk.

Lashley brushed the paper aside. He growled, "I don't believe it."

Gribemont lifted his hands helplessly. "You're a lawyer, Major. It's her own deposition. She signed it."

"You forced her!"

"On the contrary, my dear fellow. She signed willingly. As a matter of fact, she was quite spiritless about it."

The Frenchman's words made Lashley shudder. He could see her—quite spiritless, the Thémis of the courtroom, the Thémis of darkness and disillusionment, the Thémis he had reanimated and revitalized only to let her drop back into a bottomless past.

"Was she so spiritless when you arrested her this morning?" Lashley asked bitterly, wondering if the Frenchman had had the gall to look for her in his room.

"No, she was—rather upset," Gribemont said carefully. "You see, we found her waiting for you in the lobby of the Excelsior. She refused to come with us until we showed her General Marriner's order."

"Very neat," Lashley said scornfully. "And I suppose if it hadn't rained you'd have had her in Paris by now."

"Probably."

"Oh, go to the devil," said Lashley rudely, and stamped out of the office.

The rain came down with renewed intensity on the little park that surrounded the *Electrowerke* building. Lashley walked quickly to the jeep. He turned the key in the padlock attached to the steering wheel. The chain clattered to the floor board and the sound of it made him remember Steigmann. In his mad pursuit of Thémis he had forgotten all about Steigmann. He would have to see him immediately, otherwise it would be too late to put through the petition asking for a retrial. Probably it was useless to talk to him. It might save time to put the petition through now.

And then he remembered the insistence in Thémis's voice when she had asked him to go to Steigmann. It was possible of course that she knew more than she'd told him, or more likely her woman's intuition had sensed the importance of what Steigmann might say. Thémis and Steigmann, Thémis and Steigmann. Why did they always have to be linked together in his mind?

The gray monotone of heavy rain falling on sodden earth came to him as sordid music to embellish his wretchedness. He sat dull and immobile, his foot poised over the starter, lost in the feeling of complete frustration. Perhaps they were right —all of them, Gribemont, Marriner, Nissen, Kinsella, all of them. He had been deceiving himself. It was Thémis he had wanted from the very beginning, from the first moment he had set eyes upon her. And Steigmann was only a symbol—a symbol of how much he wanted Thémis. He had made Steigmann a part of his conscience because Thémis was a part of his being.

Finally he shook himself out of the mood, straightened his cap, and squared his shoulders. Thémis had asked him to talk to Steigmann—the time had come to do it.

He started the jeep and it picked up speed immediately. A guard on the front gate waved him through. He turned east, away from the city, his eyes glued to the wet, shiny pavement. The highway was clear of traffic and he could go fast, but all the speed the car could make didn't seem enough. He skimmed dizzily along the road and around the curves, and he felt a certain joy in the danger he courted.

The rising farmland to the right of the highway was shrouded in low mists. Isolated buildings loomed up ahead and floated past his vision with excruciating indolence. At last dwellings appeared in clusters on the sky line and soon he saw the wet gray walls of the medieval fortress town of Bergsdorf. He slowed the jeep and studied the side of the highway to find the turning—a dirt road which zigzagged across the farmlands toward the town. He was traveling faster than he realized, for he had to jam his brakes to make the turn. He was in second gear most of the way as he wallowed up a hill and passed through an archway beneath an ancient watchtower. He drove into a narrow street lined with low stone buildings tottering with age, past the *Rathaus* and the town's church and a graveyard crowded with figured tombstones. He crawled in low gear up a steep, cobbled street until it leveled off and he was on a cobblestoned plateau.

Here, high above the town, commanding the countryside in all directions, stood Bergsdorf Prison. A hundred years ago it had been a fortress sufficiently massive to give pause to many a conquering prince bent on plunder. There were turrets jutting out of its surrounding wall; the vacant emplacements which had once contained cannon attested to the thickness of the stone; its towers rose dismally into the dripping sky. The

Nazis had made certain alterations in its interior and had used it not long before to imprison captives of higher rank. Now the Americans had taken it over as a place of execution for war criminals.

The jeep rumbled over the cobbles skirting the outer wall and reached a narrow archway in the fortress wall. It contained a weather-beaten oak door scarcely wide enough to admit a full-grown man. Beside the door stood a sentry box and out of it stepped a sharp-eyed guard, his bayonet fixed. He challenged Lashley with rare severity.

"State your business, sir."

Lashley showed his AGO card and asked to see the commanding officer of the prison. The guard returned to his sentry box and relayed the information into a telephone. There was a delay of two or three minutes, and then the oak door opened from the inside and a corporal emerged, who because of his size and suspicious eyes might have been the guard's twin brother. He barked, "You may enter, sir, and follow me."

They walked through a dimly lit passageway and into a hall of unrelieved grayness from ceiling to stone slab flooring. The corporal led the way up a circular stairway of solid stone and they came into a narrow, bare room. At the far end of the room there was a polished mahogany door which seemed utterly incongruous in its surroundings. The corporal rapped on the door and pushed it open almost in the same movement.

Lashley saw a large and magnificently furnished office, and standing in it a tall, thin man, his hair wavy and prematurely gray if one were to judge by the smoothness of his handsome features. He wore the silver medallions of a lieutenant colonel. In a pleasant voice which might have belonged to a radio announcer he bade Lashley enter.

"The name's Sonderberg, Major," he said, extending his hand. "I'm glad to meet one of our best—uh—wholesale suppliers, though I must say I wish you didn't do quite such a land-office business."

Lashley thought the remark gauche and it made him momentarily uncomfortable, but he let it pass and stated his mission quickly and succinctly. Sonderberg blinked his eyes incessantly as he listened. Then he glanced at his watch.

He said, "I don't think there's any objection. It's just three-thirty now. That gives you a couple of hours——"

Lashley said anxiously, "Nothing happens till tomorrow morning, does it?"

"No—not until sometime after midnight, but we begin preparing them about half past five. The usual thing—the doctor gives them a quick look-over, then the hangman takes a peek, sort of for size. After that the barber—if they want him —and then they belong to the padre for the rest of the night. It's quite a business, all told."

Lashley paled. "Do they know—when?"

"Oh yes. They were told on Wednesday, I believe."

Lashley fixed his eyes on the telephone which stood on Sonderberg's desk. He studied it grimly and he thought of Nissen and the Frankfurt teleprinter at Nissen's elbow. There was still time to halt the execution. A buoyancy came into his manner and he said, "If you don't mind, Colonel, I'll see Steigmann right away."

Sonderberg said, "I hope you won't resent a suggestion, Major. You see, we try to put on a severe front for these Germans. It helps us in the long run. They get accustomed to a strict routine while they're waiting and it carries through— especially at the very end—because they've learned to respect us. It makes for cleaner executions——"

"What's the suggestion?"

Sonderberg smiled. "Don't laugh—but I wish you'd shave before you see Steigmann."

Lashley passed his hand over his chin. "I'm sorry, Colonel——"

"Won't take a minute. I've got a bowl and mirror right here, and everything you need." Sonderberg crossed the room, opened a door, and switched on a light to reveal a bathroom with chromium fixtures and a glass-enclosed shower. He said, "The Nazis certainly did themselves proud in fixing this place."

Lashley peeled off his sodden coat and tunic and looked in the mirror. His face was paler than he had imagined and he could see tiny red veins running across the whites of his eyes. His hands shook as he adjusted the razor, and he shaved with long, impatient strokes.

Sonderberg called out, "That Steigmann's quite a man."

"In what way?"

"Bravest man I've ever had in here. Didn't bat an eyelash when I told him, and hasn't given us a speck of trouble since."

"What about the others?"

Sonderberg said, "Oh, a couple of convulsions. One got paralyzed and came out of it. Curious thing, it seems to go by I.Q. Steigmann's I.Q. is 145—pretty damned high. He should have been a writer. My God, what industry he has. He's written fourteen letters and he's only been here since Tuesday."

Lashley said, "Have you read them?"

"No, I won't look at them till it's all over." Sonderberg paused. "This'll interest you. They're all addressed to the same person—that Delisle woman—you know, the one who testified for him."

The razor stopped in Lashley's hand. Only with difficulty did he resume shaving, twice nicking himself in his haste. He doused his face with cold water, then caught up his jacket and said, "All ready, Colonel."

They went down the circular staircase to the big hall and moved across it to an oak door. Sonderberg opened it with a key. They were outdoors, on a canvas-covered walk which traversed a narrow alley separating the main building from a stone structure one story high. Rain was coming down heavily, dripping like strings of beads from the sides of the canopy.

Lashley looked along the alley and saw a courtyard spreading out beyond the low stone building.

"Is that where it takes place, Colonel?" he said.

Sonderberg nodded. "You can't see the scaffold from here. It's around the corner."

A sentry was on guard before an ordinary wooden door which gave entrance to the low building. He saluted stiffly.

"This is the death house," Sonderberg said. "We call it the 'Last Roundup.'"

The interior was smaller than Lashley had imagined. Through a steel-barred gate he looked into a corridor about eight feet wide and fifty feet long which ran to the end wall of the building. Two conical flood lamps attached to the end wall threw a dazzling beam along the length of the corridor, highlighting twelve steel doors, six on each side. Each door had a tiny grating, less than six inches square, and a guard was moving along the doors, peering tediously into the cells as he passed them. Three other guards lounged at a table in the center of the corridor.

A master sergeant armed with a tommy gun and a revolver stood outside the gate. He saluted Sonderberg, then briskly eased the locks and bolts, and pushed open the heavy gate. As they went in the three guards inside leaped to attention. Sonderberg inspected them as though on parade and said, "At ease, men."

He surveyed the cell doors with a pompous formality. Finally he turned to a corporal and said, "This officer will see Steigmann."

Lashley followed the corporal to the last cell on the left side of the corridor. The corporal turned a key, slid back a steel bolt, and opened the cell door. He looked inside, shouted, "Attention! This officer will see you," and stood aside. Lashley went in.

Steigmann was standing at the side of a tiny table. He was pale, but no thinner than he had been at the trial. He wore a collarless shirt which seemed tight across his thick chest, and blue serge trousers, and slippers. His small blue eyes blinked in the flood of light that came from the corridor, and when he finally recognized Lashley he frowned.

He had been writing. Lashley was quick to see that a pencil lay beside a half-filled sheet of paper.

The cell was about ten feet by six. It contained an army cot and two blankets neatly folded at its foot, an open latrine of modern make, a chair, and the writing table. On a shelf there were some letters and cigarettes. Above the shelf a steel-wired window one foot square cast a little daylight into the cell, and next to it was a ventilation grating.

When the door closed behind Lashley the condemned man turned quickly and took a cigarette from the shelf.

"Can you give me a light?" he said furtively, in German.

Lashley said, "Are you permitted to smoke in here?"

"No. Only outside. But——"

"I'm sorry," Lashley said. "I cannot break the rules."

Steigmann sat down disgustedly on the chair. "Is there anything in particular you want?" he grumbled, looking away from his visitor.

Lashley, sparring for an opening, said carefully, "I have seen your wife—Ilse."

There was no reaction from Steigmann. He sulked in his chair and said, "What about her?"

"She has suffered a great deal."

The German made a rude gesture with his lips and said nothing.

Lashley said, "But she's more comfortable now. They have been befriended by an old man—a man called Meyersohn. Ilse went to school with his daughter, and that is why he befriends her."

Steigmann scowled in distaste. "Is that what you have come to tell me?"

"I thought you would be interested—before you die—to know that your wife is not starving."

"You think it will make me feel better," Steigmann said in a sneering tone. "You think I will be happier now that you have told me."

"One would imagine so."

The German burst out, "You are a sentimental fool!" He glared at Lashley, who was standing attentively at the side of the bed.

Watching his man closely, Lashley said, "It is not that I am sentimental—merely that I am not vindictive. You are going to die. I believe it is a correct thing to let you know about your family."

"You are an idiot! A soft, sentimental idiot!"

Lashley said with a studied quietness: "It is natural that one should be concerned about one's family."

The German came to his feet. "You dolt! You fool! I don't care about them. When will you understand that I don't care about them?"

The man's insults had no effect on the calm of Lashley's reply. "It is difficult for me to understand your attitude."

Steigmann flung back his head and gave a short, hysterical laugh.

"Of course you don't understand my attitude. You will never understand my attitude. You are an American—and I am a German, of the elite Germans, the Hitler Germans!"

He panted, half scowling, half smiling, and he studied Lashley, who stood relaxed and respectful, his cap in his hand.

"This is an unexpected pleasure," he said, pawing at his bare neck. "I did not realize it. I can tell you exactly what I think—and there is nothing you can do to me. I am going to die tomorrow. So today I can call you an idiot and a dolt, and there is nothing you can do. Nothing—absolutely nothing."

He walked in the short space between the table and the window.

"Sit down," he said with a trace of authority.

Lashley sat on the bed.

Steigmann struck a pose beneath the window, his arms folded. "I will show you the difference between an American and a German," he said. "I will show you how an American can be a sentimental fool and how a German can die. You have come here to give me comfort by telling me about my family——"

He pushed out his chin. "And I tell you that I am proud to die. If I had my life to live over again, I would live the same way and I would be proud to die the same way. Men are animals. There are superior animals and inferior animals—and I am demonstrating to you at this moment that I am the superior animal. I am less afraid of death than you are. And why not? I am not afraid to kill—therefore I am not afraid to be killed. It is the law of nature. It is the test of the superior animal that he is not afraid to kill. That is the test."

He was shouting with a curious ecstasy.

"You see how simple it is, Major. You are afraid to kill. That is why you have come here—out of fool sentiment. I have never been afraid to kill—twenty-three with my own hands. Ten of them French—five of them Jews. I kept count. Twenty-three. By my orders, I don't know how many. That doesn't matter. But by my own hands—twenty-three. That is the test of the superior animal."

He talked on and on. Perhaps for twenty minutes. Lashley didn't count the time. It no longer made any difference. He was no longer concerned with the telephone in Sonderberg's office. He listened to the man's mad ranting. Here was the proof he'd been waiting for—the guilt which Thémis had felt so sure of and guessed he might reveal. Here was the end of the Steigmann case. No longer did it matter whether Rodal was mad or sane. The petition for retrial would be filed in Lashley's wastebasket.

When the diatribe was ended Lashley said calmly, "However, Steigmann, you are not altogether the superior animal. You spared a Jew—in Paris. There was testimony at the trial."

The German became suddenly morose.

"That was not a weakness," he said. "I knew what I was doing. It was something I wanted to do. It was an affair of the heart."

Lashley struggled to contain his curiosity.

"An affair of the heart?"

"It was something I wanted," Steigmann said guardedly.

"I see. Then you have certain weaknesses."

The German said, "It makes no difference what you think. I did not consider it a weakness, and I am the sole judge of what I do and what I think."

Lashley said, "I am interested in your affairs of the heart."

"I do not care about your interest," the man said sullenly.

"Come, Steigmann," Lashley urged. "Are you afraid to tell me about it?"

The German paced the room. Lashley watched him intently. The silence seemed excessively long.

Suddenly Steigmann said, "Then I will tell you. As a matter of fact it is amusing to me in many ways. Quite amusing."

The condemned man resumed his pacing. Then he began to speak, while Lashley remained perfectly still.

"You remember the woman who testified at my trial. Thémis Delisle—that was her name. You remember her—how beautiful she is."

"I remember her."

"She was even more beautiful when I met her in Paris. It was in 1940, when I was sent to Paris as chief of the *Sicherheitsdienst.* In the fall of that year Goering came to Paris. Goering! Between you and me, he was a greedy pig. He went to all the shops in Paris and took away truckloads— and left little for those of us who were stationed there. He was a greedy pig.

"That is when I met Thémis. She was working in the Maison Potvin, one of the best salons in Paris. It was one of Goering's favorite places to buy clothes for his lady friends—and of course it was my duty, as chief of the *sicherheitsdienst,* to see that everything was in readiness for his protection. And so I met Thémis."

He walked in silence for a little while.

"Yes, I was a fool about her. Yes, I will admit it. I had a great passion for her. It is something that is hard to explain, but it sometimes happens. I did everything in my power to be attractive to her. Everything. Mind you, it was not only her body. I wanted to possess her in every way. She became a disease in my mind.

"I tried every means at my disposal. I called at the salon, at her house. I sent her gifts. For years. Actually for years— without success.

"And then I discovered why. She was in love with someone else. I assure you it was laughable, but I did not laugh then. She was in love with this Jew—this Pierre Flanders. Here I was then deputy town commandant and she would not have me because she was in love with a Jew. I assure you I did not laugh.

"Well, to get rid of this man was not difficult. As a matter of fact I had nothing to do with it. By the Fuehrer's orders, the remaining Jews in Paris were rounded up in the spring of 1944—and this Flanders was among them——"

He halted his pacing and the light from the tiny window caused deep shadows to fall across his face.

"At last she came to me. I am not a fool. I knew why. She wanted to save Flanders. There was not much satisfaction for me. But I wanted her. Even on her own terms, I wanted her more than I have wanted anything in my whole life. Yes, I arranged to have Flanders released. And in return she came to be my mistress. She was a woman of her word.

"In many ways it was the happiest spring I have known. If I could not possess her heart, it did not matter too much. At that time we knew the war was already lost. We were taking what we could—all of us. Some fools took gold, some took art. I took Thémis. It was something I would have to my dying day, something no one could take away from me—the memory of having her."

He smiled with evil pleasure.

"Then came the amusing thing. In many ways it was the supreme joke of the war. You probably know that in the last days before the Americans entered Paris we Germans had lost practical control of the city. We were safe only where we stood with our guns—and many times not even then. The underground roamed the city. Often they attacked us. And not infrequently they fought among themselves—the right against the left, the De Gaullists against the Pétainists, the Croix de Feu against the Communists. In those last days we had become in effect rather helpless policemen.

"On the very last day I was in Paris—the Americans were already in Chartres—our intelligence reported a mysterious disturbance in the area of St. Denis. There had been a gun-fight among Frenchmen. I went out to investigate. It was the usual thing. There were a few dead lying around. One of my men took a list of the names from those bodies we could iden-tify—we were very efficient to the end—and I took it back to my office in the Crillon. Imagine my surprise when I saw on the list the name of Pierre Flanders."

Steigmann stood back against the wall, threw back his head and laughed.

"There is a joke for you! I saved this Jew—and he was killed by Frenchmen who liked him no more than I did. It is a joke, no? I save a Jew and he is killed by his own Frenchmen. I think it is very comical."

His peals of laughter reverberated eerily in the tiny cell.

"You see, everybody has their superior animals and inferior animals. It happens in every nation. Only we Hitler Germans have the courage to admit it, to live by the laws of life and death, kill or be killed——"

He became suddenly serious.

"It gave me great satisfaction. Thémis did not go back to her beloved. I could leave Paris knowing that I possessed her—and that no one else did. I had kept my word. I had saved the Jew. And I imagine she wished to repay me in full. She came to my trial."

The German turned about to laugh once more.

Lashley could bear it no longer. He turned away from Steig-mann and knocked with his fist on the cell door. When it swung open he slipped out and walked quickly along the daz-zling corridor.

XVII

NIGHT HAD ALREADY DRIFTED IN AMONG THE NARROW STREETS of Bergsdorf.

Lashley drove slowly down the hill, past the ancient dwellings, past the graveyard and the *Rathaus*, and beneath the heavy stone arch of the watchtower. It was not until he came out into the open farmland that the rain sweeping across the fields struck hard against his face.

As he moved onto the highway he turned to look at the ancient fortress on the crest of the hill. He could not see it for the rain. The night had made it one with the dark sky, but in his mind's eye he saw Steigmann in the death cell, his arms folded across his broad chest, his chin thrust out, striking the pose of the superior animal. He saw the man thus, and he did not regret that he must return here at midnight.

He drove through the dark. Rain swirled in the gleam of the headlights. And his mind turned to Thémis. There was no longer a mystery shrouding her. For the first time he could see her, all sides of her, as he might see a precise point of law in all its aspects.

He could see her in the wonderful fullness of her young love, seeking her father's blessing for it and being shattered by his prejudice. He could see her in Paris, delivering herself to Steigmann, whom she hated deeply, delivering herself to him coldly. He could see her in despair when the one for whom she had paid so great a cost was struck down by the forces of darkness and confusion, marching under the banners of liberation and justice.

And he could see her in the courtroom speaking her pitiful little piece in defense of Steigmann, making her sardonic gesture to a world in which she had lost all faith, the world of the victors, to her as impure as the world of the vanquished.

He remembered anguished snatches of her conversation.

"It was something I believed I had to do.

"I hate him! . . .

"I was not trying to save him.

"Steigmann was evil, and the world judging him was just as evil. I was trying to find goodness at least in myself. . . ."

He remembered these words, and now he understood why she spoke them.

The night was cruel with rain and cold wind. He drove slowly on the dark highway, for all the urgency had gone out of him, and as he approached the city his mind churned with revolt. She was somewhere inside the dreary walls, waiting out the storm, waiting to be taken to Paris and to trial. More than ever he wanted to be with her, to tell her that her advice had been right—that the Steigmann case was at last closed. But most of all he wanted to tell her that he loved her.

He passed the gate of the *Electrowerke* building and caught a glimpse of a soldier huddled in a sentry box, his rubber coat glistening in the light of an oil lamp. The windows of the building were dark. As he drove into the city he stopped under a street light and looked at his watch. It was six-twenty. He was not due back at Bergsdorf until midnight. It might be a good time now to try to see Marriner. Not that Marriner would be likely to turn over Thémis or tell him where she was. But it occurred to him that Steigmann's testimony might alter the general's attitude. Anyway, it was worth a try. Better than doing nothing, tortured by the thought of her proximity and the walls that separated them.

The lobby of the Excelsior was thronged with officers and their girls moving in and out of the bar. In a corner Colonel

Pike was telling a tall story before a wide-eyed audience of three Wac officers. Camilla Cameron, clinging to a young lieutenant, was on her way into the dining room. Brassy waltz music floated out of the bar café.

As Lashley went to the desk to get his key Nissen pushed his way over to him.

"What's happened, Bob? Where have you been all day?"

Lashley shook his head. "Nothing's happened. Nothing."

"I mean about Steigmann——"

"Nothing. I'm satisfied with the verdict."

Nissen whistled. "That's a relief. Who changed your mind for you? Marriner?"

"I saw Steigmann."

"Confession?"

Lashley nodded slowly.

Nissen clapped him on the back. "Swell. Now let's have a drink—I'm buying."

Lashley said, "Thanks, Lance, I don't feel like it."

Abruptly he turned his back on Nissen, went over to the elevator and up to his room. He'd have to look presentable to see Marriner. He'd have to get out of these soggy clothes.

Ten minutes later he was in the lobby again, his hair combed, changed into another uniform, but his face still morose. He started toward the desk but stopped in his tracks.

Coming across the lobby were Elmer Hockland and his wife. The woman's eyes were glazed and her mouth tight with suppressed grief. Hockland held her arm, guiding her toward the elevator, and his rugged face was stern.

Lashley came up beside them as they waited for the elevator. For a moment they looked at him silently, and tears welled in Mrs. Hockland's eyes. The man bit his lower lip.

Lashley did not have to ask.

Mrs. Hockland's head moved in the semblance of a nod. "They're gone. Both of them—gone."

The man said hoarsely, "The baby too." He swallowed hard. "Born dead. A boy."

The few inadequate words that Lashley tried to say choked in his throat. He looked helplessly at them.

"You did all you could, Major," Hockland said. "Edna and I, we want to thank you." His eyes turned tenderly to his wife.

A group of officers and their girls frolicked out of the elevator amid whoops of laughter and pushed past them.

Mrs. Hockland dried her eyes. "He was a tiny thing, Major," she said in an almost inaudible voice, "and he was born out of sin and all the terrible things of war, but we could have brought him up fine—to be somebody. It wasn't his fault. We could have given him a good life——"

Hockland said, "We'd better go up, Mom."

She nodded tearfully.

Lashley watched them until the doors of the elevator closed. He stood alone. There was something fine and American in the fierce purpose of the Hocklands to salvage a life, as she had said, out of sin and the terrible things of war. They had fought and hoped and prayed, and were stopped only by death. He thought of Thémis. She too was a life to be salvaged out of sin and the terrible things of war. And she was not dead. And he loved her.

He turned sharply and shouldered his way across the lobby and went out into the rain.

He swung in where the sign read *"Eingang strengst verboten"* and rumbled along a dirt road until the gates appeared in the arc of his headlights. When a guard dashed out of his sentry box Lashley barked, "I've got to see the general on urgent business," and he gave his name in the tone of a man who does not brook refusal. He was nevertheless mildly surprised when the guard came away from a field telephone and saluted, saying, "The general is expecting you, sir."

A maid took his coat and cap and led him through the big hall. When she opened the doors of the general's living room Lashley straightened his shoulders and strode in.

Marriner was almost lost in a huge leather chair before a

sputtering fire. He poked his head forward, pushed his spectacles back against the bridge of his nose, and said, "Come in, Lashley. I want to talk to you." His voice was quiet and stern with that peculiar quality for which he had become known from Fort Leavenworth to Berlin.

"Sit down. There." He indicated a straight-backed chair a few paces to one side of him.

There was a light knock on the door and Parker came in a little breathlessly. Without looking to see who it was, Marriner said, "Parker, get the major a drink—scotch, I presume—and one for me."

Parker bustled to the bar in the back of the room. Lashley gazed into the fire, and he felt that Marriner was studying him intently.

"What are you doing there, Parker?" Marriner called out.

"Yes, sir. They're ready, sir." Parker came up with a glass for the general and one for Lashley.

"All right. Now leave us."

When the door shut behind the lieutenant Marriner said, "You've got to be at Bergsdorf before midnight. You know that, Lashley."

Lashley turned to face the general. "Yes, sir."

Marriner peered through his spectacles with firm authority. His high, scholarly brow did not appear to belong with the stern cut of his small, well-formed mouth.

"I've ordered the executions to take place as soon after midnight as possible. Sonderberg tells me if the rain keeps up he'll have to wait until morning. I don't know why. I suppose he doesn't want to get wet."

Lashley was vaguely annoyed by that remark, but said nothing.

"He also tells me," Marriner continued, "that you were out there this afternoon. Seeing Steigmann. Were you curious?"

Lashley took a healthy swallow of his drink and said, "I wanted to check on something, General. I wanted to check on whether the Steigmann execution was going to take place to-night——" He held his glass tightly and waited.

Marriner looked into his drink and his fingers played on the side of the glass. He brought up his eyes suddenly.

"Did you have any doubt the execution would take place tonight?"

Lashley had the impression that Marriner knew a great deal more than he was indicating. It was useless to avoid the issue. He tightened his lips and looked squarely at the general.

"Yes, sir. I did."

Marriner slowly removed his spectacles and laid them down on a side table.

"Will you be good enough to explain your doubt?"

Lashley hesitated. He glanced at the fire, and into his glass, and his eyes wandered to the heavy brocaded curtains covering the french windows. His mind was restlessly seeking a direct but gentle reply, for he had need of the general's good will.

He was still fumbling for a reply when Marriner said, "You may smoke."

The manner in which the remark was uttered, as if the general were pitying his dilemma, made Lashley frown slightly with resentment.

He said, "No, thank you, sir."

The general's eyebrows moved a fraction of an inch and he lighted a cigarette.

"All right, Lashley. Explain your doubt. When I issue a command I don't expect my officers to question it."

Lashley's eyes looked levelly into Marriner's.

"I told you on Tuesday, sir, I had reason to suspect Rodal's testimony. Yesterday I discovered the man is paranoiac to the point of insanity. He may have been telling the truth, but the fact is that in any American court of law he would have been disqualified. Without him, I had no case against Steigmann."

He paused to give Marriner a chance to react. The general continued to pull at his cigarette with apparent disinterest.

"This morning I prepared a petition to the JAG. I intended to move for a new trial for Steigmann, disqualifying myself as prosecutor." He fumbled in his pocket. "I've got it here—if you want to read it, sir."

Marriner flipped his fingers. "I don't want to read it. Go on with your story."

"That's about all, sir. I went out to see Steigmann this afternoon and satisfied myself that the verdict is just—even without evidence that was strictly admissible."

"I see," said Marriner in an ominously low voice. "Did Steigmann confess he was a killer?"

"He was proud of it."

"Otherwise, I take it, you would have sent the petition."

"Yes, sir."

"And you think it would have canceled the execution."

"There isn't a judge, in the army or out of it, who could ignore a recommendation from the prosecutor in a case of this kind."

"I see."

Marriner tossed his cigarette in the fire. He put on his spectacles and examined his fingers. He stroked his nose thoughtfully. He took a sip of his drink.

The only sound in the room was the low sputter of the fire. Lashley wished the man would speak. His utter calm was beginning to assume thunderous proportions.

Marriner lighted a fresh cigarette and exhaled slowly.

"You're a great humanitarian, Lashley." The inflection was clearly sardonic.

"Not particularly, sir."

"You think you have integrity?" His voice was slightly louder.

"That is the one thing I try to have. I sometimes hope I succeed. I think, sir, the problem in this case was strictly a matter of personal integrity."

"Did it ever occur to you, Lashley"—Marriner's voice was rising now—"what it would mean if Steigmann escaped execution? Do you know it would mean the death of innocent people? Do you know it would encourage more thugs to go into the black market? There are people dying of starvation every day because the black market checkmates our system of distribution. Do you know it would encourage the Nazi underground to kill more of our men? Do you know that, Lashley?"

Marriner's chin stuck out angrily. "How dare you make this a matter of personal integrity!"

Furrows formed between Lashley's eyebrows, and he came to his feet.

"I know that justice must be firm. I also know, General, that it must be straight and clean, without the morals of expediency, and that every man who dispenses justice must feel straight and clean inside himself. Ten million men died in the war against Germany and Japan in order to bring a new concept of justice into the world. It's not a matter of saving a few more lives here and there. It's a matter of keeping faith with the ten million, of keeping faith with the new world for which they died. The fight isn't over. That new world isn't a reality yet. You know it, General, as well as I do.

"And to me at least, it means that we who dispense justice have got to come into court with clean hands—into any court —the court of law, the court of history, the court of humanity.

"I had everything to gain by letting Steigmann die. Everything to gain and nothing to lose—nothing, except my clean hands, and that is the most important thing in my life, the most important thing in any man's life—the most important thing in the world."

He had made his point. And he had rammed it home hard. Marriner was gazing into the fire, his eyes blinking, reaching hard for an answer that did not seem to come quickly enough. Lashley thought: It serves him right. A soldier arguing with a lawyer on a point of justice and integrity.

Marriner continued to gaze into the fire. Finally he said, "Do you believe in a higher justice? Higher than man's?"

"I do, sir."

"Then it seems to me," Marriner said with a certain confidence, "that a high justice was operating in the Steigmann case. Take this man Rodal. What was he before the war? Before the Germans got him?"

"He was a student. A medical student."

Marriner nodded. "A medical student. Better than average

type. A man of superior education. A normal man. Probably a good man——"

He faced Lashley abruptly, and once again the note of challenge came into his voice.

"Who made him a madman? Steigmann did. Steigmann and a lot of Nazis like him. Maybe Steigmann *was* clever enough to kill everybody who might have testified against him. Probably so. And when he sat in the prisoner's dock and heard a madman's ravings send him to the scaffold, he must have known in his heart that there was a higher justice operating. Higher than yours, or mine, or Macklin's. He put the madness of perjury in this man's mind, and the madness was turning on him like the wrath of God.

"Think of it next time you run up against your conscience."

Lashley said, "We can't operate our courts that way. We've got to make justice according to the law man devised from the teachings of the testaments. The inscrutable things we leave to a higher justice—but only the inscrutable things."

Marriner got up and warmed his hands at the fire. The glumness faded from his face and was replaced by the suspicion of a smile.

"I think that's all, Lashley. You've got integrity and I've got a job to do, and between the two of us we manage a rough sort of justice. Anyway, Steigmann hangs tonight. That's the important thing."

Lashley knew he had won the argument. He remained in his chair.

Marriner repeated, "I think that's all."

There was another silence.

Lashley said, "There was a higher justice working today and it had nothing to do with Rodal."

"What was that?"

"Thémis Delisle. If Steigmann hangs tonight, you can thank her for it."

Marriner turned around. His face was once more stern.

"I had her brought to my office this morning. Pretty girl. What's she got to do with it?"

"Everything, sir." Lashley knew it was a long shot but it might work.

"I would have guessed just the opposite," said Marriner, startled. "It seems she was his mistress—signed some sort of paper to that effect. I thought just now that she was probably behind this idea of yours for a retrial——"

"Certainly not," Lashley interrupted sharply. "She begged me to let him hang."

"Oh," said Marriner, and pursed his lips.

"Furthermore she insisted that I go and see Steigmann before sending in the petition. In a curious way she aided the cause of Allied justice."

"That all may be true, Lashley, but I've got to go to dinner. I know that your interest in the girl is not entirely—let us say —impersonal. But if there's any significance in that fact, it's that I'm glad I'm a bachelor."

Lashley said with great earnestness, "Give me ten minutes, sir. Ten minutes."

The general glanced at his watch. "All right. You've got ten minutes—precisely."

Lashley took a deep breath and prayed inwardly.

"I'll begin, sir, where it began for me, on the thirty-ninth day of the trial. On that day Thémis Delisle walked into the courtroom and testified for Steigmann. I hated the woman——"

Marriner shot a sharp, quizzical glance at his visitor.

"I hated her for what she did to me. It was not her testimony —that was pitiful, futile. It was something deeper, something in her attitude. She was on the side of evil, and I was on the side of humanity, and yet she mocked me with her presence. She mocked me until I felt guilty, and I determined to find out why she came to Reschweiler. I saw the way she looked at Steigmann. I felt she hated him. And I had to know why she came to help him. I *had* to know. That's the way I'm built, sir. I *had* to know.

"I began to find out on the night you showed me her dossier. She came to see me that night at my office . . ."

In brief, bitter sentences he told of Thémis and her father, of the man's fabulous patriotism and of the anti-Semitism that flamed in him to his last breath.

ᐟ His voice cracked with outrage, for the story in its bald recounting was becoming even more repellent to him.

Marriner sat deep in his chair, peering into the fire. His forgotten cigarette burned almost to his finger tips.

He said quietly, "But she didn't tell you why she became Steigmann's mistress."

"She didn't tell me. She was in love with me, and she couldn't bring herself to tell me. There was only one other person in the world who knew the story. At Bergsdorf this afternoon I heard it—from a man who was happy to tell it, because the telling of it gave him the last satisfaction he will have in his lifetime. . . ."

Lashley gazed vacantly into the fire.

"Yes, she was Steigmann's mistress. She became his mistress early in 1944 . . ."

Rapidly and with a rising indignation he put into words the scene in the death cell. And as he spoke he could see once more the gray cell, and the glimmer of light falling from the tiny window on the swelling chest of the condemned man, and he could hear the thick voice and the hysterical laughter.

". . . When I left the cell he was still laughing. He was laughing at me, at our victory, our hollow victory. He was laughing because he knew in the end he stood to win, because hate and killing and the doctrine of the superior animal were still triumphant. That's why he was laughing——"

"He won't laugh much longer," mumbled Marriner, glancing at his watch.

Lashley came away from his chair and stood, his back to the fire, facing the general.

"And what of Thémis? Are you going to let them take her?"

Marriner passed his hand across his brow and over his eyes.

"We'll have to depend on French justice, Lashley. They're a great race, the French. They've got all the humanities given to any race, and more than most. I'm sure we can leave her safely to French justice."

Lashley shook his head earnestly.

"We can't leave her safely to French justice, any more than we can to American justice or British justice. They wouldn't understand if she got up in court and told them we are as evil in our furtive ways as the Nazis. They would laugh if she pleaded that she testified for Steigmann because our victory was a mockery. And yet it's the truth. We talk of liberty, equality, fraternity. We fight under the banners of freedom. We die for it. But do we believe in it? We don't. The French won't admit that Nazism lives and is growing in France, just as we won't believe it lives and is growing among us in America. But it's there, and it's growing, and we are blind to it, and refuse to recognize it."

Marriner nodded briefly. "Well, the French have got her and there's nothing——"

"There's something we can do, sir. Something you can do. A simple request to the French to release her, to drop the charges, while she's still here."

"And the reason?" Marriner said sharply.

"Services rendered. Rendered to France, and to us. Rendered to the Allied cause. The Allied *cause*, sir. Few people know what that word means. *She* knows. She didn't save Steigmann. She condemned him. She deserves your help."

Marriner took hold of Lashley's arm and walked him to the door.

"I'm a soldier, Lashley. My father was a soldier. I was brought up and trained to fight for my country. That's the tradition of soldiering. You fight for your country and you don't ask many questions beyond that. Matters of humanity and a new world—things like that you leave to the men in the cutaway coats. That's soldiering.

"Well, it's changing now. I can feel it. The old style of soldiering is slipping away from me. New problems are coming up—problems we were never trained to solve. We come up against questions we can't find answered in the manual of tactics.

"Frankly, I have a nostalgia for the old style of soldiering. I liked it. It was a good, simple life, sometimes a short one, most times a long one. I don't know exactly what's causing the change. Maybe it's this new world they talk about. Maybe it's really coming along. It must be, because the old world of soldiering doesn't exist any more. We don't treat troops like troops any more, we treat 'em like human beings. And even enemy populations. We don't treat 'em in masses, we treat 'em as individuals who have a right to live.

"I'm up against a thousand new problems, and this is one of them, this thing about the Delisle woman. I don't know, Lashley. I'll have to think about it. I'll have to hear that Steigmann is dead. And when that action is over, maybe I'll tackle this one. I don't know."

They were at the door.

"There isn't much time, sir," Lashley said. "They fly in the morning."

Marriner swung on him sternly.

"I give orders, Major. I don't take them. Good night."

"Good night, sir."

SATURDAY

XVIII

LASHLEY REACTED SLEEPILY TO THE HAND THAT WAS PUSHING at his shoulder. He strove to open his eyes.

A voice said, "It's time, Major. Wake up."

He had been dreaming of someone shaking him and ordering him in just such a voice to wake up, telling him that it was time.

"Wake up, Major. Wake up. It's time," the voice repeated.

The man standing over him was just such a man as he had been dreaming about. A huge man with thick muscles running down the sides of his neck, a hard, expressionless face, cleanshaven but still darkly shadowed. The man wore a steel helmet.

Lashley looked about him. Bright lights shone from the ceiling. He had been sleeping in an armchair in Sonderberg's office.

The sergeant standing over him had a tommy gun slung over his shoulder and he was saying, "It's four forty-five, Major. They'll start in fifteen minutes. Better get ready."

Lashley shivered with a sudden chill. He stretched his arms and flexed his muscles.

"All right, Sergeant. I'm with you."

He went into Sonderberg's bathroom and doused his face with cold water. He looked in the mirror with no sign of enthusiasm. Then he took up his cap and coat.

"I'm ready, Sergeant."

They went down the circular staircase into the big hall and across to the oak door which the sergeant opened with a key. They were outdoors, in the narrow alley separating the main building from the squat stone death house. Lashley saw that six men carrying rifles with bayonets fixed stood in line before the small door that gave entrance to the death house.

It was not raining. The sky was alive with stars, and to the east it was trimmed a lighter blue, as if rain had caused the dark to fade on the horizon.

They walked along the alley between the buildings and came into a huge courtyard, almost the size of a training square. Perhaps it had been a training square, Lashley thought. There were no cobblestones underfoot. It was paved smooth.

The courtyard was in semidarkness. A few dim lights imbedded in a high surrounding wall gleamed lonesomely and cast a pale light over the scene.

In a corner of the courtyard, contained in the angle made by a shed and the outside wall, stood a scaffold. From a distance it looked curiously small and inoffensive. It reminded Lashley of a square bathhouse which used to stand on the peninsula which jutted out into Lake Erie, differing only in the fact that it had a steep staircase mounting to its roof. When he approached closer he saw the superstructure—two beams sticking up perpendicularly, joined by a heavy crossbeam. A shiny steel ring almost as big as a horseshoe was attached below the crossbar. Two men were on the scaffold, leaning against the beams. There were a number of persons standing about the base of the scaffold and they were unnaturally hushed.

Abruptly the courtyard was flooded with light, coming from at least a dozen searchlights attached to the top of the wall and the tower of the main building. The scene was suddenly brought into sharp relief. The two men on the scaffold came away from the beams on which they had been leaning and began to converse. One of them—a short stocky man of middle age who wore the stripes of a master sergeant on the sleeves of his jacket—carried several loops of heavy rope on his left arm. He was demonstrating to the other—a skinny young soldier—the strength of the knot that formed the noose.

The crowd at the foot of the scaffold numbered about twenty-five. There were three colonels and a sprinkling of junior officers. Farther back Lashley saw Van Tyne of AP and Gubbins of UP, and next to them was Camilla Cameron, looking exceedingly smart in the same coat and hat in which she had arrived. There were three other men in correspondents' uniforms. Lashley did not know them.

He looked about for Sonderberg. Not finding him, he moved around behind the spectators and took a place against the wall some twenty feet from the scaffold. He was beginning to feel a heaviness in his chest.

Then he saw Rodal and Maria. They stood huddled against the wall a few paces from him and closer to the scaffold. The Czech was whispering in the girl's ear. She nodded her head and screwed up her nose and tittered in a way that was both sweet and mad.

The men had already fitted the rope through the steel ring. Now they stood on the ground on the left side of the scaffold, attaching the long end of the rope to a boxlike mechanism. The noose dangled low on the scaffold, almost to the floor boards.

The murmur of muffled conversation floated across the courtyard. It was as though no one dared speak above a whisper.

Lashley felt cold. His shoulders were shivering. He pulled up his coat collar and buttoned it high on his neck. He continued to shiver and he knew it was not the cold.

The hum of conversation died abruptly. The master sergeant ran up the steps and stood at ease at the back of the scaffold, facing forward. One of the spectators up front—a captain—came weaving through the crowd and leaned heavily against the wall. His face was a dull green.

Lashley glanced at his watch. It lacked one minute of five. He craned his head but could see nothing to occasion the sudden tension. Then he heard deep intonations in German and the sound of cleated boots marching slowly across the pavement.

" 'I am the resurrection and the life, saith the Lord . . .' "

A strange procession came around the corner of the death house. Sonderberg marched alone in front, his arms stiffly at his sides. Behind him were two soldiers wearing steel helmets and carrying rifles. Swinging out on the flanks were two more soldiers, and farther behind the gleam of bayonets indicated there were four others.

The condemned man walked in the center of the solemn group. Lashley wondered if he was Steigmann. He could see only the white of the man's shirt, for a pastor was walking awkwardly in front of the man, occasionally turning toward him.

" '. . . and whosoever liveth and believeth in me shall never die . . .' "

It could not be Steigmann, Lashley thought. Steigmann would not have asked the services of a pastor. Not Steigmann with his belief in superior and inferior animals, and killing and being killed.

The group was momentarily lost behind the scaffold. There was a shuffling of feet and a sharp command, "Forward march!"

A gray head appeared over the edge of the platform and then a figure came into full view. It was the pastor, and his voice rang out strong: " 'I am the resurrection and the life . . .' "

Lashley felt his stomach contract and move up like a hard ball into his chest. He breathed deeply and held his breath as long as he could. He was conscious that his teeth were hard clenched.

It *was* Steigmann. He came off the narrow staircase closely attended by two guards, each a foot taller than he. His arms were free and his fingers stretched taut. Under the bright lights his face was marble-white. He held his chin high, his mouth an expressionless line like a short stroke drawn by a heavy pencil. He blinked, looked down on the crowd for a fleeting moment, then stared straight ahead.

Even the wind seemed to have halted its murmur as the condemned man stood on the edge of the platform, savoring his last moments of life.

The guards seized his arms briskly and shoved him to the center of the platform. The pastor glided in front of him, eagerly studying his face, intoning, " '. . . he that believeth in me, though he were dead . . .' "

Steigmann's mouth twisted and he murmured something. The pastor bowed his head, then walked dejectedly away from the condemned man and left him with the two guards standing at his side and the hangman behind.

From the base of the scaffold Sonderberg called up: "Are you Otto Steigmann?"

Steigmann jerked his chin affirmatively.

Sonderberg said, "Do you wish to say anything before you die? You may speak for thirty seconds."

Steigmann lowered his head and looked directly at Sonderberg. For a moment he glared in silence. Then a sneer came to his lips and he uttered an almost inaudible *"Leb' wohl."* A wisp of his sparse hair waved in the wind.

Sonderberg signaled with a wave of his left hand. The guards suddenly produced two leather straps, pinioned the man's hands behind his back, and his legs at the ankles just above his slippered feet. They did this work with lightning speed. They had scarcely moved from the shackled figure when the hangman appeared behind him and clapped a black hood over his head. Without a second's delay the noose was over the hood and snug around the neck. The hangman raised his right hand.

The low whine of hemp sliding over steel filled the silence.

Lashley did not see Steigmann fall through the trap. At one moment the German was standing on the platform, and faster than the eye could record it, he had disappeared. A thud like a bag of marbles falling on velvet assailed the ears, and seconds later, so it seemed, one last sound—a sound almost like a grunt of defiance—came from beneath the platform. The rope swung gently from side to side.

Someone close up front was retching. Lashley saw it was Camilla Cameron.

At his side he heard a high, delirious voice. Rodal was whispering rapidly in Maria's ear. His lips and chin palpitated with his excitement, and the girl's eyes rolled in ecstasy and her mouth was wide with uncontrollable mirth.

Lashley leaned against the wall and shut his eyes.

He could hear Camilla Cameron retching. He was content that she was retching. If she were back home, not seeing this, she might be writing a brave, biting piece for the newspapers, filled with easy flowing phrases—phrases decrying the long-drawn-out trials, demanding a prompt settlement of the European problem so the world can get back to normal.

Now she was retching. Perhaps she would know that killing in cold blood does not come easy, that it is not done with a few glib words on a typewriter, that it is a huge and desperate job to kill a man, that it has fallen to Americans to do the job and do it honestly.

He opened his eyes. The rope was no longer swinging. It stretched taut from the steel ring and moved straight into the blackness beneath the trap.

Rodal and Maria were watching it with eyes that rolled and gleamed in the blazing light. Maria was asking in German, "Is he still dancing? I can't see him. Is he dancing?"

This was the new Europe, Lashley thought. He wished Camilla Cameron would stop retching long enough to study these people. Perhaps she would know that settlement in Europe is not contained in a series of clauses drawn up on beribboned parchment by men in cutaway coats. Perhaps she would see that Europe is a sea of traumatic minds. Like Rodal and Maria, stark mad from torture, delirious with revenge, filled with the greed that flows from starvation and fear.

The feel of death was about him, and his mind fell on the Hocklands. Sitting on their Iowa farm, he thought, they little dreamed that their future would someday be bound up in the fate of a postman's bedraggled daughter living in Reschweiler; as millions everywhere little dream that the future of each of them flows down into a strong single stream which draws its elements from strange and unwitting sources far off as an Iowa farm and drab as a cellar on Thaelmannstrasse.

Ten minutes passed. Two German war prisoners carried a pine coffin out of the shed and placed it on the ground in front of the scaffold.

The hangman pushed aside a canvas curtain and entered the interior of the scaffold. He came out almost immediately. A captain and a lieutenant then went in. A loud voice could be heard saying, "I pronounce this man dead."

The captain and the lieutenant came out. The hangman signaled to the war prisoners and the three entered. Ten seconds later they emerged bearing Steigmann's body, placed it in the coffin, and carried it into the shed.

Someone murmured, "Johann Bacher."

Sonderberg marched stiffly toward the death house.

The sun was still below the hills when Lashley drove into the city, but the sky was crystalline blue and the air was soft and mild.

He climbed out of his jeep at the Excelsior and stood looking at the ruins of the *Operahaus*, breathing deeply, seeking to free his lungs of the air he'd been breathing. He knew now how much strain he'd been under from the moment he walked into the dim courtyard until the sixth man had swung from that lonely scaffold.

He raised his eyes above the ruins. The sun was edging over the hills and the horizon was dazzling bright. It was such a morning as he remembered from his childhood when all the cares of the world seemed to have disappeared.

He glanced at his watch. It was seven-thirty. The plane for Paris did not leave for an hour.

He thought about Marriner, at breakfast now in his big house behind the sign *"Eingang strengst verboten."* Sometimes he liked him and sometimes he hated him. But this was the mark of a good soldier who must be loved and hated by his men at certain times. And Marriner was a good soldier and also a good man. Marriner knew a great deal about life, a great deal more than the stiff traditions of the service allowed him to betray.

Today he was sure he would like Marriner. Sure that the general in his shrewd way would arrange things with the French authorities. This time he was not going to worry. He had no need to worry.

He saw her when she was still some distance away, her hair shining in the morning light and her head raised high, as if reflecting his own mood.

And now she saw him. She began to run, her hair tossing from side to side, her skirt flying. Her hands came up now as though reaching for him, but she was still a long way off.